THE LOOP

A Convivial Comedy for Delirious People

DYLAN THOS. GOOD

Trash Raiders Media

THE LOOP

Published by Trash Raiders Media
www.trashraidersmedia.com

First Printing: November, 2022

This is for Sumner Erickson.
Thank you for taking care of your big brother.

...And to my high school English teacher, Mr. Dormann.
Or Dormouse. Dorstop? Whatever your name was.
Thanks for making fun of my writing in front of the entire class
that one day.
How do you like me now, you worthless fuck?

THE LOOP

ACT THE FIRST

[AN INTRODUCTION TO FRIENDS AND ENEMIES,
WHEREIN WE DELIGHT IN THE CONTINUING
ADVENTURES OF A TOILET PLUNGER AND
DISCOVER JUST WHERE TO STICK IT]

Now, it was that *other* season on the coast of Oregon.

From July through October, no one could blame you for getting lost in the green. The smell of cedar, fir, and spruce twisted in and out around the branches. Kites were everywhere. Your shoes sank into the feathery beach sand, and each briny sea breeze had a smile for you. There never seemed to be a reason to doubt these wonders were your dearest friends.

Until that motherfucker November rolled around.

Before you knew it, Mother Nature was back on the rag, and all that communing-with-nature shit became nothing more than a soggy, foggy, blustery memory. Sure, all the kids of Beaver Lake asked Santa Claus for bikes and video games every Christmas, but all they ever seemed to get was amoxicillin. It was either that or an airborne garden gnome up the ass.

As his Firebird shifted into overdrive, Junior Berrick smiled and ripped his throat hoarse in an effort to appease the Tiki Gods. His mix-tape of Hawaiian Christmas songs rattled the speakers, front and back, and soon nothing outside could compete. Not the busted, swinging tree branches, sideways sheets of rain, or flapping layers of rooftop tar paper. None of it could trump the marimba ring that took him away to his version of paradise.

Troughs zigzagged across Highway 101's deepening puddles, and soon the turn signal was clicking. The resulting gold beacon reflected off a white and blue sign lit by two floodlights Junior had wired himself: *LeisureFace - Executive Timeshare Condominiums.* Underneath was the prized tagline—*The 21st Century Look of Leaving It All Behind!* Despite the fact that most people thought the new century started January 1, 2000, it wouldn't actually arrive for another five weeks. Nevertheless, Leisure-Face had already been flogging the slogan since the summer of '99.

The first person Junior laid eyes on each morning was Cles Gubbins. There he was, shuffling out to the mailbox to get the day's *B.L. Mirror,* the puny local newspaper. Even on a good day, it was no bigger than a tabloid. Gubbins was a subscriber simply because there were periodic articles trumpeting how wonderful he and LeisureFace were for the local economy.

In the cold reality of it all, Gubbins was a blue-ribbon shit stain of a human being. He was self-aggrandizing to the end, and arguably the Holy Grail when it came to stereotypically despicable CEOs. Racist, elitist, sexist, and probably a few other things that end in 'ist,' Androcles J. Gubbins—everyone immediately assumed the J stood for "jerkoff"—abused power from inside a pair of gray Haggar slacks and a pink Oxford shirt in ways not seen since the Roman Empire.

One morning not long ago, Junior had witnessed Gubbins berate the Native American fellows tending to the rose gardens lining the entrance of the property (*"you wagon burners don't understand a damn thing!"*), slyly escort a young Asian housekeeper into his office (who was quickly unemployed a few days later, probably because she didn't swallow) and, whether it deserved it or not, kick his wife's dog in the back.

All before 10 am.

There he stood on the porch of his on-property Craftsman home, waving his hand, nose in the air, and raising his brow in that subtly superior way. It was enough to make any self-respecting member of the human race want to stomp Gubbins' face until his lips caved in.

The only reason Junior hadn't yet done it himself was because Gubbins had taken a chance on him, hiring a kid with no work experience whatsoever, all those years ago. Yep, it's true. Horrible racial slurs, sexual harassment, and animal abuse, but *that* was the realization that made Junior sickest.

The broad, red snout of the Firebird swerved and sniffed out the same parking spot it had since before Junior graduated from Beaver Lake High School. At 18, he'd taken the thankless and lonely swing shift Maintenance position at LeisureFace for a back-breaking/bank-breaking $4.50 an hour. Nearly ten years on, he was now the manager. A bigger paycheck, which came in handy for taking care of his dad, a better shift, and commanding some respect were the rewards for hanging in there that long, but sometimes he still felt as lonely as when he watched the sun set during that first evening on the job.

Toothy Goodyear treads rolled to a stop as Junior hit the brakes and twisted off the ignition. He was thankful for winter's impending arrival since it slowed the sap from dripping onto his windshield.

Steve, the night auditor, was heading home, and Junior gave him a quick wave as the 'Bird's door swung wide. Steve was a nice enough guy, but took his job a little too seriously. Not that there's anything wrong with earning your pay, but Steve's paycheck didn't even come close to justifying the spiffy two-piece suit he always wore. The only people he ever got to show it off to were the occasional drunk or insomniac who stumbled into Reception as he was crunching his nightly numbers.

Now, like most mornings, that suit was rumpled and creased with boredom, and its only use was getting Steve across the parking lot on a tired charge to his car.

An oversized double garage aside the main guest building served as HQ for both Housekeeping and Maintenance. Junior zipped up his jacket and headed for the door as Steve's headlights carved around the trees and buried in the murk.

Berta was there at the garage entrance, leaning against the door-frame and having a cigarette. Already. That couldn't be a good sign. Junior's spidey-sense tingled enough to tell him to tread lightly. As he got closer, he could smell the spout of wind-whipped smoke that blew out from between Berta's olive-skinned cheeks.

"I told your Secret Santa to bring you a windproof lighter this year." Junior thought his opening line was pretty charming for first thing in the morning, but Berta's expression didn't change much.

"S'okay. For the winter, I'm thinking of moving up to a blowtorch I found on a military surplus website." There was a fun kick to Berta's words. It's too bad it hid behind a sad irony that extended beyond her disappointment in holiday gift possibilities.

Junior repositioned his hat, suddenly feeling the prick of the humidity. He figured he had better step it up. "You alright?"

Berta nodded her head and sniffed. "Yeah."

Junior knew it was bullshit. He had only just gotten to work, but was certain she'd already washed down at least six pills on her way to approximately 50 by the time her head hit the pillow that night. Five years on, and Berta's health wasn't any different. Not any worse, but not any better. Just a rerun that someone hit the pause button on.

She continued, "I'm just waiting on Dorena and Casey. They won't answer—"

Just then, the walkie-talkie on her hip began to chatter. The voice was young and clear, unfettered by a slur of the usual static. "*Casey to Berta.*"

"This is Berta. Hey, I need someone to take a deionizer to 314— there's butts a-plenty up there. You or your sister near HQ?"

Up in a room on the second floor, Casey's short, blonde ponytail was slugged over her sweaty shoulder. If there was a smoking room to take care of, she knew her sister would already be up there. Her enthusiastic thumb nearly cramped as it shoved in the walkie's button.

"Just finishing up here in 216." Blue eyes rolled over the room. The fast, young brain behind them tried to tally how fast she could check the room off her QC list. "Can be down in a minute." She knew it would be at least three.

"*I think there's one right by it in the linen closet on the third floor,*" Berta chimed through the walkie-talkie's rash of static.

Casey never heard this. She was too busy doing a little dance around 216's kitchen, celebrating the fact that she was about to go on break. Her quick hand reached for the back pocket of her jeans, calmed by the bump of a cigarette lighter. Three minutes premature, a penciled X lodged itself onto the QC sheet.

Casey didn't need to hurry. The third floor's linen closet hung wide open, just a hop from room 314. Behind its locked door, the deionizer sat on the kitchen island, its plug hanging off the edge as a rough cough barked through the room. Dorena shook her head, the curly, dark thickness swinging back and forth as she tried to right the wrong of her inhale.

Three knocks stabbed at the door. Jaunty, sloppy knocks that could only come from a tiny set of knuckles like her sister had. Just to be safe, Dorena slid up against the door and knocked twice in return. One more came from the other side. The bolt lock sprang back.

"Where the fuck have you been?" Beneath Dorena's slightly blood-shot eyes, little ganja sprigs stuck to her lip and all over the front of her white apron.

"What?!" came Casey's high, defensive retort, raising a hand to brush off her sister's greenery. The Morris sisters embodied the typical story of a sibling relationship. Love always won out, but on certain mornings like this one, you never were completely sure.

"Gimme your lighter," Dorena commanded. "I'm over here trying to blaze a bowl off an electric stovetop. Nearly killed myself."

The lighter flew through the air, with Dorena catching it so coolly.

The flat, unblemished alabaster of Casey's forehead wrinkled, con-fused as she saw what her sister had tuned in on the entertainment center's TV: a bumpkin-sounding starfish jumped up and down with what looked like a piece of yellow cake wearing shorts and a tie. What. In. The. HELL?

Dorena, finally appeased by getting a good hit out of the pipe, circled around the kitchen. She held up a saucepan sporting a spiraled, copper-colored burn.

"Ya know, I'm getting high on the job, and even I remember how to boil water." The pot bounced back up on the counter. A short-tempered aluminum clang rang out for a merciless second.

"Alright, my turn," Casey demanded.

"Bullshit, dumpling!" Dorena contested in a hot blur, reaching again for her little sister's lighter. "I just got here! I already stopped for the deionizer—I know that's why Berta's sent ya up here!"

Unfair anger started to circle Casey's pouting face. "Let me have it or else."

Dorena's smoke blasted out with a cannonball of sibling defiance. "Else what??"

"I'll tell Petey," Casey's soprano deepened and tolled as she thought, "that you tried to abort him at eight months."

"Where do you get this shit?" Dorena's cheeks raised and wrinkled, the smoke bracketing her foggy lips. "It was six!"

"Eight!"

"Fucking seven—TOPS!" Dorena conceded. "Alright, I'll tell mom you got your belly button pierced."

"Right, like she'd even care." Casey wasn't a very good liar, but there was just enough of a neglected crackling in her voice to make it believable. Well, at least to anyone but her big sister.

"She'd shit a purple Twinkie! You remember?" Dorena got closer, her sneakers slicking up static from the freshly vacuumed carpet. "Huh? You remember what she was like when you pierced your own ears? We weren't allowed to have thumbtacks in the house for five years after that!"

Casey's porcelain features burnt over black as she laid down her winning hand. "I'll tell mom that Paco moved back in."

"You wouldn't fuckin' dare," Dorena hissed.

The blue eyes stared down the bigger, bolder, and bustier frame in front of them. Hands on hips and with no words, Casey held her gaze for as long as she could.

Inevitably, the possibility of how much her little sister could fuck up her holiday season quickly made its way to Dorena's baking gray matter. The pipe sailed out of her hand. "You little bitch."

Casey's palm burned as she caught the blown glass pipe thrown her way, emitting a tiny "Owww!" as even more of the little green sprinkles popped out of its shallow bowl.

Dorena turned back at the doorway. "Alright, but I'm coming back for it after I do 323."

"Fine!" Casey just wanted her sister out of the room so she could get a hit and calm down. Because of how close they'd always been, she hated fighting with her. She had to admit to herself, though, that the rare victories were pretty damn sweet.

"And no readings!" Dorena ordered. "We don't have time for that shit today. You can do it after we get home."

"It's my break, I can do what I want," the younger sister's assertive whine shot back as the front door opened and closed with a *whuuush*.

Casey's arm swept everything to the right side of the coffee table as her tiny hand pulled the big, silk-wrapped stack of tarot cards from her pocket. They had been with her longer than any of her friends, and for almost as long as her family. When she and Dorena's parents had gone through a divorce over ten years ago, she clipped a mail order coupon from the back of a magazine in hope of finding some light in those dark days. From the moment she opened that plain, brown-paper package, Casey began to memorize the meaning of each card. Drinking in all the symbols, the patterns, and the insight. Years later, that hopeful curiosity had turned into a thirst, a persistent need to second-guess the turns and potholes of one's own life path.

The blue and white backing on each card danced and skidded as she shuffled and shuffled.

One tumbled out face-up and upside-down from the pack. A seated man clung to four shields emblazoned with stars. Four of Pentacles reversed. Financial instability. Delay. Loss. Lots of things that make you sigh. Just like the short, irritated one Casey did just then.

"Yeah, you gonna tell me something I don't know?"
Back into the deck it went.

Back at Maintenance, all the walkie-talkies chirped "*Front desk to*

Ernesto" in quadraphonic sound. Junior unplugged the loudest one from the charger dock simply so he could turn it down. The voice at the end belonged to Stacey-Lynn down at Reception—her clear, friendly tone was just as plump and full of life as she was. "*Front desk to Maintenance.*"

Junior slid in the button. "Yeah, this is Junior."

"*Hey there, Junior, do you see Ernesto anywhere?*"

"No, he's probably hitting some of the landscaping on the 'A' building by now. What ya need?"

"*Oh okay, could you tell him to swing by if you see him? We have two more dead VCRs here at the front desk, and Gubbins needs at least one of them fixed for the holiday party.*"

"I'll send him down to grab 'em when I see him," Junior offered, clipping the walkie to his belt loop.

"*Thank yoooou much!*"

The band went silent as the raindrops began to whip harder against the windows. Just then, the gusts bolted in, spilling Ernesto's tall, lithe form into the corridor. Tools on the pegboard rattled in the forked breezes until the door was closed again. Dots of white rain floated on the top of Ernesto's afro, and the black branches of his fingers held up a couple of slick, tapering oak handles. They were just like the ones bolted to the gas barbecues on each guest room patio.

"You see this?" Ernesto's voice cracked, at least an octave higher than usual. His boss was trying his damnedest not to laugh. "This is the fourth pair of handles I've found in the past hour, man!"

"Where are you finding them?"

"On the ground! These folks put their damn Thanksgiving turkeys in the barbecues for ten hours until the lids melt and the handles drop off!"

Junior's smile broke through. He couldn't keep it away any longer. "That's right, you didn't start till January. Yeah, we keep the part number on file."

"They do this every year??" Ernesto was probably up two full octaves by now.

"Every year."

"'A'ole pilikia, my brother." Ernesto's voice was back down to its normal register as he shook his head in vague disgust. "I'm on it."

"Stacey-Lynn's looking for you."

"Yeah?" Ernesto stopped dead. "What she want?"

"Two more VCRs waiting for you at the front desk."

"Shiiiit," the young Black fellow slurred, almost to himself, as he started to shuffle off. "We need to go back to laserdiscs or somethin'."

Junior caught a reflection of himself in the window. He looked tired and his eyes were stained with worry. His still-hadn't-been-cut hair hung limply from out underneath his Hawaii cap, slathering around the collar of his branded LeisureFace jacket. Unfortunately, his best friend noticed, as well.

"Junebug, man. You okay?" Ernesto's pitch wavered with concern.

"Yeah." Junior steeled himself. The truth was getting harder to dish out these days. The humidity was getting to him again, and Junior shoved a few fingers under his cap to give his scalp a scratch. "Dad was up in the middle of the night. He thinks the raccoons are rearranging the patio furniture."

Ernesto smiled. "Hey, that's a step up!"

Junior scrunched up his face. "You serious?"

"Word! Last time I was there, he talked to me for 20 minutes about Shakira bein' the one who would start World War III." Ernesto continued, his eyes locking onto a toilet plunger across the way. "Your pops is off the wall. For reals. I gotta pay him a visit again soon."

There was a respect in Ernesto's voice that was most appreciated. "Definitely," Junior agreed. "He'd like that." A glance to the dusty wall clock above the pegboard jolted him into action. "Damn, I gotta check cee-oh-two levels before Gubbins does."

Ernesto was quick to empathize. "Dude, we gotta find that motherfucker a hobby." His words growled out softly with a hard-earned resentment he was barely able to contain.

Being the only one who knew of Ernesto's past, Junior had to be the firm voice of reason. "Easy, brother, you don't need any more court appearances."

"Hey," a dark, defensive cadence rang back, "I don't talk about that shit anymore. You know I was just protecting my moms." Ernesto's intrinsic and very warranted fear of law enforcement could clearly be heard in his coda. "Fourteen months out of twenty-four years isn't a fair yardstick to be measured by, man."

"Yeah, I know that," Junior leveled, "but a lot of folks aren't gonna see it that way if you get yourself in that kind of situation again."

"Which is why I'm stuck with jobs like this for the rest of my life," Ernesto lamented. "No offense."

"None taken." Junior remembered he was running low on pH drops down at the pool's maintenance room. In his haste, he rattled some vials on the supply rack until he could find a few to stuff into his jeans. "You down for some A-building deep cleans after I pick up the QC sheets from Berta?"

"Yeah." Ernesto's brows raised as he nodded his head good-naturedly, and for that Junior was thankful. Racism is a sticky subject, and talking about his unfair criminal record made Ernesto's black skin turn even blacker.

"You got the truck?" Junior sighed.

"Yeah. Hold up, hold up." Ernesto snatched the toilet plunger he'd been eyeing. Junior pulled his hat brim farther down and the figures of both spry, young men sped back out into the downpour.

Down under the front entrance awning, Ernesto pumped the soft brakes of the work truck to a stop. Dirty rain sloshed around the grooves of the LeisureFace long-bed as the rotors squeaked out a quick chirp.

Junior saw Dorena coming, and despite the hairbreadth of time he had to get to the pool and at least begin to look busy, he just sat there...looking around the passenger side wiper blade and through the speckled windshield. Looking. Surveying the confident pout that rose and fell through the smashed curls of her damp hair. Junior was getting worse and worse about tearing his eyes away from her. He knew he wasn't fooling anyone anymore.

"Nigga, you don't have time for pussy now," Ernesto's voice honked. "Go, man. Go!"

Junior fumbled with the chrome handle and shouldered open the door. The raindrops smacked off his eyes and nose as he ran off into the main lobby.

Sitting behind the wheel as his broad smile shone through the late-November murk, Ernesto could only shake his head. A randy giggle spurted out into the cab. "Don't mean I don't have time for pussy, though."

He swung back the driver's door and popped up the plunger from the truck bed. Dorena was busy rummaging through her pockets, and Ernesto knew exactly why.

"Shit, girl, I bet you just had a cigarette. I'm gonna tell your mama on you."

Dorena tilted her head to the side, bubbling up a defiant smirk. "My mama saw yo' mama at bingo last night."

"That's 'cause yo' mama's a bingo ho!"

"Hey!" Dorena smoothly wiped her grin off as her pointer finger struck out at Ernesto. "Don't be callin' my mama no hos, muh-fucker." She bent down and whipped a handful of wood bark at him.

Ernesto retreated, mock-screaming like a girl as he made his way past Reception, which is where Stacey-Lynn's poofy, dishwater blonde hair and chubby, blusher-scrubbed cheeks sunk a bit each minute she struggled with the call rattling into her ear.

"No!" Her voice echoed around the sofas, cups, and coffee stirrers. She looked around to see if anyone had heard her, self-consciously dropping her volume. "I don't want to talk about this now. I can't." Stacey-Lynn's husband, Fitz, was berating her for already being asleep, legs closed, when he came home last night at about 2:45 AM, reeking of Jack 'n' Coke and sporting a semi-lump to the left side of his zipper.

"I have to go." Hot verbal squiggles continued to smack her eardrum as she noticed the elderly couple heading towards her. Thank God they were enchanted by the bright colors of the lobby's complimentary tea cart, slowly setting down their luggage for a few extra seconds. Stacey-Lynn's boiling whisper begged her ratty hubby once more for a kind of temporary truce. "It's my break, that's why. I have to do it before check out, and I'm not spending the entire 15 minutes listening to this. Again!"

A few filtered words shook out above her silver earring. Two of them were 'selfish' and 'cunt', one of which Fitz had already flung to his wife just moments before. Stacey-Lynn's fingers hit a button, any button, and an outside line cut off Fitz in mid-shit fit. The receiver clobbered the switch hook, and that happy, customer service face came back up into place. She reminded herself to suck in her gut and sit up straight, as Stacey-Lynn recently saw a news article that mentioned good posture being a sign of being better educated and more cultured. After just three minutes on the phone with Fitz, he had, yet again, completely depleted her self-confidence.

"You folks need some help?" Her voice cracked a bit as she addressed the old couple, but she recovered fast. Years of practice paid off.

"Oh no, pumpkin!" The words crooned out around the white hair and rosy lipstick. "We're just going to sit for a bit." A shaky, tender hand held up an insulated paper cup, brimming with the couple's newfound treasure. "It's not often you find oolong!"

"I know, huh!" Stacey-Lynn's hands slid a LeisureFace-embossed sign onto the counter: *Your Leisure Is Our Business—Be Back Momentarily!* Her walkie-talkie was already in hand as she swept around the corner.

"Stacey-Lynn to Casey."

A few clicks of static pranced across the signal in the wake. Finally: *"Yeah, Casey here."*

"I'm heading on break," Stacey-Lynn's voice wrapped shrill and urgent around the core of its pleasantness. The happy face was already starting to slip. "Can you just keep an eye on the desk? I'll be back in a couple of minutes."

"No problem!" Casey's accommodation was music to her ears. *"I'll head dowwwwn...right now."*

"Muchas gracias!" Stacey-Lynn breathed out in relief as she hit the exterior doors of the side corridor. She didn't even have the walkie's 'off' button in position before her hand was on the door handle to the water heater room.

The grated door swung back, and she stepped inside. As usual, the juicy mouth descended on her. She drowned in his darkness, his scent, his passion. In the dimness, a tongue brushed past her earlobe, sending the perfect fifty-fifty mix of sensuality and fun down to what waited between her thighs.

"Oh, baby girl," Ernesto pleaded in earnest. It was one of those tones women loved to hear. One that could whisk you away to anywhere in the world and care for you till the end of time. One that will take you down, and that's right where Stacey-Lynn's LeisureFace khakis were headed—down around her ankles. The forceful shadows forgivingly hid her fat rolls, even though her lover told her a long time ago she didn't have anything to be ashamed of.

"I know you want it." Ernesto's words crushed and breezed sideways as she pushed against his mouth, literally taking his breath away.

An unladylike "Yes!" breached the hum of the water heaters, tumbling gracelessly out of Stacey-Lynn's wanting lips. It was like magic, and her attention paid no mind to the snapping of rubber gloves or short, hissing sprays of WD-40.

To this day, Stacey-Lynn has no idea that her first double-penetration was courtesy of a toilet plunger.

Out in the pool's maintenance room, Junior was pretending to be busy. He slung around some pH balancers and tapped his pen on the carbon dioxide tanks. A hollow, pinging sound ricocheted around the back corners. One such corner housed a graveyard for inflatable pool toys left behind by guests from the past five years or so. The other was a grimy, bolt-locked door that no one had ever found the key to.

He could hear the coming footsteps. Cles Gubbins' voice bent and waved, unintelligible from too far away. Junior had just enough time to throw the pool water's pH sample into the floor drain.

Boss man's sentences could begin to be made out in full—"Why, you certainly look special today, little lady!"

Junior knew Gubbins could only be talking to Casey. You could practically hear the asshole's heavy breathing every time he was near her. For some reason, probably denial, she hadn't picked up on it yet.

Junior raked the wall-mounted skimmer off its hooks from above the CO_2 tanks. He shot an eye to the surface of the pool, which, mercifully, looked cleaner than usual.

Gubbins' white shoes clapped louder and closer on the cement outside the doorway. Junior's opening line was a gift from God.

"Whoo! Helluva lotta floaties this morning, Mr. Gubbins!"

The CEO fell for it—hook, line, and skimmer.

"Not surprising, young man!" Gubbins cast a jaundiced eye over the length of the pool, noticing one light that was burned out in the deep end. A nervous finger flicked in its direction as a haughty scowl rose on his face. "I want you to get that colored fellow..."

"Ernesto." Though he hadn't kept count, this was the fourteenth time Junior had prompted Gubbins the name of someone who'd been with the company for nearly a year. No one's memory is *that* bad.

"That's the one!" Gubbins smiled. His teeth looked like tiny white Chiclets—the kind they sell near the register at Rite Aid. "Want you to get him in there and swap out that light before we close the pool for the season."

Most people would have wondered if Gubbins was serious. Junior knew his hesitation could be read all over his face. Then, Gubbins' beady hawk eyes squinted and a big, airy guffaw puffed up from out of his pink polo shirt. "Just kidding! Of course!"

Junior smiled, wilting at the waist as the weight of the skimmer dragged him over, relaxing more than he should have.

"His type can't swim!" Gubbins reasoned in his own skewed fashion. "Their bones are too heavy—that's a fact!"

Stunned by the tartness of the comment, Junior couldn't even lift his head as Gubbins continued.

The CEO offered a playful pat to his employee's ribcage. "You go ahead and see that gets done, wontcha?"

There was no concession in Junior's voice as he looked up. "We'll get right on it."

Gubbins gave a wink and another tap on his subordinate's back. It reminded Junior of how the CEO patted his wife's dog. When he wasn't kicking it, that is.

The randy exec rocked back on his heels, probably to get one more gander of Casey at the front desk. In everyone's best interest, her small frame was tucked out of sight.

Gubbins turned and headed out the gate that led to the beach. He'd seen just enough of Casey's cleavage to successfully rub one out in the south side alcove less than five minutes later.

Junior let the skimmer smack back into the corner, threw the padlock on the door, and slipped out quickly. As he headed for House-keeping to catch up with Berta, something popped off the brim of his Hawaii cap and plopped into the pool. Distracted, he looked up to see Dorena hanging over the second-floor balcony. Most of her front was stained a pasty green.

"Hey!" she grunted through the battered smoke of her cut-rate cigarette.

Junior could only grin. Even though her huge cleaning gloves went up to her elbows and made her look like the monster from a 50's drive-in movie, she was a hot mess to Junior. Emphasis on hot. "Hey, what?!" he called back.

"I signed up for winter deep cleans," Dorena quipped, "not a fuckin' life sentence up here."

"Sliding scale." Junior's smile got bigger the more he craned his neck. "I don't know what to tell ya! Room's gotta look good—that could be the one you stay in the night of the Christmas party."

"You pay your fifty bucks yet?" Dorena asked, alluding to the 'discount' price all LeisureFace employees needed to pony up for a room of their own so they didn't have to drive home drunk.

"Last week," Junior nodded. "Bargain at twice the price, ain't it?"

"Yeah, almost. My walkie-talkie is dead," Dorena's voice caught the heavy, soaking wind as she heaved a rainy chunk of hair from out of her face. "Can you tell Berta to slip me some more Soft Scrub when she's this way?"

Junior pointed up the path. "Heading there now to grab QC sheets. Be right back."

The Cleaner from the Black Lagoon shouted out her thanks as Junior's feet crunched the shale, making his way past a few guests bound for the hot tub. His soggy steps swirled over the linoleum on his way back through Housekeeping to Berta's office, which was actually just a desk shoved against the farthest wall of the cleaning supply closet.

"Berta?" Junior blurted out before looking up. When he did, his footsteps turned to slush.

Berta was sitting there, picking at some sliced strawberries behind her second pile of morning pills. The left side of her face was wet. "Hey," she called back without making eye contact.

Junior knew tears when he saw them. "What?"

Berta shook her head, trying to keep her face out of sight.

Junior pressed on, "What is it? I could tell there was something wrong as soon as I saw you this morning!" His voice screeched to a halt, trying to walk the line between badgering her or seeming too concerned, both of which he knew would just make her clam up.

Berta's eyes finally swung upward, locking in. "I was cleaning Gubbins' office..."

Neither of them knew whether or not she wanted to continue.

"Yeah, so?" Junior was imperative, almost mocking. It did the trick, though, because Berta's broken words were set into motion.

"We're done. He's selling LeisureFace to StileCorp. They're wiping us clean. Bringing in their entire crew."

Junior's face clamped up around his eyes, which squinted shut under the weight of a cagey type of misunderstanding. It was too much to compute all at once. "StileCorp?"

Berta tried to jog his memory, but her brain was too much of an emotional clusterfuck to hash out the best details. "You know, the ones who owned the Beach Time Resort? Up in Astoria?"

It all got clearer as Junior got angrier. The words, quick and desperate, came to him on the fly. "That fuckin' place folded two months ago! Don't all those people have new jobs by now?"

"Winter on the Oregon coast," Berta's voice raised and whistled, searing into the skin of Junior's ears, "what do you think?"

"Alright, alright." Junior took a couple of steps back. The nape of his neck burned as fate told him to keep his mouth shut for at least a few seconds more. The cramped quarters suddenly seemed unbearable. Against his better judgment, he asked something he just had to know.

"How long we got?"

"Monday, the first of January," Berta calmly said, her forehead rising up from the lace of her joined fingers. The tired, watering eyes paused above a droll set of drawn lips. "Happy new year."

Arithmetic pounded up Junior's temples. "So, pink slips around the 15th?"

Berta surrendered, shrugging at what sounded like a good approximation.

"Well, now we know why the Christmas party's early this year." Junior's foot smashed against one of the shelving units, and a mélange of plastic bottles, steel wool, and paper boxes took their turns shaking loose and bouncing off the linoleum below. One of the casualties was a new bottle of Soft Scrub. Junior shoved it into his back pocket and slumped on a huge stack of laundry tubs that were awaiting the absolution of an acid-wash cycle.

Berta had flinched at the clamor, turning away as her tearing eyes squeezed tight. The phlegm in her throat rasped at each one of her words as they came out.

"Even with COBRA, I'm gonna lose most of what I've saved trying to keep up with my meds." Berta couldn't say any more. Actually, she didn't need to. Her hopelessness was so real.

Junior got to his feet—that bottle of Soft Scrub hurt like a son of a bitch, anyway—and knelt down at Berta's side.

"No. No, it's gonna be okay." Junior's arms slipped around Berta. She seemed so small. He tried to hold her close enough to muffle her cries because, if nothing else, he couldn't bear to hear them. Sure, he could go off and walk into damn near any maintenance position between here and Eugene, but Berta would be screwed six ways from Sunday as soon as she lost any part of her medical coverage. The arithmetic started up again. A lot of guestimated rent figures, expensive propane heating bills, and cold necessities that munch away at your bank account each took their turns pinging a nanosecond at a time in Junior's head. Right now, though, the only thing that took precedence was something of a morbid, trivial curiosity: "So, how much is he selling LeisureFace for?"

Berta broke away and wiped her nose. To Junior, it seemed she regretted not having the answer he was looking for. "Gubbins was coming," she whispered, "I didn't get to see. Junebug, how are we gonna tell everyone?"

It wasn't really a matter of how, but rather when. And though it was tough, Junior and Berta had foisted whispers and hard pauses on their people by quitting time that day, pulling them into dark corners or supply closets to stammer out the sordid details. Appetites were ruined at lunch, tempers flared in vain during smoke breaks, and a lot of 'shits', 'fucks', and even a 'goddammit' or two peppered the air, some of which were caught by the guests, but to hell with it. What did they have to lose? Their jobs?

Each of them took it to heart in a different way.

Ernesto sat for hours on the couch, nursing a Rogue Ale beer and staring at the television, which wasn't even turned on.

Dorena slumped on the patio and huffed cigarette smoke out into the drizzle. She saw this whole thing as yet another hurdle in getting back custody of her kid. Casey stayed inside and pretended to not see the reversed Four of Pentacles when it fell out of her tarot deck for the second time that day.

Stacey-Lynn warmed herself by the pellet stove, hoping what Ernesto told her as she was leaving for the day was alarmist bullshit, and that there could still be a chance someone got their facts wrong.

Fitz wouldn't be home until late. She tried to convince herself that the sooner she told him, the better. She sat and waited. And waited. But she just couldn't bring herself to tell him that night.

Berta pulled out her insurance papers that evening and pressed a lot of rubbed-off buttons on her Texas Instruments solar-powered calculator. The total that kept coming up was pretty much the same, and it was never close to being enough.

And as optimistic as he could be, Junior, the last to leave that evening, sat in the driver's seat of the Firebird entertaining the fantasy of twisting the key, stomping the pedal, and driving away forever. His dad, the omnipresence that had always held him back from everything, good and bad, was right there at the front of his daydream like a human roadblock. As he drove home, he looked a few times into the rear-view mirror to size up the huge hatchback. He wondered just how much stuff he'd really be able to squeeze into it if he ever found the courage to live his own life, and not just the one that had been foisted on him.

Crawling to a stop in between the flaky, painted lines at the side of the townhouse, Junior reached down and slid the needle on the Firebird's transmission up to 'P'. For just a second, he sat there, suddenly tired at the thought of how much effort was going to be burned up looking for another job. The pause wasn't long, though. He decided not to step too deeply into that puddle of self-pity, twisting off the snarl of the five-liter engine. Raindrops pattered down through the forested cul-de-sac's obstacle course of dark trunks and leaves, with only a chosen few destined to slide down the pasty windshield.

As usual, the calm only lasted a heartbeat or three for Junior. A few seconds later is when his dad snuck out onto the patio with an opened can of cat food.

Cyril Aldrich Berrick II, simply known by his surname to everyone lucky enough to have crossed paths with him, adored his home state of Oregon. Why? The raccoons. As a pre-Vietnam kid in the late 1950's, he'd spent far too much time talking to them by the ground-down fir stumps in his backyard. A weird trust formed, and soon they were following him around the neighborhood. Now, as a shell-shocked, certifiably-insane, post-Vietnam adult, he'd spent far too much of his government assistance buying his fuzzy pals the tasty canned cat food they seemed to love. The man was proof positive that, even after you become nuttier than squirrel shit, your hobbies, and your friendships, can still endure.

Berrick needed to be told at least three times not to do something before he considered acquiescing to the request. In reality, his son has already pleaded with him five times in the past month to not waste any more of his scant money feeding the local wildlife. Since Berrick's potholed intellect told him he'd only heard it two of those five times, he continued. Not surprisingly, Berrick never even saw his son's huge Pontiac parked within a dozen feet of him as the bottom of the aluminum can gently scraped the concrete. The slippered feet tiptoed back in through the door, which slowly slid closed again.

Junior pushed out the long red door and heaved it shut again. His license plate—"NUGGETZ"—vibrated loudly for a few seconds as he headed up the walk. He told himself that, at least, the cat food was better than what he dealt with last year...when the electric bill skyrocketed before he could discover the space heater his dad put on the patio to keep his furry friends warm at night.

One of the many diagnoses given to his father over the years was Obsessive-Compulsive Personality Disorder, and Junior could already hear the piano tinkle of the theme to "The Fog" before getting the door unlocked. A happy Berrick had just gotten the movie in the mail the other day, the shipment being an absolute necessity after he'd successfully destroyed two previous copies due to overuse. Well, one was overuse. The other was rendered unplayable after Berrick took it in the bathtub with him, but that's another story for another time.

Junior stepped inside. A catastrophic John Carpenter score and the smell of Fancy Feast Mixed Grill wafted around his entrance.

Berrick didn't look up. Judging by the small mountain of gold tinfoil on the coffee table, he was working on his twentieth chocolate Hanukkah coin. No, the Berrick family had never been anything within spitting distance of Hebrew, but Junior was certain his dad would convert, if necessary, to continue his holiday confection tradition.

"You wanna see fog," Junior twisted his neck to the slider doors, "just look out the window."

Berrick leaned up, beaming, pointing at the screen. "Do you know who that is, son?"

Junior didn't even have to look at the screen. He had answered this question a hundred times before, but never as flat and unenthused as this. "It's Adrienne Barbeau."

"Fifty-one years old! Fifty-one! And she just gave birth to twins!"

"She a very gifted woman, dad."

"Junior—"

"I told you not to call me that."

Berrick steamrolled right over his son's lament. "You're a good boy, so you don't know this, but you know what happens to a woman's snapper by the time she's fifty-one?"

"I really don't wanna know."

"It's like that...that thing! Ah, hell!" Berrick's memory twisted and turned as his sheepskin slippers pounded on the floor for mercy. "That—*whatchamafuckit*!! That thing I got you that we put the lawn sprinkler on!"

"The Slip 'N Slide?"

"That's it!" Berrick cracked his palms together, his enjoyment tumbling his tinfoil pile a little lower on the coffee table. Junior immediately wondered if his dad had eaten anything that day that wasn't kosher-certified chocolate. "Those kids probably shot out of her like those t-shirt guns at the Trailblazers games!" Berrick's knees flew up in the air. "BOOM!"

"Dad!"

Junior flung his Hawaii hat onto the dining room table. His mother had bought it at the Honolulu airport right before they all had come back home from the best vacation he'd ever had. Three weeks later, she was gone...passed away...or whatever euphemism people were using these days to describe that thing we all fear. He suddenly missed her very, very much.

Berrick pivoted, shooting his second imaginary fetus way up into the top tier of the living room bleachers. "BOOM!"

"Dad!!"

"What, boy?!"

Junior dropped his tone, trying to sneak some sense and reason through the back door of this conversation. "You eat anything today? Other than a fortune in pocket change?"

Berrick held up his plastic pot of gold. "Ten dollars! That's all they wanted for these. A hundred for ten dollars! That's a dime apiece!" Berrick was undeniably wacky, or at the very least 'entertaining', but he had a well-greased penchant for numbers. He knew the exact release date and running time of every movie he watched, and could add up all his Yahtzee dice before the damn things could even stop tumbling. "A dime...and they're the size quarters! How do the Jews stay in business? Oh! I made you dinner."

"Oh, yeah?" Junior quipped, discovering at that moment how much of an appetite you can work up learning that you'll soon be unemployed. And there it was on the counter: a plain hoagie roll, propped open with a spoon. Junior closed his eyes for a lazy couple of seconds, wishing it would suddenly have some salami and big sandwich pepperoni in it when he finally lifted his lids again. He turned around and slyly shook the grindless grinder at his father. "You didn't really...make dinner."

"Yes, I did! I mean, I may not be able to fart butterflies, but I can work some magic!"

Junior's fingers dragged down the roll as if he was showing it off during a "Price Is Right" showcase. "There's nothing in it!"

"Well, I opened it for ya!"

Junior was getting nowhere fast, and he was more concerned about his dad's Hebrew riches, anyway. "And I told you I'd pick you up whatever you need on the way home. I don't want you walking down to Circle K anymore."

"I didn't," Berrick swung his attention back to the homicidal fog, "I took a cab."

Circle K was about 150 yards away.

"You took a cab?"

"Ooh, Jamie Lee Curtis!" It wasn't that Berrick was ignoring his son, it's just that there was so much juicy celebrity gossip to share these days. "People Magazine says she might be a man, but I don't care!"

"You took a cab? To the end of the street?"

"Really, I don't care! I'd love to suck her dick."

"You're embarrassing me," Junior's groan was buried under the low aside, "and we're not even out in public."

"Hey," Berrick's hands pushed out in front of him, "It's not like I'm sucking Gwyneth Paltrow's dick or something! I'm not weird. 'Shakespeare in Love'? My rosy butt! 'Shakespeare in Drag' is more like it."

Junior's asides continued. "I'm losing my job and he's taking cabs to the bottom of the hill."

"What?" There was a sharpness to the word that only a protective parent could hone.

Junior wouldn't say anything. He just sat there with his naked hoagie roll and his head down because he couldn't look his father in the eye. That's when Berrick forgot all about the screen in front of him and held out both of his hands to his son. "Come here, son."

"I found out I'm getting fired, dad." There was anger in the young man's tone, balanced with a saucy fear that still kept him away from his father.

"But you haven't done anything wrong." Berrick's empty hands still wanted to touch his son. "I know you haven't."

Junior's nose began to run and the carpet he was staring at began to quiver under the rising damp of his tears.

Seemingly accepting that his son wanted to stay strong in front of him, Berrick let his arms drop. He had a genuine interest in another detail, though. "What about that girl?"

The confusion that ensued behind Junior's gritty hairline was something he was actually thankful for—it distracted him enough to let the tears hide for a little while longer. "What girl?"

"That one you like. Dora, Dana—"

"Dorena."

"That's the one!" Berrick's little epiphany actually made both of them feel better, but only for a second.

Junior succumbed to the notion that, not only was he losing the job that kept the roof over his bed, but he was also losing the reason for getting out of it in the morning. "I don't know, dad."

Junior stood up, and Berrick took it as a good sign. The sound of dusty, rough denim sloshed as Junior walked by and plopped down on the cushion beside his father. At first, the young man thought it was because he needed the moral support of his father, but in reality, it was because it was the only option for him at the moment. Junior knew he wouldn't be able to sleep tonight. He wasn't hungry anymore, and he sure didn't feel like talking about this another second longer.

As Berrick rested his head on his son's dirty bicep and ugly zombie lepers made Jamie Lee Curtis scream better than anyone with a penis ever could, Junior could only think of one quasi-self-help phrase: *It's always darkest just before dawn.*

But he knew it was a hell of a long time until morning.

Eventually, morning did come. Not a bad one, either—sunbeams crept through a curl of lumpy cumulus clouds, haloing that hilly cage of trees east of Highway 101. The site was just promising enough to tickle Gubbins into manhandling his golf bag into the trunk of his Mercedes. By December, almost all the courses were shut for the season, unless you had the kind of money Gubbins did. When you had wealth, your whole life was like summertime.

Irons rattled against woods, and rubber grips thumped in unison. It would have been a hell of a lot easier if he hadn't been doing business at the same time. He felt it best to take a break from the clubs in order to release the cordless phone from searing into his shoulder. Though it seemed StileCorp was holding all the cards at this point, life always seemed to deal swine like Gubbins a pat hand, saving their fat, curly-tailed asses from the meat grinder to live another day.

"Well, that's just what I'm talking about, you know what I mean?" Gubbins' mock civility wasn't the reason to hate him. It was because his scheme was working exactly as he'd planned it. "I'm very considerate of your international board, and that's the kind of thing that I'm looking to present at LeisureFace's annual Christmas, excuse me, holiday party this year."

Gubbins took a breather from being despicable as his StileCorp liaison rambled on, agreeable with his lead as they danced the Corporate Jitterbug. It was a simple two-step—stroke and get stroked back. Usually, no one gets off, but you can rest assured they all get paid.

The CEO looked down over the driveway to his timeshare kingdom while the strokes came faster.

"Yes, we're all very happy to be doing business with you, Mr. Gubbins" segued into *"You seem to have a well-honed sense of our commercial mission here at StileCorp, Mr. Gubbins"* before naturally escalating into something like *"Do excuse me, Mr. Gubbins, I have shit all over my nose and I need to take just a moment of your time to wipe it off."*

The whole conversation easily reiterated the notion that clueless people with too much money are the most dangerous thing in the world.

"And you're very intelligent folks, so I'm sure you can appreciate my intentions of celebrating not just our partnership," Gubbins cooed, watching his Housekeeping and Maintenance minions bound around the property, "but the partnership of all our brothers and sisters on the planet. Hanukkah! Yalda! Christmas!"

His beady eyes slid over to Ernesto's black figure as it shoveled a fresh layer of topsoil and wood chips over the shrubbery roots near Housekeeping. Gubbins' smile shone perfectly, belying what he felt in that bowl of sour grapes he called his heart.

"...even Kwanzaa."

Things down in the main building were even less enjoyable. Did you ever see the aftermath of a 76-year-old woman with a bowel problem who didn't quite make it to the toilet fast enough? Casey had! As she slammed shut the door to room 102, she made a double-pronged silent pact to herself that (A) she'd never go in that room again, and (B) she was quitting, right then and there.

She may never become an actress or be able to make enough coin doing tarot readings, but Casey was absolutely certain she didn't have to take this shit, either. She rolled her fingertips over one another, feeling the grating, sandy sensation from washing, re-washing, and washing again in water hot enough to boil lobsters. All this surely wasn't worth the $7.75 an hour she was getting for the next three weeks until she and everyone else got canned.

Just then, her sister breezed by. Casey could tell by the way she was checking her pockets that Dorena was about to go on a smoke break.

"No go," Casey grimaced. "We're going to have to replace the caulking, too."

"I read that, by 2010, adult diapers will outsell baby diapers," Dorena offered, seemingly out of empathy. After all, she was the one who originally found the mess this morning. "But if they want me to go back in there, they're gonna have to give me a jackhammer and some Everclear first. Break time at the water heaters?"

Casey could see and hear Dorena's lighter rattling anxiously behind her fingers but couldn't look up. Her eyes would've given her away, and she knew her big sister would talk her out of the plan she had in mind. "No," she shook her head, "I gotta go give something to Berta."

Dorena noted the queer little stoicism in her sister's voice. Before she could lock eyes with her, Casey was already heading back to Housekeeping.

"Alright, later." Dorena knitted her brow, but the nicotine jones she was having whitewashed any suspicion she may have had as she rounded the corner. She threw back the door to the water heater room. Junior was inside, and both of them recoiled.

"Sorry," Dorena forcibly decompressed, her face draining from a dark red to a prettier pink. A spry yellow flame rose from her fingers and touched her slightly bent cigarette. "I didn't think anyone would be in here now."

Suddenly, Junior recalled a study on some news show his dad has been watching the other night that said women are more attracted to guys who don't talk much.

"Nah, it's cool." Three syllables—if less is more, Junior thought he was off to a good start. Without another word, he pushed one of the upside-down buckets towards Dorena, who took a seat on it.

Her lip spewed up a thick and sexy wisp that drifted Junior's way as she looked at him a bit cockeyed. "What you doing here so early this morning?"

Junior could only shrug. "Easy to be on time when you don't sleep all night."

Dorena twisted her butt around on the bucket until she wasn't so uncomfortable. "Yeah, I feel ya." The empathy in her voice was unmistakable.

"Everyone's feeling it," Junior nodded, trying to keep his words to a minimum.

"So..." Dorena's pause pushed its way around Junior's ears, "you going to Hawaii to look for a job now?"

Junior shook his head, almost too fast in dismissing the idea. "Nah."

"Why not?" Dorena teased, pushing her innocent eyes up the walls. "How do you say 'unemployed' in Hawaiian?"

Junior smiled. The oppressive thoughts about his dad flew away, and he was able to take pleasure in his own cleverness. "Bro-oh-oke."

Oh man, the laugh. That laugh that came out of Dorena was fucking *bliss*. Junior floated on it for as long as he could, but reality came back to nag him like the bitch that it is.

"You gonna go back to work as a caregiver at Golden Cedars again?" Junior asked.

Dorena shook her head, evasive. "Nah, I can't do that shit anymore. It's just..." She looked out into the bright contrast of the grey coming in from the shoreline. "I can't deal. I know I can't."

"Why not?" Junior didn't ask it to make Dorena feel bad. He had an inquisitive nature about him, even during the odd moments when he wasn't consciously trying to butter up the housekeeper of his dreams.

"I learned a lot at that job. But," Dorena paused, her lips pinching down hard on the filter, "I couldn't handle everyone dying. The empty beds. Boxes of their belongings. The sounds of their families cryin' in the hallways. That smell. All the time, that goddamn smell. It fucks with your head. If you let it." Her last sentence suspended a type of screened self-loathing in front of her eyes.

"Well, I know Berta's really gonna miss you and Casey." Junior tried to be consoling, but wasn't sure whether or not he pulled it off.

Dorena's eyes rolled as grey ash flicked off the cherry of her smoke. "Man, you can't even *talk* to Berta this morning."

Junior agreed. "Yeah, but I pretty much expected that. I don't wanna know what's going through her brain, considering what she's got to contend with."

There was something in the way Junior said it that obviously piqued Dorena's interest. "What?"

Suddenly, Junior's quest for cool got sidelined by a greater need to form a bond with the sultry mouth he wanted to kiss. That thick frame his fingers had waited so damn long to caress. And the fur-soft field of burnt auburn that poured down and curled over her shoulders. The thought that both of them were days away from their respective pink slips pushed Junior to work faster than he was used to, and that's the real reason the secret came out.

"Ever see all those meds she takes?"

Dorena nodded, her eyes fixed on him. "Yeah."

"She's got HIV."

Dorena's dark eyebrows pushed up as she heaved her nicotine cloud to the ceiling. It rose softly and folded around the myriad of pipes. "Mmm-hmm, I know."

"You knew?" The minute creases on Junior's face smoothed away as his eyes went wide for a second.

Dorena bounced her chin up and down. "I recognized a few of the pills one day." She turned and stared Junior straight in the eyes for the first and only time that day. "Used to know someone who had it."

Junior's understanding look awaited Dorena. "Someone?"

"My ex. His name was Mark. He didn't tell me about the affair he'd had until after I'd gotten pregnant with Petey. So, I made a deal with God and promised that if my cement mixer of a uterus somehow delivered our son, I'd leave him as soon as I could get out of the hospital bed."

"You didn't break your promise and piss off the Lord, did ya?" Junior razzed.

A sideways smile came. "No. I didn't have to keep my promise." Then the smile faded away. "Mark died of pneumonia six weeks before Petey was born."

Junior suddenly felt dirty. Not just from Dorena's candid confession, but it was if he'd betrayed Berta's confidence, too. "I'm sorry," Junior issued aloud as penance for everyone involved.

Dorena continued. "Without much of a plan B to fall back on, I ended up with Paco. A few of his small-time busts later, and before you know it—bam!—you don't have custody of your kid anymore. It turns out God only lets you parlay your deals so far."

Speaking of God, he must've been getting bummed out right about here, so he sent Ernesto to bust in and liven things up.

"Aw, dag," the lithe fellow jumped back, "so this is where everyone is!" He twisted his wrist to catch the time before shooting a look to Junior. "F.Y.I., it looks like Gubbins went golfing, but Junebug, you on deck in five, nigga."

Junior glanced at his watch and pushed his back against the wall as he gave a good stretch. "Yep, and I want you to finish that last VCR this morning, too."

"Indubitably, boss!" Ernesto nodded before turning his attention to Dorena. "Hey lady-friend, I thought you'd still be in 102!"

Junior winced. "You mean the Brown Planet?"

Ernesto waved his palms out. "Hey, hey! We classy in this joint, right? We prefer the term 'Senior Stool Sanctuary'."

Dorena piped up, sickened as she looked back to Junior. "I blew out a half-can of deodorizer in there."

"Not the vanilla cream, I hope." Junior's moan was steeped in exasperation.

Dorena was curious, but couldn't help being a little defensive. "Yeah, so what?"

Junior's decade of experience in maintenance was about to explain something Dorena never learned in science class. "You mix those two smells together, the room smells exactly like hot dogs the next time you go in."

The notion was so repugnantly absurd, Dorena naturally let out a simper. "Gross! Well, that caulking around and behind the toilet is gonna need redone because that shit ain't comin' out. Literally."

"Brrr!" Ernesto blurted as a shiver attacked his body, and he slyly tried to move for the door. "Alright, well, I have a VCR to fix—"

Junior let loose a nauseated laugh. "Nice try, cracker! I'll give you a call later so we can knock it out."

"Wait a minute," Dorena overlapped, turning to Junior as she prepared to extinguish her smoke. "Why do you call him 'cracker' and he calls you 'nigga'? With all due politically-correct sensibilities, shouldn't it be the other way around?"

"Yeah, but if we do it our way, we don't end up in HR," Junior reasoned.

Ernesto slapped his white brother five. The cracking echo sprang around the curved metal of the water heaters.

"Meantime, niggas and niggettes..."

"Oh, thanks for including me," Dorena drolly added.

"...I've already been here for two hours bustin' landscaping ass, so I'm breakin'!" Ernesto began to pop-n-lock. Some people wish 1984 could have lasted forever. "Aw yeah, one of y'all motherfuckers get me a refrigerator carton!"

Dorena laughed and threw her crunched, speckly-tan butt at him. "Get outta here!" she barked beneath a serrated series of giggles, and Ernesto's smooth moves slid him out the doorway.

Junior knew he had to get going, but couldn't tear himself away from Dorena just yet. He could run flowcharts, interview her co-workers, and still not have this kind of alone time with her again for weeks, maybe months. Strike while the iron is hot, they say, and he needed to do it now. Dorena was already shuffling through her pockets and twisting on her bucket in preparation to leave.

"So, no plans yet for another gig?"

"Nah." Despite the sadness in her voice, the smile Dorena wore was a valid enough reason to fall in love with her. "If I didn't need the money so bad, I wouldn't even bother till spring. I just wanna get this week over, go to Eugene for the day with Paco, and forget about this." The crinkly pack and lighter slid back out again. Junior figured one cigarette just wasn't going to cut it for Dorena right now, but she seemingly relented and returned them to the snugness of her jacket pocket.

Junior smirked, "Go to Eugene—yeah, right!"

"What?" Dorena was busted and tried to hide her face a bit.

"There's only one reason anyone goes to Eugene!"

Dorena's sideways smile came back. "Yeah, well, never dip into your own stash. It's bad luck, you know what I mean?"

Junior's grin stepped up, trying to match the beauty of the one in front of him. "No, I don't!"

"Good boy," she commended. "Keep it that way."

"You still with Paco?" Junior didn't even know how he said it. It just kind of came up from his heart and out his esophagus, without his permission.

"Mmm-hmm." Out of shame, fatigue, or another such reason, Dorena offered nothing more.

Junior suddenly felt self-conscious and couldn't bring himself to ask for details. He wouldn't have gotten them, anyway, because, just then, someone new crashed their party.

The craggy face and sandy red hair that slid up to the doorway escaped Junior entirely, but Dorena had definitely seen him somewhere before. Probably in Eugene.

"Where's Stacey-Lynn at?" The words were curiously mucous and curt from Fitz's mouth, and the thick wad of tobacco spit he sent into the bushes was the reason why. His approach immediately rubbed Junior the wrong way.

"Well, she's the receptionist, so—"

"Yeah, I'm real aware of that, pencil dick." Fitz's spit rose up around his teeth again, and his beady eyes locked onto Junior. "She's not there. You wanna tell me where she is?"

Since Dorena was sitting there with him, Junior suddenly found his nerve. "Not particularly, no."

Fitz bristled, his feet beginning to slide over the metal threshold of the doorway. He pressed his eyelids down to glare a little deeper into the slight maintenance man, studying Junior's features—the young, defiant brow, the Firebird patch on his jacket, the reserve in his knees as he braced himself against the wall. "It's probably a good idea to rethink that, tough guy."

Just as Junior sat up with wide eyes, Dorena held up her hand. She blew out her smoke as she looked up. Though no one planned for it to go straight into Fitz's face, it was a serendipitous way to drive her point home. "If she's your wife, then you probably know she goes on breaks, right?"

Fitz backed out of the doorway.

"Why don't you just have a seat in the lobby?" reasoned Dorena, her forehead stretching flatly as her eyebrows rose. Fitz hung on the door jamb, pissed, but staid. "Relax," the housekeeper suggested, "she'll be back."

Dorena took another drag off her cigarette, seemingly as a way of shutting her mouth and censoring herself. Junior could see the intolerant flash in her gaze and was starting to feel his heart rate return to normal. At least, that was until Fitz narrowed his eyes once more and shot a look back to him through Dorena's grey nicotine haze.

"Must be nice having your lady do your fighting for ya, eh? Tough guy?" Fitz began to slink away but not before hawking a lung oyster full of chew all over the aluminum siding that flanked the door.

Dorena turned to Junior with a self-effacing smirk. "What can I say? Some people just have bad taste in men."

Whether or not she intended it with a double-meaning was something Junior thought about for days afterward.

Fitz headed back to the lobby, passing room 114, then 113, and then 112, which was the closest to the north side of Reception. Inside, Stacey-Lynn and Ernesto stood face-to-face behind the closed door. They hadn't planned it, but like everything else they did, it was touched by kismet. Stacey-Lynn had just checked out the room's guests and listed it as a forthcoming deep clean. Ernesto, now on break, just happened to stroll by. Now, here they were in the middle of the room's clutter. Lights off. Towels piled into the bathroom sink. A pot full of tepid coffee on the kitchen island. The still-warm iron and its board in the middle of the living room. It was all theirs. A brief, private heaven. But they still bolt-locked the door just in case.

"I don't wanna go on like this," Ernesto professed.

Feeling a swift punch in her heart, Stacey-Lynn mouth's trembled as it served up a single word. "Why?" It was far from an original response, but it was an honest one.

Ernesto's dedication burned into her eyes and his smile grew in degrees. "Because I don't want to have to hide you anymore. My love for you is proud, baby, and it's bright, and it's time everyone saw it. You deserve it all."

The confession allowed Stacey-Lynn's heart to flutter back to life, and all the darkness that flirted with her head cleared away.

"I just realized the only time I'm not afraid is when I'm with you." Stacey-Lynn surprised herself with her own sincerity, but by admitting this, she gave Ernesto a reflection of his own feelings. Ernesto confirmed it, nodding as tears began to run out the corner of his eyes.

What was intended as a short and tender morning connection between the two then somehow grew and shifted. Though each of them knew they didn't have the time for this right now, the world nevertheless spun them into each other's arms. Soon, their footing tilted and they whirled back on to the bed. Thankfully, it was one of the few that that hadn't yet been done up by Housekeeping that morning.

Stacey-Lynn pulled open her wet lips as Ernesto entered her. She squirmed in a tizzy of pained delight as he stretched and pounded her, again and again. The two tore at each other to try and, somehow, be even closer than they already were. Their breaths chipped off in ragged gasps, piling up and tumbling down, and neither could last much longer. The orgasm that broke and gushed over both of them was the stuff of dreams, but Stacey-Lynn's ankles were bent back so far, she smacked herself in the face as she came.

A stone's throw away from the festivities of room 112 was the main parking lot where Casey was planning her quiet escape. She threw her battered lunch bag onto the passenger seat, which cradled the shiny, silk-wrapped deck of tarot cards, as well. She fussed as her hair caught on the feather-trimmed roach clip hanging from her rear-view mirror. This gave Fitz the time to slither up to the young girl without being noticed until the last moment, scaring her half out of her mind.

Casey's fear showed plainly on her face, whittled sharp by a keen annoyance. However, there wasn't a trace of intimidation in her voice as she regained her composure. "What are you doing here?"

"That's what I was about to ask you." Fitz maintained his masculine stance as he smoothed his hand over the sopping hood of Casey's old Toyota. "What? Is this it? Is this what you do for a living?" His tone didn't change. The words hung and bled with a perverse, tantalizing edge—the kind of shit you only hear from drug dealers.

His cackle of laughter came right on time, and Fitz's superiority complex was something any woman could set her watch to. It was there to dig, burrow, and displace. Like a weed. Which, coincidentally, was exactly what he was looking to sell.

Casey began to explain. "To be honest, no. I just—"

"You holding? I am." Fitz's eyes fluttered, but it was his smile that was truly awful. It was a gaping, broken window that allowed his poisoned intent to blow through unfettered. For a knucklebud of pot or a simple teener bag of meth, Casey was sure Fitz would sell his own mother into slavery. Hell, for all she knew, he already had. Maybe that was the reason Stacey-Lynn never mentioned anything about having a mother-in-law.

"Don't need any. Paco and Dorena are already supplying half of this town." Casey rolled her eyes, giving away more than she cared to in regards to how she felt about her sister's part-time career choices.

"And we could be selling it to the other half!" Fitz contested, as if he'd been waiting to say it.

Fitz used to have some of the best shit in town, but lately he'd been resting on his reputation. Casey decided to call him out on it. "The last thing I bought from you was some kind of bullshit San Fran bunk reefer. It was cut with so much oregano, it smelled like a Papa Murphy's pizza."

"That was nothing like this, girl." That's when Fitz's latest special blend came out of his coat. The dude had more herbs and spices than Colonel Sanders, and each new conjuring upped the ante just a little bit more.

Casey had just a bad enough day to begin the bidding. "Ten."

"What??" Fitz's voice cracked like cheap plastic. You could have sworn his indignation was real. "Is this fuckin' coupon day at Safeway? Ten?!"

Casey's hand went for the chrome flap of the Toyota's door handle. "You don't like my offer, sell somewhere else."

Fitz's red sausage fingers pushed the door shut again. "Twenty-five."

Casey started to get scared, but she couldn't show it. "Fifteen."

The salesman's words got slower, more forceful. "This is worth...twenty-five...to you." The sausages started squeezing into their doughy palm. "Understand?"

"Fifteen." Casey wouldn't be broken. She was always at her strongest when her cards weren't in front of her, and, right now, they were about five feet away on the passenger seat. The blue silk looked slick and false out of her peripheral vision. She pulled the exact amount out of the front of her jeans. "Not a penny more for you, Fitz."

A ten and a five were held up in front of Fitz's glower for a mere second or two before being snatched away. The little Ziploc bag smacked off Casey's chest as she caught it.

"You know," Fitz, livid and insulted, bit off his words for a pause, "only stupid bitches would be here cleaning up crap instead of making coin out in the real world with this." He pulled another bag, a much bigger one, out of his pocket to boast his standing. "Take that ten bucks you just saved and go buy yourself some dignity, kid." He started to walk away, but guys like Fitz are never satisfied with merely getting the last word. They just don't know when to stop. That's what makes them salesmen. "And tell Stacey-Lynn to get her ass home right after work!"

Casey sighed slowly and peacefully through her teeth as the door swung wide and she plunked down into the driver's seat. She grated the key into the ignition and turned it, with the sluggish starter refusing to turn over the motor.

"No." Casey half-closed her eyes, shaking her weary skull from side to side. "Not now. Just get me home." She tried it again, and the starter repeated its glub-glub nearly word for dying word.

This is where her resolve finally caved in.

Casey pulled the key from the ignition and reached for the silky deck. Thin fingers slid up and down the thickness of the pile until she felt that familiar tingling; it started at her scalp and melted down her shoulders.

The card she pulled was Temperance.

Thankful, Casey slammed the key into the ignition once more and the motor coughed to life. She let up off the clutch as her hand moved down to wrench the car into reverse.

The Toyota puttered happily up the driveway as Junior popped out under the awning at the front of the main building. He wound his way around the dark, soaking concrete sidewalks, heading into House-keeping. A chorus of dryers sang in monotonous drones as their cousins across the way sloshed around their guts with a series of discordant clanks and clicks.

Berta was at her desk, eating cereal and trying to keep the milk from falling onto the QC sheets she was stacking up for Junior. The small black-and-white TV/radio combo atop the desk clamored for her attention like a little kid. On it, a grizzled cartoon gold prospector and his trusty mule went dancing across the miniature screen. *"New Arizona Munch! Dat tasty oat cereal with 'leven vity-mins 'n' miny-rals—so the only ones who love it more'n kids are da grown-ups!"* the prospector promised.

Another fast-talking pitchman stepped in. *"Now yoooou can be a forty-niner and WIN the reeeeal gold bar inside specially-marked boxes of Ar-i-zona MUNCH!"*

Berta shook the cereal box on her desk. "I'm trying, goddamn it!"

Junior walked in right as the commercial was finishing up. The prospector picked up a butterscotch gold nugget and a chocolate pick-axe, stowed 'em in his saddlebags, 'n' rode off on the dunkey into what would have been a sunset if the screen had any color. Dancing block letters spelled out A-Z...M-U-N-C-H. Berta bobbed her head to the goofy music as it faded back into Bob Barker and his long, phallic microphone.

Understandably, Junior was confused. "What the hell was that?"

"They're giving away a real gold nugget inside one of the boxes!" Berta chewed heartily. "Worth forty-nine grand. People are buying it by the ton, and it's really good, too!"

Junior picked up the box, scrunching his face up as he checked out the pitchman prospector and his mule. "Ass Munch Cereal?"

"Arizona!"

"A! Z! Munch!" Junior pointed right at the letters as he said them. "That's ass munch!" Junior couldn't believe what he was seeing. "Ass Munch Cereal! There's a donkey right on the box!"

"You gonna get your mind out of the gutter and help me eat some of this cereal, or what?"

"They're really selling this to kids?!"

"Technically, their parents, who are the only ones who love it more than kids." Berta was starting to sound like she'd gotten a new job working for the cereal company. "Come on, I got three more boxes last night."

"Nah, nah, that's okay." Junior chuckled as he started paging through some of the QC sheets to the side of the desk. "These ready to rock?"

"Mmm-hmm." Berta swallowed a mouthful of butterscotch and chocolate deliciousness. "I think both those ones on the top have stove burners out."

"Great," Junior frowned, "now if we can just get them off backorder." His tone went low but mischievous. "You do any more cleaning in Gubbins' office lately?"

Berta nodded. "You were right. Supposedly the 15th is black Friday. Or should I say pink Friday?"

"At least Gubbins is giving everyone the Christmas party this Saturday," Junior rationalized with a modicum of sadness. "You wanna go?"

Berta grabbed her cereal bowl and gave a blustery scowl as she rolled back and stood up from her chair. "You kidding? I'm not giving that bastard the satisfaction."

Junior had an idea that he didn't make immediately clear. "Wait a minute. Think about it."

"I can't go there and act happy and pretend I don't know what I do!" Berta protested loudly. She put down her cereal just long enough to hoist a load of warm, crinkly sheets from the dryer. "As much as I hate to admit it, I'm just not that good of a sport, okay?"

"Exactly." The soft smile that floated to the surface of Junior's lips was telling, giving Berta a perfect snapshot of what he had in mind. "Let's be brats about this."

"No, no, no," Berta folded, stacking the big square sheets for Dorena's next pass by the laundry room.

"Come on! Vengeance is a beautiful thing!" Junior was getting animated and strangely vindictive, especially for a guy who, due to his youth and experience, would probably be first to find a new job.

"Junebug, look, when you get to be my age, you'll find that the best revenge is living well. I can't do that if I piss away this job reference."

"Oh, that's bullshit," Junior dismissed. "Like anyone's gonna call Gubbins for a reference."

"You don't know that!"

"The same Mexicans sharing social security numbers at housekeeping jobs up and down the coast have been doing it for years without incident." His emotions started to show, and Junior's voice got belittling as a result. "You think anyone's gonna care enough to check on you?"

Berta's face sank, hurt, as Junior bit his tongue a sentence too late.

"I'm sorry. I'm sorry, you know I didn't mean that the way it sounded." Junior reached out to hug Berta. Thankfully, she accepted.

"I know you didn't." Berta slipped away and responsibly moved the sheets to their proper spot on the edge of the folding table, closest to the door. She picked up her cereal bowl and headed to the supply closet for more detergent. "It's just I'm behind the eight ball, not only because of my health, but because of my age. As long as I have Casey and Dorena, I'll be able to get done what I need to finish. Then I can get the hell out of here looking good enough to give me a fighting chance to find something new."

And that's when fate shit all over Berta Mancari.

The supply closet door swung back, revealing a handwritten note stuck crudely to the door by our well-traveled toilet plunger. A ring of keys rocked daintily back and forth on its handle.

I know you got a lot to lose, but I don't.
I'm sorry.
I'll miss you.
- CASEY

Berta closed her eyes for longer than a blink. It was as if she was taking the fleeting few extra seconds to try to figure out what she was going to do next.

"Berta, this is our only chance. Our last time all together," Junior intoned. "Let's have some fun, man. Go out with a bang."

Berta's eyes opened. She gave an almost imperceptible nod of her head. "Let's do it."

The puckered plunger made a squeaky *pop!* as it fell off the door, clunking to the floor below. Casey's keys skidded across the linoleum.

ACT UP

[FOR THE WANT OF NARCOTICS & GROCERIES, AND WHERE TO BUY THE BOTH OF THEM]

Down on the ground level of the A building, the front door to one of the rooms stood open. Unbearably crisp winds blew in, rattling the window blinds, local restaurant menus, and even the free kite LeisureFace issued to each of its guest rooms. These distractions were all but ignored by Ernesto, who was working up a sweat trying to reason with the locked-up capstan of a VCR. He was coming dangerously close to losing his cool, but the mechanical beastie let loose the tip of his flat-head screwdriver just in time. The machine offered a mechanical raspberry as its heads slid into their default position, the whirring automation scaring Ernesto for a second.

"Hey! Now, I know you don't wanna start no shit!"

He was too preoccupied with the satanic video player to see Gubbins, fresh back from golfing, strolling by the open door. A quizzical look crawled up the CEO's face as Ernesto wrested with the capstan for one last time.

"NO! You dirty, made-in-China motherfucker!"

The VCR bounced off the bottom of the kitchen trash can just as Gubbins walked in the door. Ernesto turned around and ratcheted down his temper on demand, kicking the thin, snaking electrical cord out of sight.

"Hey, Mr. Gubbins. How were the links today?"

"Fine, young man, fine!" Gubbins' ugly-ass, patent leather golf shoes slid over the carpet. Ernesto could hear the static tickling the expensive, tan leather soles as he got closer. "How are things in Maintenance this week?"

"Busy," Ernesto nodded, as the bullshit got hip-deep. "Busy. Some deep cleans are going on. We're working with the Housekeeping ladies on that one. Usual maintenance QC keeps us out of trouble, of course."

Ernesto paused, wearing his best salesman smile. Unfortunately, by now, Gubbins was peering around his tall form to give the exorcised VCR his full attention.

"And, as you can see," Ernesto patly concluded, "I've been doing some work with the guest suite electronics. You don't want that kind of thing to get a foothold."

"No, of course not." Gubbins' finger tapped in the direction of the trash can. "You think we might be able to—how should I say it?—'cannibalize' the parts from this poor fellow here to keep costs down and wages up?"

Ernesto's voice cracked. "Cannibalize? Naw, naw, you see, this is an old model."

"Old model?"

"That's right. Plastic parts—all of it! Totally incompatible with the newer, much more durable models." Ernesto was already trying to think three steps ahead of Gubbins. And himself.

"Well," Gubbins rationalized, "don't we have existing older players that might be helped by these parts in the garbage?"

"The possibility is minuscule," Ernesto effectively scoffed with an elite air. "We've nearly finished with upgrades, and keeping these bulky systems around will take up a needlessly large footprint in our facilities."

Gubbins scowled. A short, piercing scowl that can only be done by people who know they're untouchable. Those holier-than-thou pricks with their nose in the air, sniffing at everyone else because their shit don't stink and never will.

But, then it happened.

The scowl dried up, and all of Gubbins' middle-aged lines went away for a glorious moment as he laughed. To Ernesto, it was a scary laugh. Not because it was 'evil scientist' bad, or 'meat clever massacre' bad, but because it was convincing, and very, very good.

"I like you!" Gubbins confided, his grin placed perfectly.

Something in Ernesto's brain told him to smile back. It probably came from the part that helped him pay his bills. "That's awfully kind of you to say!"

"A fellow like you is someone I enjoy working with."

Ernesto would have punched the bigoted fuck had he not been so surprised at what he was hearing. "Really?" he asked, now totally confused.

"You bet, boy." Gubbins' schmoozing continued, "You know, I've had a bunch of people coming up and asking how we keep the rhodies so purple and the hydrangeas so blue around here."

"Yeah! And all that blackberry shit out of it, too!" Ernesto proudly exclaimed, freezing his smile in place to try and cover up what just came out of his mouth. Gubbins' expression didn't change, so he figured he was in the clear.

"Precisely. LeisureFace—that first word—leisure! This is the place where even the workers can go home, turn off the ringer on the phone, loosen their belt, and get comfortable in their off hours!"

"That so?" There was a touch of challenge in Ernesto's voice, but it didn't bother anyone.

Gubbins nodded. "It's that kind of life and work balance that makes LeisureFace a step above in the industry! To our workers, and, more importantly, to its owners who come from all over to visit us. That's why our annual holiday party is going to be especially important this year." He turned and looked right in Ernesto's chocolate eyes. "And you can be a big part of it."

When he considered all the rumors flying around the past week, Ernesto had no idea what to expect at this point. "Me?"

Gubbins went to the window and looked out over the Pacific. It growled and fidgeted but was surprisingly blue for early December. Majestic whitecaps kept getting prematurely shorn off as they headed for the shore. "Just look at that! People from all over the state—the world!—come to see our little piece of heaven."

Ernesto swaggered over closer to the window, belying the mixture of distrust and subservience he felt. There was no denying the five-star view, though.

"Yeah. They do, Mr. Gubbins."

Though it should have been a prideful statement, Ernesto's voice was laced-up at its end by defeat. These days, the pain in his gut called 'doubt' was keeping him from believing anything.

Gubbins kept his eyes on the sea. "You know about the StileCorp take-over, don't you?"

Ernesto was smooth. And cool. But he was too honest of a guy to act. "Yeah."

"They aren't our kind of people," Gubbins vowed. "People like you and me, we overcome, but them... They want everything handed to them. Employees are just money to them."

Ernesto thought it was a strange thing to hear from a CEO. He tried to keep his discomfort under the radar for at least another few seconds, praying to be enlightened with some load of tripe that would, somehow, get him off the hook.

"I'm gonna fight them." Gubbins' hands balled up. "Show them that my staff is heads and shoulders above any crew they could bring in here." He was either being very noble, or the smarmiest, most hypo-critical turd ever shat out of the hospitality sector. "And you can help me do it!"

The ebony head tilted a bit, the eyes filling with equal parts suspicion and patience. "I can?"

"If we can show them what we're made of, they could keep the status quo! You. Berta. Junior. Even that little housekeeper we have, Casey!" Right after saying her name, a gleam came up in Gubbins' eye, but since Ernesto wasn't a mind-reader, he was spared the reason for it. "At the holiday party, we need to show them our solidarity. Our diversity! I've got an idea that might help all of us, and especially your wallet."

The needle on Ernesto's bullshit meter was jumping all over the place. He didn't trust Gubbins or even like him, but the reality was that the jobs weren't going to open up until Easter. That was another four long months away. The notion kept tapping the back of his brain like a ball-peen hammer. It was the pacifier that made him ask the question that followed.

"What you have in mind?"

"For you to do an authentic African presentation. You sing right?"

"A little." Ernesto wondered how Gubbins knew. Or if he just guessed. Correctly.

"Spirituals? It's the essence of where you're from!"

"I'm from Myrtle Beach, man."

"No, no—Africa! We all should be proud of where we're from, and this month is Kwanzaa! It's the perfect time for it." Quick in his step, Gubbins' optimism brightened more and more as his deal continued. A convincing, heady tone rose immediately in his voice. "And if you step up for our team, there just might be a little something extra in your paycheck next week!"

A wink and a nod—the suitable capper to a deal proffered by a rich man. One who got rich by pulling off this kind of thing countless times before. But do you know how difficult it is to say 'no' to a rich man's deal? If you make $8.25 an hour, you would.

Up in the Maintenance area, Junior was wiped out. As he watched Berta's car sloppily splash through the puddles of the parking lot, his fingers began to brush down over the light switches. Shadows quickly sprang up around him, signaling the end of another long day. It was already ten after six, and there still wasn't any sign of Ernesto. Weird. The guy was a tireless beast when he was on the clock, unaffected by downpours or 95 mile-per-hour gusts, but Ernesto's car was always the first one heading north on 101 when quitting time rolled around.

More grimy, orange glows from the overhead incandescent lights bedded down for the night before Junior hooked up his walkie-talkie to the charging station. Ernesto didn't have keys to lock up, so Junior was stuck here until he got back. He figured he might as well throw a couple of his tools into the hatch of the Firebird as he waited.

For some reason, Nuggetz was sitting lower on one side. Junior's features squished up into a ball as he narrowed his eyes on the rear passenger tire. It had a clean slash, about two inches long, through the R of 'GOODYEAR'. It only took a few seconds before he correctly deduced his sidewall's assailant.

That's when Ernesto shuffled up. He was holding one of those crinkly, see-through garment bags, like the kind you get from the dry cleaner. This may have been the reason for his delay, so Junior was more confused than ever.

"Where you been, cracker?" Junior asked. "It's almost a quarter-after." He could vaguely make out the clothing through the plastic—ostentatious gold and coral feathers, and a repeating series of green, black, and rust schemes on what looked like a thin cotton robe.

"You ain't gonna believe this shit."

"Probably not," Junior nodded, now more concerned about Ernesto than the question of how he was going to get home. "You got everything you need before I lock up?"

Ernesto pushed up his eyebrows. "We'll see." He pushed his chin in the direction of Nuggetz's flaccid rear tire. "What's this about?"

"I'm willing to bet good money it's Fitz."

Ernesto's voice went up an octave. "Stacey-Lynn's husband?" He played it cool just in time to bring his pulse back down to normal again and not tip his hand to Junior. "Oh. I hear he's a stone-cold douche nozzle. You piss him off or what?"

Junior shook his head, looking out at the surf. "How'd he know which car was mine?"

"That." Ernesto struck a finger out to the Firebird patch on Junior's jacket. A groan piped up at the easy answer. "You got a spare?"

"It's at home," Junior sheepishly admitted. "Fixed a dent on the donut rim. Hadn't put it back in yet."

Ernesto's keys jingled as he opened the door to his Saturn, which was parked a few spots away from Nuggetz. "Then go lock up and jump in. Let's get the hell out of here."

To Junior, it certainly looked as if Ernesto had a lot on his mind. He wasn't the only one.

The knife Fitz used to slice Junior's sidewall was now flicking seeds out of his stash. They skidded across the dining room table, in amongst Zig-Zag papers, crumpled baggies, and a worn-out grinder. Northwest Cable News was blabbing in the background about more winter rains and an increased chance of flooding in the usual places. The sound of the electric can opener whirred, and the smell of frying hamburger was starting to get overpowering, turning Fitz's stomach as his patience wore thin.

"Turn that shit down, please," he barked, "I'm working here!" With a spasm of nervous energy, Fitz sucked the slurry of tobacco spit between his clenched teeth.

Stacey-Lynn sighed. She'd gone through this nearly every single night around dinner time, which is the reason she kept the remote close to the stove. The channel jumped to another, slightly quieter station as her flipper danced ground beef around the rim of the pan.

Fitz turned around, his face locked up in a peculiar grin. "Hey, honey."

Stacey-Lynn either ignored him or couldn't hear him over the happy poppin' and snappin' of the pan. The marking pen Fitz used on his Ziplocs flew past her and rattled off the flour canister on the counter. She turned around with a glower.

"What is it?"

His wife's attitude surprisingly made no dent in Fitz's weird smile. "Baby, go get me one of your cunt sticks."

"Fitz!"

"Come on!" The smile was falling from Fitz's lips, and his voice was tightening by the syllable, the anger rising again. "I got my hands full here. You want me to make extra-special money? You gotta have an extra-special product." Anticipating the next step in his handiwork, Fitz pulled open his lower lip and tipped his chaw into the trash.

The flipper slid into the frying pan as Stacey-Lynn grabbed her purse. She rummaged through it quickly, plucking out a single tampon and throwing it carelessly to her irate husband. His fingers smoothed it out lovingly as he checked for damage.

"Swear to fucking God, if you broke the paper..." Fitz muttered hotly, but, upon a closer inspection, everything looked fine. The sharp tip of his knife cut through the end of the tampon paper, and his fingers quickly got to work. "Ya know, I've been busting my nuts for years to build us up to this point. Everyone else in town? That fuck, Paco?" Fitz's fingers continued to press, roll, and repeat. "Gonna sprinkle this soggy, wetback shit he's pushing with some high octane and sell it right back to him and his bitch!" Fitz cackled, unable to catch his breath. "Nobody has anything this good."

Stacey-Lynn found it easier to go against her husband's grain when she wasn't looking right at him. "I work with that bitch. She has a name, you know. Dorena. She's actually very nice, and so is her little sister." Her defiance died out as she braced for Fitz's next wave of anger, but it didn't come. He was too engrossed in his work.

"Nobody," Fitz repeated, entranced by the details he was getting just right. His tongue slithered out to wet the paper a bit more. He turned back with his finished achievement sticking from between his knuckles—a single joint with the word "TAMPAX" perfectly centered down the middle of it. "Nobody."

Stacey-Lynn barely saw it as she removed three crammed buns from the toaster oven. "That's great, baby."

"Fucking equidistant—look at that lettering! Best one all month."

Plates crowding Stacey-Lynn's hands threatened Fitz's working space. "Yeah? Well, we need this place to eat, so please—"

"No, no, no, no!" Fitz squealed, his eyes nearly bulging out of his head. "We've got at least two people waiting on this, don't touch a god-damn thing!"

The plates clattered down loudly on the tiles of the countertop. "Fine, you can eat at the coffee table." The dinnerware finished chattering, and Stacey-Lynn found just enough courage to fill the space with her own request. "Maybe your latest stash of tampon magic will give us enough money to actually go somewhere for a change. It took me two years to save for that camera, Fitz, and it hasn't been out of the house once yet!"

Fitz wasn't listening. He could swear he smelled Manwich. "Aww shit, Stay, not sloppy joes again!"

"Yes!" Stacey-Lynn's eyes didn't fill with the tears of aggravation, but fear. She knew the dam was about to break, and to hold it for any longer could mean she may never again get her head above water.

"You cooked the same thing two nights ago!" Fitz's face was turning a passionate pink as spittle gathered at the middle of his lower lip.

"Just eat it."

"The fuck is this shit?" Fitz griped, his elbow on his knee.

"Well, it may be all we have for a while!" Stacey-Lynn screamed, spinning round to stare daggers straight at her husband.

Fitz furled his expression so tight, he could barely see her. "What the hell's that mean?"

Sloppy joes, with golden brown, perfectly toasted buns, were placed neatly on both plates. Two for Fitz, one for Stacey-Lynn. "Just eat. Please." She moved each plate in front of their respective chairs. The plea fell on deaf ears as Fitz knocked his plate out of the way and pointed a finger straight at Stacey-Lynn's nose.

"Answer. My. Question."

She couldn't control it anymore. Fate sent the tears down. She could feel her mouth opening, even though she didn't want it to. The words formed.

"There's a take-over bid for LeisureFace," Stacey-Lynn cried. "A company up in Astoria wants to replace all our staff at the beginning of the year." She blew her nose into her napkin. "I guess Berta saw the details on Gubbins' desk last week."

"You've known? You've known for days and you didn't tell me?" It was like clockwork. Fitz's abusive personality immediately shifted to blame the victim. That way, it was always easy to gain the upper hand.

"I'm..." This is where fate's words dried up. Stacey-Lynn bowed her head and sobbed. She wanted to apologize but didn't really know what for. She thought she might have been brave enough to say, "It's not my fault," as she cried but wasn't entirely sure. Her heart hurt, and she wished Ernesto was here to help. The thought of not having him in her life as much, possibly at all, was more than her brain could calculate right now, especially in the wake of the wrath Fitz was brewing up across the small table.

"Do you know what this is going to do to us?" Fitz queried, with only his wife's slowing tears coming as an answer. "You have a ninth-grade motherfucking education. You know how lucky you are to have this job? To have me? You ARE smart enough to know that?"

Even sensing the danger all around her, Stacey-Lynn couldn't bring herself to agree. Her perceptions all abandoned her, and she was left to struggle with commanding even the smallest retort. But it was somewhere there inside of her. Growing.

"Tomorrow," Fitz continued, "you're gonna go down to the employment department and—"

Stacey-Lynn's windpipe shivered as she spoke. "I've already looked on the WorkSource Oregon website and there isn't much right now."

Without a hint of consideration, Fitz steamrolled over his wife's intent before she could put the period at the end of her sentence. "You are going to go down to the employment department and find something new. Tonight, you're going to give me your house keys. When you find another job, and you can pay your half of the mortgage, you can have them back again."

Stacey-Lynn couldn't believe what she was hearing. Something was making her shake her head, making her rebel. "You can't do that."

"I can," Fitz nodded, totally secure in his power. "If it weren't for the fact that you opened up your legs on our first date...you'd be in the gutter right now."

"I'm not giving you anything," Stacey-Lynn pledged. "This is half my house, too."

Fitz demanded, "And when you get a job again, you can get your half back."

Stacey-Lynn bolted out of her seat. "Then I guess half of this is your fault!" Sloppy joe flew off the table, spattering the white of the refrigerator. "And this is half of your mess!" Buns bounced and rolled as the sturdy plates hit the floor and gave a sickly, hollow rolling sound as they came to a rest on the linoleum. "And in a few weeks when I don't have a job, I'll have a LOT of extra time to clean up my half—!"

Fitz's arm shot like a cannon to bury in Stacey-Lynn's thick, sandy hair. Her knees buckled as the wrist locked and pushed her toward the garbage can.

"Take it. Take it. Take it. Take it. Take it. Take it. Take it." Eyes closed, Fitz repeated the words. Even after his pained wife had taken hold of the trashcan. After she'd hastily grabbed a dishtowel to sop up the smears of peppered tomato sauce that dotted the kitchen. The phrase and the grip continued, over and over. It wasn't until Stacey-Lynn had done a satisfactory enough job that Fitz's fingers were allowed to slide away from the roots at her scalp.

She knew Fitz was never more irrational than when his speech was collected and even, and that's the exact tone that came from behind her.

"Now, I know where you keep your keys, so I'm going to go get them." The lack of malice in his voice belied what clunked along in Fitz's simian brain, making him even scarier than when he was out of control. "Until then, you go ahead and put another three buns in the toaster oven and try a little harder this time."

There was a part of Stacey-Lynn that wanted to block her husband's stroll to the heart-shaped key holder by the front door. Ultimately, she figured it was a much wiser decision to stay where she was, at least for the moment. Drying sauce cracked over the back of her hands, and the failing strength in her fingers, little by little, helped her shift her weight.

When she finally got to her feet, the open package of hamburger buns was there on the counter waiting for her.

Hamburger buns were what Casey was picking up at the Safeway across town at that exact same time. Her eyes made a quick pass across the ingredients before she realized she was too young to be worrying about things like that. She held them up to Dorena, who was down the aisle debating Planters Cheez Balls. Her big sister nodded, so the package flew into the cart. Since snack food companies have the bad habit of filling half their bags with air, the buns landed in a soft pillow of Doritos.

"Can't believe you're ditching me for your boyfriend," Casey lamented. Her mock doldrums were just pathetic enough to make Dorena lean back and give the latest in a series of guilty groans.

"I'm sorry. Alright? I never thought Paco would want to go to an office Christmas party, but once he heard we can barbecue, he was all in."

"He's just going in hopes of making a score off one of your co-workers," Casey tossed off, her jealous feelings surprising her.

Unable to refute her sister's assumption, Dorena seemingly backtracked on the conversation. "And those were potato buns, weren't they?"

"Yeah, yeah."

"I can't believe you're flippin' me this much shit about it." Dorena always found her little sister's separation anxiety both flattering and a nuisance. She prodded the cart farther down the aisle. "Why do you wanna go? You're not even an employee anymore."

"I know. It's just... I've been feeling bad for leaving Berta like that."

Casey studied her sister's body language now. In all honesty, the remark seemed to intrigue her a bit. There was a kernel of maturity sprouting up through the soil of Casey's personality, and Dorena seemed to embrace the change with a welcome relief. "Well, it's cool. I talked to her and we're making it happen without you. I mean, it's gonna be light until Christmas and New Year's, anyway."

"Still," Casey contested. She couldn't find the words to explain herself any further, but she wasn't going to be given the chance, anyway.

Cles Gubbins and his goddamned mint-green golf pants rounded the Safeway Customer Service counter and locked an eye on each of the sisters. He cut through a closed express check-out stand to greet them.

"Casey. Dorena. It's good to see you, girls!" He may have addressed them both, but Gubbins barely took his eyes off of Casey, who was too uncomfortable to notice. "How are you doing this evening?"

"Very well, Mr. Gubbins," a sly Dorena acknowledged, with her typical quiet cool firmly intact. "Thanks for asking."

"Casey, we sure miss you at LeisureFace." Gubbins was getting better and better at his game these days. "I never got to say goodbye."

"Beg your pardon," Dorena interrupted, "but I'm going to snag a place in line. I'll let you two catch up."

Casey swore she saw Dorena grin as she pushed the cart past an end-cap of Mentos. She headed toward the closer of two open check-outs, presumably so that she could see and hear everything that happened. And to gloat, of course.

"Oh, that's no problem. See you soon, Dorena." Gubbins turned back to his captive audience of one, trying not to make too much eye contact with Casey's enchanting, gorgeous, captivating, watery-blue irises that looked as if they rose from the sun-drenched sea itself. As Gubbins continued in earnest, he tried not to trip over his tongue. "What was your reason for leaving us? Have you thought about coming back?"

"Not without being dragged and handcuffed," Casey muttered, realizing a second too late the sexual connotation of her flippant remark. Her gaze darted up to see the grandfatherly expression inches in front of her melt and run with adoration.

"Oh!" Gubbins exclaimed. It was all his dry mouth could muster as his pulse battered away in his ears.

The back of Casey's hand fluttered around in front of her face as if to try and clear the careless air she'd just contributed. "I mean, it...it was just time. Don't worry, though, I have a few other things that are looking like they might pan out soon."

Convinced she had saved face, Casey soon found herself trying to keep her pretty blue eyes from popping out of her head. Dorena had grabbed a magazine from above the impulse-buy section overflowing with candy bars and Tic-Tacs. An Allure cover story trumpeted, *"Age Is Just a Number! – Dating an Older Man"*. Dorena did a silent 'ooh' and 'ahh' as she leafed through the pages. Meanwhile, her tortured little sister was too busy nodding her head and trying to remember Gubbins' topic. It turns out, Casey shouldn't have smiled as widely as she did. It only made things worse for her.

"I'm glad to hear that, Casey," Gubbins commended, but it was clear he was crushed. You can't keep a good scam down, though, and he perked right back up to continue his cockeyed flattery. "Everyone liked you so much, I was hoping we could try to find you some other position sometime."

The praise bolstered Casey's strength a bit. It was just enough to allow her to finally look at her sister again, who was performing mock fellatio on a tube of Rolo candy, her eyes rolled back in ecstasy.

"Oh." Casey's train was close to jumping the track. "Oh, that's sweet of you to say, thanks."

"Are you coming with Dorena to LeisureFace's big holiday bash this year?"

Gubbins turned around to motion to Dorena, who slammed the candy bar back into place, getting herself together just in time to sling-shot back an innocent smile to both of them. Casey took advantage of the split second to push up her middle finger for Dorena to see before Gubbins could turn back. She was positive she saw the cashier smile.

Casey shook her head. "Nah, I think she's bringing her boyfriend this year."

The more embarrassed Casey got, the more Gubbins thought of her, and he was about to prove it. "Well, that's okay. Umm..." He meant to stumble on purpose, for effect, but it turned out to be genuine as his heart went jogging up his windpipe. "You could come with me."

Casey did everything in her power not to duplicate the immediate, slack-jawed expression that cannonballed its way onto Dorena's face.

She looked away for just a second to shake the shrapnel from Gubbins' bombshell out of her brain.

"Oh, you don't have to do that," Casey cooed, trying to keep from looking straight at Dorena. Her big sister jumped up and down in ways unseen since long before her child-rearing days. There she was at the check stand, nodding her head maddeningly fast, and egging Casey on to take the bait, all in the name of fun. She knew Dorena had a vengeance streak a mile wide, and it couldn't have been more obvious than right now.

Gubbins' intentions shifted into reverse, if only to gain more traction. "I didn't mean to impose! It's just..." His voice quavered ever so slightly, perfectly hitting its mark.

"It's okay," Casey's plaintive, supportive voice remarked with a shade of pity. By now, Dorena was out of control, flailing wildly on a bender of middle fingers, choking gestures, and sodomy pantomimes.

"I'm sorry," Gubbins continued with the lilt of regret in his voice, "it's just that my wife will be out of town this year for our party. I don't have anyone to invite, and I figured since you were a member of our team most of the entire year, it would be the right thing to do."

"Oh." Casey stopped, forgetting all about her sister and opting to absorb the compliment. She couldn't tell if she was caving to her sister's well-honed sense of revenge, or because of the gratitude that was being pushed her way. It couldn't be that bad. Could it? "That's really nice of you to offer. When is it again?"

"This Saturday, the ninth, at seven o'clock." Gubbins' nerves started to fray, and the rest of the party's details eluded him for the time being. "No funny business. You don't have to if it'd be uncomfortable for you."

Casey was looking down and, therefore, couldn't see Gubbins brace for the hit, privately cursing himself for offering the succulent young thing a last-second escape after nearly having her in his clutch. She stole a glance over to Dorena for support, but she was busy handing a small stack of raggedy coupons to the cashier. Without any sibling guidance or persuasion, Casey Morris was free to make up her own mind.

"Okay, yeah. That's fine."

"Do you need a ride?" Gubbins winced, just slightly. The head of his dick started to balloon up, pressing against his mint-green zipper. Thankfully, the object of his affection kept eye contact for the rest of the conversation.

"What?" Casey queried. The double entendres were now too many to count. Then again, maybe Gubbins was just being nice.

"Do you want me to pick you up?"

That offer didn't sound any better to Casey's ears, but at least it didn't come off as crude as his first attempt. She shook her head as an offbeat smile hopped across her lips. "No, I'll just get a lift with Dorena."

Gubbins' feet slid, starting his gait a little too fast. "Great! I'll see you Saturday then."

"See you then, Mr. Gubbins."

Gubbins intended to add to just call him 'Cles' but didn't have the time. Less than 45 seconds later, he was jerking out his load in the men's room. Hell, he undid his belt so fast, it swung and made a dent in the stainless-steel toilet paper holder. It's still there today—second stall on the left.

With a cartful of bagged-up groceries, Dorena waited at the foot of the checkout with the biggest shit-eating grin in history. Casey finally exhaled, shaking her head. Her feet tiredly scuffed the floor as if her last three minutes with Gubbins had totally spent her.

Dorena's grin refused to budge. "That was...*so sweet!*"

"Oh please," the younger sister protested.

"You blind? He totally likes you," Dorena suggested with a quick mix of authority and irritation as she dug around inside her coat, grappling for her lighter. "I haven't seen drool like that since Homer Simpson. Oh man, this is gonna be so cool."

"What do you have in mind?" Casey's voice was shrill and angry. "I mean, he's got bucks, he's got the jobs, and he probably could blackball both of us for fifty miles up and down the coast! What's the worst we can do to this guy?"

"Guys like him? It's either hit 'em in the wallet or the ego," Dorena rattled off with aplomb. "It's simple."

"How simple?" Casey challenged.

Dorena lit up her cigarette just before the automatic doors breezed open. "Let me explain..."

Something told Ernesto this day would be coming, so it was no surprise when a six-pack of beers was broken out of the trunk of his Saturn. He and Junior were already four deep, and so they saw no harm in polishing off the set.

For the most part, the mesh of the lawn chairs kept dry due to the overhang of the townhouse roof. However, each joint of the tubular aluminum was dotted with a rusty bolt, and every one of them threatened to squeak when you so much as breathed.

"How the hell'd I get myself into this?" The question Ernesto asked was more to himself than Junior. "Tell me."

"Then don't do it." Junior's retort sounded defensive, but it wasn't meant to. Truth be told, he was enjoying trying to help out his best friend. Inside, his dad was behaving himself, at least for the moment, so that made life even better. Junior could tell by the music cues, though, that the latest showing of "The Fog" was almost over. "Screw Gubbins. I don't get why you just don't take off. Now's your chance. There's nothing here."

"No, man. Not yet," Ernesto argued flatly.

Junior noticed that the lei slung around his weather-resistant outdoor Buddha statue was sopping wet from the recent showers. The polyester flowers had turned into colorful blobs, pasted flat to the happy deity's resin chest. "Let's face it, your mother isn't getting any younger."

"I hear ya."

"You told her last year you were coming back and you didn't," Junior reproached as he draped the lei around his own neck, fluffing up its synthetic petals with a few flicks of his fingers.

"I know. I'm just not ready yet."

"Cracker, you don't even really like it here. I'd miss you, but there's nothing for you—"

Ernesto broke and sputtered like an ashy volcano. "Not yet, alright?!"

He was immediately regretful for the outburst, taking his final swig of suds for the night and depositing the empty back in the cardboard six-pack holder. "Sorry, man. It's just tough right now."

"What is it?" Junior was soft but insistent. "Really?"

Junior could see a cloak of doubt wrap itself around Ernesto. His buddy shifted in his seat for more than a second or two, feeling the squeezing weight only a crisis of conscience could put on you.

"Stacey-Lynn."

Junior about fell out of his chair. "Excuse me?"

Ernesto dropped his head, pushing his fingers over his chilly ears. "Nigga, you heard what I said."

"How long?" Junior felt he was overstepping his boundaries, but his curiosity just couldn't do without the details.

"Six months." Ernesto's eyes were moist with pride and sentimentality. "Six months last week. We hooked up at the Memorial Day picnic."

A troublesome tone latched onto Junior's interrogation. "Fitz doesn't know anything?"

"This point, I don't give a fuck if he does. He doesn't deserve her. I do." Bitterness tore at the edges of Ernesto's pledge. "But, if I don't come up with some cash and a plan for our future soon...," he trailed off, the lump in his throat competing for air, "I know I'll lose her."

Junior's mind was a blur, but he tried to remain focused enough to be supportive. "You don't know that."

"Yeah, and I don't wanna risk it, either."

Just then, Berrick slid back the patio door, poking his head out. "Did you find your donut?"

Junior reached behind him, pulling out a temporary tire on a shining and nicely reconditioned 15-inch wheel. "Sure did, dad."

Berrick turned to Ernesto, who was still slumped over in his chair. "Look at that! Now, that's a nice rim job, isn't it?"

"Dad, it's just a rim. Rims! Not a rim job."

This was probably the only thing in the world that could have made Ernesto start to laugh, and a heavy, slow chuckle fell out of the corners of his mouth.

"You staying here tonight?" Berrick asked Ernesto.

"Nah. Thanks, Berrick, but I'm gonna get going in a few minutes. Me and Junebug got work tomorrow."

"Come on! Let's watch a movie," Berrick pouted.

Ernesto busied himself dropping the finished beer bottles back into their paperboard holder. "I'll be back again soon. Don't get all sad and shit."

"Be sure to take those empties, too. That's thirty cents right there!"

"I'm on it," Ernesto reassured.

Berrick went back inside and drew shut the door. Junior recognized the sound of "The Fog" restarting.

"You headin' out?" Junior asked.

"Mmm-hmm. I'll tell ya, I'm burnt, bro."

Junior started to smile. "Well, there's something I haven't told you."

"Yeah?" The muffled clink of the bottles came to a halt.

"I've been talking to Berta."

Junior's smile was infectious, popping and foaming like the strong head on his beer. It found itself now being transferred, bit by bit, to Ernesto's mouth.

"Yeah?"

"We've decided the Christmas party is on. We're getting rooms. Food. Booze. She's got the bud. High test all the way."

"Serious?"

"As a heart attack." Junior's smile got even bigger. "You in?"

"Fuck to the YES!" Ernesto howled as his arm swung from the side and clapped his palm against Junior's. "Now I can't wait to give those StileCorp jugheads the best Nubian Halftime Show they ever seen!"

A lone raccoon looking for cat food, and possibly beer, chittered in reply as it walked by the patio.

A copy of "*101 of the Cruelest Practical Jokes!*" was nudged aside as

Berta's grocery bags pushed onto the dining room table. She'd spent all last night studying the best of the book's candidates, and all tonight shopping for them. She only had about $20 to spend and actually came a dollar or two under.

Crayons. Duct tape. Life Savers candy. Chicken bouillon cubes. Zip ties. She smiled at the potential each of them had as they came out from the bags. A new box of Arizona Munch followed. Berta considered opening it to see if she was a "49er" gold-bar winner, but was too tired to deal with that right now.

Next to last to be unloaded was a fat Tupperware tub full of seaweed that she'd scooped up from LeisureFace's beachfront on her way out to the car. She peeked inside to check. The pungent blast of salty rot forced her to snap shut the lid even faster than her curiosity had opened it.

The final victory for the evening was a single Morton turkey TV dinner. She slid her finger under the side tab and grabbed a fork to stab holes in the plastic over the potatoes. Into the microwave it went. It was already a quarter past nine, and she didn't have the luxury of cooking up anything more substantial. There was something scrumptious about those mashed potatoes, anyway. Mmm.

From out of the bathroom, Berta retrieved surely the biggest pill organizer anyone would have ever seen. Her fingertip brushed over the remote control button as she walked past the living room. Beavis and Butt-Head giggled in the background as she began to fish out the pills remaining under today's "PM" section of the organizer. There were so many, she sometimes couldn't close the lid unless she first shook them down for a second or two.

She paused to crack out some ice from the freezer trays and grab a clean glass from the cupboard. After a quick stir of the potatoes, Berta began washing down pills as she emptied her pockets. Car keys, Kleenex, and a receipt all dropped onto the dining table. She had to switch pockets before unearthing the pull tabs she had bought. Berta had picked them up—along with a quick glass of wine—at the bar of the Sandmark Lounge, which was on the same business loop as LeisureFace.

The ubiquitous mascot for the state of Oregon's biggest pull tab jackpot in history was a cool cat with an afro and sunglasses. 'Gimme Five' were exorbitantly-priced, five-dollar-apiece shots to win $55,555. Hell, that was even more than Arizona Munch was offering, so Berta took the plunge and was about to give it a try. When else was she going to get the chance to find a new job without going broke paying for her meds? Sure, it was less of a payout than Powerball, but with five chances on each card, the odds were a lot better.

The microwave beeps shook her away, slipping the ticket into her prank book for safekeeping. Berta had the good sense to grab a pot-holder at the last second—the boiling juice from the diced carrot compartment attempted to trickle over the sides of the tray and onto her hand. She picked up the fork and made her way to the computer. Soon, the sloshing and beeps of the dial-up connection swam around the Bubble Jet printer, which was also clunking and righting itself in hopes of being used that evening.

Berta's eyes slid down over the jobs on the WorkSource Oregon site, but there was next to nothing to click on tonight. The tail end of her sigh turned into a cooling blow onto her potatoes, relishing in the creamy heat of fake potatoes and even faker butter. You put enough salt on anything, it'll taste fabulous.

The faithful Bubble Jet was called to the front lines as a new blank document with the words "SIT ON MY LEISUREFACE" were copy-and-pasted over and over again, filling up the whole page. After a few more clunks, its physical twin began to pop, line for line, out of the printer. Berta smiled, sliding her scissors out from the drawer as she swallowed a sodium-packed mouthful of dressing, washing down a few more pills as soon as the savoriest notes had dissipated.

Berta made the evening's shower hotter than usual, if nothing else to help loosen up her back. She'd already taken enough goddamned pills and really didn't want to add a Doan's to tonight's list if she didn't have to. She took her bedtime wear—sweatpants and a long baseball shirt—from the back room without even turning on the light.

The row of lush indica plants that overpowered the smaller of the two bedrooms would have astounded any law-abiding guest. To Berta, they'd become an intrinsic part of the landscape. She once likened them to common houseplants. Houseplants that needed a lot of box fans and grow lights, and she had the electric bills to prove it.

Over the years, Berta had become careful not to divulge her address too frivolously. Sure, Beaver Lake wasn't exactly Detroit when it came to crime statistics, but she didn't need the hassle of nosy neighbors or local stoners looking to score. Probably the best scenario she could ask for was the rare, blessed nights such as this. Nights when she was feeling good enough to pass them by, and not be needled into putting their buds to good use before she bunked down.

Though she had made great strides in her party plans this evening, Berta couldn't help but page through the prank book a bit more as she eased into bed, searching for only the cruelest of the cruel. There was one about baking a dead squirrel inside a cake. Some inventively cruel hijinks there, without a doubt, but she really liked her layer cake tin and, undoubtedly, would have to throw it out if she decided on that one. She hadn't seen any squirrels for weeks, either.

Since she was post-menopausal, the one with the bloody tampons and maxi pads was a non-runner, as well. Then again, there were always the sanitary napkin dispensers in the LeisureFace ladies' rooms...

A few others, like the vomit-filled soda bottles, sounded good on paper but ultimately seemed messier than they were worth.

Exhausted, Berta plucked the Gimme Five pull tab from the book. Three fives in a row were all she needed. The first tab cracked back. No dice. Same with the second one. And the third. The fourth slowly unearthed a big yellow 5. And then another.

It was then Berta noticed that her fingers were just barely trembling.

A banana rounded out the trio.

"Shit!" she growled quietly into the peace of the bedroom.

The fifth tab at least gave Berta an instant win of two dollars. It wasn't even half of her five-dollar investment, but she preferred to think of it as getting tonight's dinner for free.

Paco always did his deals behind the community swimming pool, simply because it faced the opposite way of the police precinct. All the cop cars always just pulled straight onto 101, never bothering with the fairly affluent and semi-residential area behind it. The fact that the pool had ample parking and was closed most of the time was just gravy.

Fitz wasn't going to bother getting out of the car. He was about ten minutes late and couldn't have been happier about it. The first light of another dreary December morning coated his car hood as Paco swaggered up to the window through the headlight beams. Like a couple of track stars with a baton, the deal was passed off in seconds and with no words. Fitz made sure to see four twenties before handing off the meager baggie, fuller of air than product. He did everything he could not to snicker too loudly as he rolled the window back up and drove away.

Waiting for Paco back home were Dorena and Casey, both of them still in their sleep shirts. Those dorks on "Good Morning America" were blathering on, second-guessing what the next Furby or Tickle Me Elmo was going to be for this holiday season.

Kicking off her velour slippers to the far end of the couch, Dorena rolled her neck over its padded arm. Her back crinkled and cracked just enough to let her do housekeeping for another day. She sipped half-heartedly at her mug every couple of minutes, but mostly it was just there to make the coffee table look purposeful. Smoke rippled out of her nose as the smell of searing cigarette paper lifted, mixing in to perfectly round out the checklist of the apartment's typical morning smells.

Casey nibbled at a Pop-Tart, periodically slapping her fingers on her thigh so as to not get strawberry crumbs shuffled into her outsized tarot deck. The blue plaid backing blurred as she tumbled them one over the other, cutting the deck with as much precision as her little hands could.

"How long does it take him?" Dorena grumbled as she shot a look to the clock by the front door, which read only three minutes later than the last time she glanced up at it.

Six cards—three over three—were what kept Casey from answering. It was her go-to layout. The past cards to the left were full of bad shit, judging from the pictures of people bound, blindfolded, and crying amongst a profusion of swords. Loss, separation, helplessness. But a transformation was afoot in the two present cards situated in the middle, leading to a much sunnier outcome in the last two cards on the right where happy folks partied and danced under rainbows.

"I didn't get to talk to Petey last night. How is he?" There was a hook on Casey's line, but her sister was still too groggy to catch it.

"Good." Dorena sounded a bit surprised, but thankful. "You wanna go see him this weekend?"

"Yeah, that'd be cool." Casey's pupils swelled and shrank as she dove deep into the meanings of each of the six cards.

Dorena decided to get up and start getting ready for work, rather than catching yet another curveball of self-pity while she sat on her ass waiting for Paco to get home. But then her sister's tone—*that* tone—the one that came out flat, entranced, and calm when she was at the peak of her powers, stayed her intentions for just a little longer.

"I think you're going to get him back soon," Casey said.

One word came out of Dorena. It was deep and croaky and full of more hope than anything she'd said in months: "What?"

"Page of Pentacles, Ten of Cups." Casey pointed to the progression as each of her phrases were dug up like little buried treasures. "Dark-haired little boy. Inspiration. Reunions." Her voice turned increasingly persuasive, pointing at each card as she went on. "Ten of Cups—happy endings! Especially how it morphs from the present with the Eight of Cups, which is transition, sadness, solitude."

"Do it again," Dorena commanded, quietly. She was so intent on it, she actually put out her cigarette in order to give Casey and the cards her full attention.

The cards immediately began to pile together, stacking back up again between Casey's palms. "Yeah, let's try for more details with a Celtic cross—"

"No, the six-card Hungarian!" Dorena lowered her voice a bit, almost as if she fashioned it as a form of apology. "Just do it again."

The deck was placed squarely in front of Dorena. "Cut 'em," Casey instructed.

Dorena's hand dropped and then reconsidered, rising high on the stack before lifting it off and putting the remnants on top.

Casey shuffled and flipped out another half-dozen cards representing her sister's predicament. It wasn't much different from the first layout.

"Fuck me!" a shocked Dorena intoned as she touched the Ten of Cups, which, yet again, showed up in its exact same slot.

"It's damn near the same thing! This time it's the Magician." Casey pointed to the thin paperboard rendering of a red-robed man.

Dorena had naturally absorbed every card's meaning simply due to Casey's omnipresent deck. "Wisdom and skill are used to change your future," she reminded herself.

The front doorknob began to rattle, and Paco stumbled in. His cap was on backward, making him look even stupider than he already was. The brim accidentally knocked against the door as he shut it, finally succeeding after a series of sloppy, unsuccessful tries.

"It took you an hour and a half to do a fifteen-minute deal?" Dorena queried, her anger dropping Petey from the front of her intellect for a moment or two.

"Shit's good, ladies!" was Paco's vociferous introduction. His eyes could barely focus, and he probably couldn't give a fuck less at this point. "We got any more Pop-Tarts?" He meant to sit down on the loveseat but fell forward into the couch cushions.

"Did anyone follow you?" a nervous Casey asked, scooping up and discarding her deck into their wrap of blue silk. She went and looked out the front window and saw Paco's car parked almost entirely sideways, taking up three spots in the parking lot. "For fuck's sake! Did you save us any?" She sounded just as angry as Dorena and pinched the bolt lock into place.

Paco unfurled the baggie from his jacket. It hadn't been anything remotely resembling full to begin with, and now it was damn near empty. Only a few joints remained from the scanty purchase. "A little something for everyone!" he cracked, trying to keep his vision focused.

Dorena snatched the bag, yipping like a mutt in a meat grinder when she saw the contents. "Oh great, the Tampax Bandit strikes back! Dumbass, you know Fitz hates us. You could get rolled doing this kind of stupid shit!"

Casey picked right up where Dorena stopped. "Fitz is looking for any excuse to swing in and step on your dick. You've already turned a bunch of people onto him, and it's not like Beaver Lake is a cottage industry."

Dorena's furor caught its second wind. "Pac, I'm sick of this bullshit! We could have sold this in town for more than you got it for, but now we can't even make a trip back to Eugene to make a profit, because you smoked half of it before you got a foot in fucking door."

Paco didn't even realize he was being torn a new asshole, but it's not like the girls didn't have a point. Their operation was getting sloppy— the quality of the buds was getting milder, the free samples were more frequent, and Fitz's reputation was starting to rise, which was a luxury they couldn't afford anymore.

Paco pulled up Dorena's slippers to use as a makeshift pillow. "Do we have any more Pop-Tarts, Dorrie?" He didn't even open his eyes to ask.

Dorena headed into the bedroom. "Screw it."

"What are you doing?" Casey asked, a bit concerned. She hadn't seen her sister this pissed off in years. Well, at least weeks.

Dorena tore off her sleep shirt and tossed it onto the rumpled white sheets of the bed. She threw the neck hole of her LeisureFace shirt over her head and began to pull on a pair of bleach-stained jeans. "I'm going to work! Only person in this house who has a job, so that's where I'm going."

The words stung Casey badly, and guilt instantly shaded her fair complexion. She had meant to look at the want ads yesterday, but the odds were high that it would have been useless to do so, anyway. "You want me to make the chili for dinner?"

"No, we got three sets of leftovers we gotta do something with," Dorena reasoned, belying the fit of steam that you could almost see piping off her head. She ripped the car keys from sleeping Paco's hand. He snored just loud enough to be heard over the commercials on television. The baggie was thrown Casey's way. "Here, load up. Hope to fucking God Berta's gonna bring her stash to the party. Lock this behind me."

The door slammed shut, and Casey did as she was told. With a grimace full of shame, the baggie was tossed onto the loveseat as she sat down on the floor. The cards slipped back out of their wrapping. She took a deep breath, holding it for only a second before a familiar voice broke through Paco's nasal whinny.

It belonged to Cles Gubbins.

"*Want something more than just a getaway? Then come and see the twenty-first century look of leaving it all behind. Right here—at LeisureFace!*" There he was. The same gray slacks and pink Oxford shirt. He hadn't even changed after getting back from the links. "*All oceanfront condominiums in the heart of the world-famous Oregon Coast.*"

Suddenly, Gubbins was in a room. To be exact, it was 112—Casey could tell by the view of the pool behind him. She never knew it was the same room in which Ernesto pounded Stacey-Lynn senseless a few days back, but it sure did photograph nicely on T.V.

"*Relax by the fire to watch the waves, or let yourself melt in any one of our warm, inviting Jacuzzis and heated swimming pools. Whether you're delighting in the colors of the annual kite festival, having a bite at one of our great salmon bakes, or just in the mood for combing our miles of peaceful beaches, LeisureFace has just what you need to leave it allll behind.*"

Unconsciously prompted by Gubbins' last word, Casey defensively grabbed her own ass. She looked away, knowing exactly what was on the screen. She could almost hear him smiling. A new voiceover popped up to help her wash away the previous 25 seconds.

"*LeisureFace Luxxxury Condominiums, off the Highway 101 business loop in beautiful Beaver Lake!*"

And, just like that, it was over. The next commercial came along, and life returned to something seemingly normal. The prospector and his mule began to do-si-do as that Arizona Munch song bounced its way through the length of the living room.

The next reading she would do was going to require some help.

Casey's hands stopped working the deck and grabbed for whatever was left in the baggie on the loveseat.

As the virtual Gubbins faded off Casey's screen, the real one was in his office finishing up his first business of the day. Naturally, it was his last courtesy call up the coast to the big wigs of StileCorp, all of whom were due in town in a little over 48 hours for the LeisureFace Christmas ("Holiday") Party cum Corporate Take-Over Celebration.

"We're ready for it!" Gubbins' voice ramped up at the end, barely able to contain himself. The possibility of the take-over and having Casey on his arm as it happened was too much for him. He'd spent half of the morning with at least one of his hands thrust into the front pockets of his golfing chinos. The fact that he had recently gotten his handicap down to eight was nearly forgotten in the excitement of the past few days.

The celebratory voices on the other side of this three-way call were giving all the typical praise for the property, which Gubbins volleyed right back at them.

"You gentlemen have delivered a fair price in a fair deal, and we can't wait to rock your world on Saturday."

Gubbins gave a geeky laugh and bid the makers of his golden parachute goodbye for the meantime. Once he saw Berta walking past, his keen senses shifted priorities to grab some QC sheets he'd personally been toiling over off his desk. Even a casual observer could tell there was something special about them, what with the color-coding and overall neatness Gubbins had employed drawing them up since the first minute he'd arrived that morning.

The glass door to the office breezed open. "Berta!"

Her head swung around just casually enough to make Gubbins believe she was starting just another day. "Yeah, Mr. Gubbins? Do you want your office cleaned now?"

"No, no. Not now." Though the answer wasn't what Berta was hoping for, Gubbins nevertheless was about to unwittingly give her a stellar opportunity of a different sort. One she'd been waiting for all week.

"Can you see that you and Dorena give some special TLC to these rooms by close of business tomorrow?"

"Sure thing. She should be here in just a few, so we'll get started on them then."

"Great. These rooms really need a woman's touch."

And with that sexist remark, Berta knew she was going to put into effect the things she'd gleaned from "*101 of the Cruelest Practical Jokes!*"

"You know I got that in spades, Mr. Gubbins." Berta was proud of herself for not tipping her hand as she said it. This whole act was making her stomach ache in the same way the medication sometimes did. Her want for a homemade joint was quickly pushed aside.

"Sure do," Gubbins agreed before his conscience moved on to the next item on its to-do list. "And have you seen Ernesto?"

"Yeah, he's doing the pool readings with Junior. You want me to tell him to come by?"

Gubbins shook his head. "No, it's okay. I'll catch up with him later."

Berta gave a parting smile and immediately headed for Reception. Straight away, Stacey-Lynn noticed the look on her face. "What?"

Berta held out Gubbins' QC sheets. "Could you make me a copy of these, please?"

The shifty vibe took over both of the women as the papers slid through the fax machine.

Berta offered up another question. "Dorena isn't in yet, is she?"

The receptionist peered out at the parking lot and shook her head in response to Berta's question as the QC sheets fell out of the fax machine. Stacey-Lynn knew something was up and was busting at the seams to find out what it was. Like all gossip, the take-over rumor had assumed a life of its own, becoming LeisureFace's latest and final employee of sorts, and its presence was getting everyone in a vengeance-minded mood.

Berta was handed off the copies, which weren't as colorful as their original counterparts. She gave Stacey-Lynn a quick thank-you and was on her way, missing Dorena by only a few seconds.

Outside, Paco's borrowed car braked angrily, its screeching brakes sliding it the last foot of the parking space.

Stacey-Lynn heard the car door swing closed with a heavy slam. After the nutty exchange she just had with Berta, she was hungry for dirt and hoped that Dorena would give her some. But anyone who'd watched the late arrival get out of the car could have told you that she was heading straight for the water heaters to have a cigarette, despite the fact she'd already crushed out two butts into the car's ashtray during the commute.

The door to the water heater room slammed back. The metal knob banged loudly against layers of drywall tucked aside the door jamb, and Junior's butt nearly fell off the overturned bucket it was sitting on. Sure, the clatter was unsettling, but the thing that really scared Junior was the thoughts of unemployment, the Christmas party, his father's impending check-up appointment, and a hundred other things dancing over his gray matter, fighting for attention.

As Junior caught his breath, Dorena raised her brow. "Why are you always hiding in here?"

"I could ask you the same thing, you know." Junior's voice had just enough edge on it to steal Dorena's interest.

Her eyes pitched a glance over the parking lot and then back towards the ocean. The dark, tumbling waves somehow unlocked what Dorena had penned up inside of her. Or maybe it was just the fact that Junior actually gave a shit. "Good place to smoke when you're stressed. You?"

Junior shrugged, surrendering to honesty. "It's a good place to talk to you." He was suddenly too warm and flipped up his Hawaii cap to give his scalp some air.

Dorena came forward, and the door slid closed behind her. There was a doubting smirk on her face made even more sullen and cryptic by the light from the single bulb above them. She leaned against the wall, burning off the tip of a fresh cigarette.

"So, why are you stressed?" Junior wondered aloud. He looked up to see if Dorena had heard it, and, judging from the way her face slid into a steely pout behind the nicotine steam, he was certain she had. Dorena waited for an agonizing pause before finally opening the tap and letting her troubles flow out of her.

"You want the short list or the long one?"

"The short one," Junior decided. "Gubbins wants me to start cleaning up the rec center in about ten minutes."

Dorena gave something approximating a smile, appreciating Junior's candor. In a way, though, he just said it because he knew she wasn't going to want to go into the details of the long list, anyway.

"You ever discover the only reason you're with someone is because you're both in the same business?"

Junior shook his head. "I hope I never do." It was said with one-half relief, one-half fear of the possibility. That's probably why he kept talking. He knew the girl in front of him made him happy. Period. But to have her, he had to show her the way to her own happiness, too. "Maybe you need to find another business. Maybe what you have is holding you back."

"I know..." Dorena pressed on through her self-doubt. "It's just hard being strong for other people sometimes."

Though Dorena never saw it, Junior nodded with a pearl of shared wisdom, his stare fixed and distant as his thoughts flew and scattered. It was that moment when he decided he had to have a little talk with his dad tonight. At the age of 27, Junior Berrick was a prisoner to his other job: caretaker. In reality, it was the first one he'd ever had. One that required of him everything from cleaning up cat food cans when the raccoons were done with them to massaging his father's sweaty, graying temples so he'd fall back asleep after waking up screaming, convinced he had seen V.C. faces and guns sticking out of the trees.

"How's your dad?"

The likelihood of Dorena being psychic was slim, so Junior relented to the probability that he was getting worse and worse at hiding his thoughts these days. It brought a sad smile to his lips.

"Okay."

Dorena wore a look of quiet surprise on her face in response.

"Alright, maybe a step or two below okay." Junior's self-effacing confession at least wiped the melancholy off his mouth.

Dorena approved, her teeth showing from behind the fibrous smoke. "Hey, that's better than three steps below."

"Trying to get him into the doctors soon, but the waiting is getting brutal. I'm hoping I don't have to start taking him to Portland, or some shit like that."

"*Berta to Dorena*" spilled out of the walkie-talkie at Junior's hip. Dorena's eyes got big, and she immediately crushed out her smoke as Junior unclipped the walkie and pushed it her way.

"Dorena here. What's up?"

"*Could you meet me on the top floor?*" Berta's disembodied voice requested over the squawk box. "*Up here doing finishing touches for the StileCorp rooms.*"

"On my way," Dorena said into the plastic grate. She promptly stood up and sent the walkie back in Junior's direction. "Shit, I gotta run."

"Keep it. I'll just grab another one."

"Sweet," Dorena exhaled with a little cough as she stowed her smokes. A slender envelope of muted daylight came into the room as she stopped at the door and turned back to Junior. "Thanks for helping keep me sane. At least for one more day."

Dorena took off and the door closed quickly behind her. For the first time ever, Junior didn't feel a longing sickness after talking to her—there was so much in the previous three minutes to celebrate. And with a rejoicing fist pump, that's precisely what he did.

The day turned out relatively sedate for Ernesto. Notes that Gubbins had left at the Maintenance department outlined areas that needed touch-up paint, beauty bark, a series of greenery, or other assorted ass-painery. What started as an annoying assembly line of c-level kvetching turned out to be a peaceful godsend. Ernesto was left to his own devices to try and put his bullet train of thought on a slower track.

As he dodged swim-suited retirees to brighten up the gloss-white gates of the Jacuzzi area, he wondered how his mother was doing, and cursed himself for not phoning her the past couple of weeks. While he tried to reason with numerous free LeisureFace kites caught in a row of trees facing the beach, he crunched numbers and tried to forget the needling, finer points of his puny savings account. And, as he gently dropped some sword ferns around the perimeter of the parking lot near the end of the day, he was able to look through the front doors and see Stacey-Lynn wiping her brow. She was constantly on the move, busy as a plump little bee, as guests secured reservations for the end of the month. He hadn't gotten to talk to her all day, and numerous parts of him were starting to get lovesick.

"Hey, buddy."

Ernesto knew the voice, but the choice of words threw everything off-kilter. He turned and saw Gubbins looking down at him. It definitely wasn't a buddy, but Ernesto was too tired to summon a grudge. His throat was dry from not talking to a soul for hours, so the response came out a little scratchy and weak. "Hey, Mr. Gubbins."

"I love the beauty bark you added by the rec center!"

"Oh, cool." Ernesto raised his eyebrows, taking the compliment well. "That new stuff isn't exactly organic, but the kind of red, rusty hue looks nice with the white rails and the greenery."

And now, the real reason Gubbins was here: "You try on the costume yet?" The question was low and raspy, with his eyelids pressing together just slightly, in a diabolical kind of way.

Ernesto hadn't touched the costume since he made a folded pile of it on the side of his bathroom counter. "Uh, yeah. I don't think there will be a problem." He still had a tug-of-war going on in his head about whoring out himself in front of the people responsible for the pink slip he'd be getting next week.

"Well, let me know if it needs any last-minute alterations." There was a pissy insistence in Gubbins' voice before that low, raspy tone swung back around. "I can get them done tomorrow if we need them."

"Nah, it's alright. We'll make it work out just fine." There was something sneaky in the way that Ernesto said it, but Gubbins was too wrapped up in his own plan to notice.

The CEO clamped a hand on his worker's bicep. "That's what I like to hear." He went to walk off but popped back around the façade of the entranceway. That secretive tone came with him. "You're going to be a wealthier man next week!" he whispered with a wink. "We got another big day tomorrow. See you in the morning!"

Ernesto began to wonder just how much extra would be in his paycheck for this Negro Public Relations stunt when all was said and done. Everyone has a different idea of wealth, but, somehow, Gubbins' affluence gave Ernesto the superficial notion that everything would work out just right, belying the intimidation and shame he felt deep inside.

He took a quick look at the front desk as Gubbins passed it. Stacey-Lynn had already left without coming to see him on her way out, presumably due to not wanting to conspicuously wedge herself into a conversation between him and the boss. He looked around the parking lot, but her car wasn't anywhere to be found. The shovel slung over one of Ernesto's sad and sloped shoulders as he sulked back to Maintenance.

Berrick had an audience today. His ramshackle copy of the Kama Sutra was held together by Scotch tape and sheer will—even the horniest silverfish wouldn't go near it. However, if you have students, the best thing to do is teach them. Two raccoon sows sat at the edge of the deck with their fluffy tails wrapped around their haunches. They didn't need sexual guidance, but figured they'd deal with it in order to have a chance at the tin of cat food that lay at Berrick's feet.

"Alright, girls," the lesson began, "there's only one sure-fire way to get ahead. Prostitution! It says here that to obtain money, erotic attraction may be real or simulated. You know what that means—fake it till you make it!"

The two students shuffled around the grass and rewound their tails, getting closer to the tin sitting on the concrete. Both of them broke their attention to watch the arrival of Nuggetz as Junior pulled to a stop inside the spray-painted lines on the other side of the deck. This angered the professor.

"Now listen, damn it!" Berrick tooted, glaring over the top rim of his reading glasses. "I gotta tell you the next part about pimps, because you can't do all this yourself!"

Nuggetz's heavy door went shut, and Junior shuffled his feet over the grass and up to the patio. The two schoolgirls moved just enough for him to get by.

"I'd ask what you're doing, but I probably don't wanna know."

Berrick threw another curt look over the top of his glasses, but this one was directed at his son. "I'm teaching the ladies about life and love."

One of the two classmates chittered in agreement. They really wanted that cat food.

"You know, I can't take you with me to the party if you're going to do things like this." Junior knew damn well that the LeisureFace Christmas party, stuffed full of its soon-to-be-canned employees with nothing to lose, had a propensity to get even more batshit than his dad already was. However, that was precisely the problem—it's hard to raise hell and enjoy yourself when you're serving double duty as a role model.

"You don't have to worry about me!" Berrick's reassurance was, somehow, little comfort to his son. "By tomorrow, I'll have some more scripts for my chronic kookiness you hate so much, and will probably be asleep for most of it."

The thick slab of acrid self-pity that was stapled to the back end of Berrick's transparent grump went unnoticed, for just a moment, in the wake of something Junior found more pressing.

"What do you mean 'by tomorrow'?"

"The doctor's office called. I can get in tomorrow morning, so I took it." Berrick paged a bit further ahead in his book, seemingly more interested in the whoring arts than arguing.

"What time?" an exasperated Junior asked.

"Nine-thirty. It'll be fine. Just leave a message right now and tell Gubbins you'll be a little late." The rusty, defensive edge on Berrick's words refused, out of pride, to be sanded away. His indignant finger slapped the corner of a wilting, smutty page.

"Wish you would've told me today before I left so I could have—"

"Well, I didn't. And if I had, you woulda belly-ached about it, the same damn way you're doin' now when I didn't tell you. You're only there for another couple of weeks, so there's no use in walking on eggshells with people who don't give a fuck about you anyway."

Berrick was clever at twisting things around to take the heat off himself, but, for once, he had a point in doing it. A good one.

Junior fumed, heading for the patio door. "No one's gonna get the message till tomorrow, anyway. I'll just call in the morning and Stacey-Lynn can tell him I'll be late."

Berrick's intended final jab stopped his son from pulling back on the screen.

"I'm nuts. Not dumb. You need to be reminded of that once in a while, Junebug. I'm not any worse than I was thirty years ago."

Junior wanted to cry. The frustration was too much, and it all came out at once. "You're reading the Kama Sutra to raccoons! You watch the same movie over and over. You can't be trusted to walk down the street by yourself. You can't make a goddamn sandwich anymore, dad!"

"Well then maybe I shouldn't go Saturday night and embarrass you?" Berrick's suggestion was calm. Too calm. "I know that Dorena girl's gonna be there, anyway, and I don't wanna cramp your style."

"You..." Junior caught himself just in time. At least, he thought he did.

"I already have." Berrick could have posed it as a question, but he already knew the answer. "I know. That's why I jumped at getting these meds tomorrow." His voice slowly chugged upwards, resolute and gaining steam. "But just because my brain works a little different than everyone else's, I can't go to one of those places and rot for the rest of my life. That's the only thing I'm ever gonna ask of you." You couldn't yet see Berrick's tears, but you could hear them. "*Mākou 'oe i kekahi kime!*" Unwavering, he beat his fist down on the arm of the deck chair. It was the first time Berrick had ever perfectly nailed a Hawaiian phrase, so there was no excuse for his son not knowing exactly what he had just said: We're a team.

"We'll always be a team, dad."

Junior went inside, unable to say anymore.

Soon afterward, Berrick dismissed his class.

The headlights on Stacey-Lynn's car bounced up and down as they neared the trailer. During this time of year, the driveway path to the carport was riddled with shallow puddles full of slop and would probably stay that way until at least May.

Her trunk was full of groceries—she figured she may as well stock up now before her paychecks stopped at the beginning of the New Year. She had lied to Fitz and told him she found a new part-time job at a hotel up in Waldport to get him off her back and have him return her keys. Something about Fitz confiscating them enlightened the view of herself. She knew Fitz could be a controlling fuckhead, but the basic idea of not having the keys to her own home frightened her. It was a victimized, chaotic feeling. Those very keys jingled as she pulled them from the ignition. She lifted the small tab aside the driver's seat and the trunk breezed open, the whipping winds making the plastic grocery bags inside shiver and whisper.

The carport didn't offer much shelter at this point. The rain began shifting sideways as Stacey-Lynn loaded up each hand with plastic handles that stretched under the weight of milk jugs, ham shanks, and sloshing boxes of mac and cheese. Her tired feet clomped the few steps to the front door, which flew back in turn.

Fitz's expression was that of alarm, irritation, and preoccupation, and his eyes were wide and dotted with tiny pupils. These weird qualities made him look like a replica of her husband. Stacey-Lynn was about to find out that her estimation was, for all intents and purposes, pretty much right on the money.

"The hell are you doing?" Fitz wondered aloud from behind the sticky whites of his eyes. "Why are you being so loud?"

Stacey-Lynn tried to hand off the bags around her left hand but couldn't disentangle them. "Can you help me, please? The trunk is full!"

"Full of what?" Fitz still hadn't blinked once yet.

"Groceries!" Stacey-Lynn tried to hold up her hands a little higher, but her wrists were starting to give out. "Fitz, I'm getting soaked!"

Fitz pushed past her and began to hoist out the rest of the load from the trunk. Stacey-Lynn hurried over to the kitchen counter, which caught her bags just in time. Pulling the windswept hair from her eyes, she noticed deep red bands around her wrists. She shook out her fingers, trying to deaden the ache.

Stacey-Lynn heard the trunk slam shut as she turned to glimpse a pair of half-made joints on the kitchen table. A bag of light brown powder was nearby. At first, her crazy head thought it looked peculiarly like the beef gravy mix you can find in foil packs near the Stove Top stuffing.

From the look on Fitz's face when he came through the door, Stacey-Lynn could safely bet the powder on her kitchen table wasn't made by McCormick.

"What is that?" Stacey-Lynn's voice cracked under the weight of its naivety.

Good money would have bet on Fitz squirming his way into the topic in a slow, defensive fashion, but instead, he went full-tilt-boogie. An entrepreneurial pride jumped onto his face, and he abandoned his shopping bags to give his wife the sales pitch.

"Horse, baby! You know how good my last ones did? Well, these A-bombs are gonna blow the lid off the whole state! We're talkin' money, Stay. Big fuckin' money like we've never seen."

Stacey-Lynn didn't take her eyes off the bag. "I want this out of my house." Soft, with no anger. It was said with a directness any man would have admired. Any man who wasn't on heroin, that is.

"No, no, no. You're not listening." Fitz's arms swung around as if controlled by someone else. "You want out of this place? You want to stay home and work on your photography? I want that, too, I want that, too!" Fitz took Satan's gravy mix and suspended it in front of his wife's face. "This is what's gonna get us where we wanna be."

Tiny, red pinpricks dotted the back of his hand.

Stacey-Lynn finally had the reason for her husband's darting, needle-point pupils. Her suspicions didn't need confirming, and she knew if she asked, it would just make everything worse. "I don't know where you got it—"

"Think about it. Just...think about it a second." Fitz closed his eyes. A dumb, elastic grin of perfection sat down on top of his face. "We can get a new house. Get some newer cars, I mean, not right away, but hey! You can stop working these stupid fucking jobs you take, and...and...and take some fucking pictures instead. All of it!" His eyes flashed open and skimmed evenly over the room, never resting. "We can feel so alive!"

That's when his penis made an appearance. Not that Stacey-Lynn had never seen it before, it's just that she wasn't expecting to see it in the middle of an argument about the Schedule 1 drugs on their kitchen table.

"Come on. I want to share this. I wanna share this with you!" Amazingly, Fitz was already half-hard. Stacey-Lynn yelped as her blissed-out hubby scooped her up and whisked her down the hall. He never realized how close he came to smacking her head on the hallway corridor, but, in the state he was in, he wouldn't have cared, anyway.

Stacey-Lynn landed face-down on the bed, which was just what Fitz was hoping. Drugs are bad, and you probably shouldn't do them or sell them or make them, but in this case, they were a romantic godsend. Despite the fact she had worked a nine-hour shift and that this was the first time all week that she hadn't been on her period, a dazzled Fitz was convinced that his wife's snatch tasted just like strawberry pie. He lapped it up with enough conviction, it made a believer out of Stacey-Lynn, whose thoughts soon went to Ernesto. Her clothes ended up somewhere at the foot of the bed, and Stacey-Lynn eased back into the cold, supple pillows waiting for her.

Fitz got in between the familiar pair of thick, milky thighs. He began to mumble sweet nothings as he ran his fingertips through her hair. Or, at least, attempted to.

"Aw, motherfucking Jesus! Go brush your hair, Stay! You know I love to run my hands through your hair. Go!" Fitz rolled over onto his back to wait, his wet-tipped pecker slapping and rolling in protest. "Hurry the fuck up."

Stacey-Lynn got off the bed, her nakedness suddenly hitting her as a chill swept over each shoulder. She twisted the dial to the bedroom's forced air heater as she headed for the bathroom. Reaching for the sink's tip-out where she kept her brush, she opted for a quick pit stop.

"What are you doing?" Fitz finally whined.

"I have to pee," Stacey-Lynn admitted, mid-stream. She finished her business and then took to brushing her hair, understanding why Fitz had protested. The winds had been crazy this evening, turning her hairdo into a flattened, knotted snarl. The fancy brush worked its magic and soon Stacey-Lynn headed back around the corner, relishing a rush of warmth from the heater grate.

This is when she discovered yet another effect of heroin: nodding off.

He wasn't quite asleep, but Fitz wasn't anything close to crisp, either. He lay there on the bed with his eyes mostly shut, his mind and body cocooned in a narcotic embrace.

"Fitz?" Stacey-Lynn went to touch him but stopped. A part of her was alarmed, shaken by how distanced he looked, but an even bigger part of her was offended by his selfishness and the lovingly anesthetized grin under his nose. He let out a little sigh, turning his head away to stare through the latticework of his eyelashes at the light of the nightstand lamp.

Stacey-Lynn retreated to the bathroom. She flipped open the tip-out to replace her hairbrush, but instead found her fingers slowly removing all its items. One by one, they were lined up on the countertop. With a sweep of her hand, they all fell into a sturdy shoebox she kept under the sink for her sewing notions.

She didn't stop there.

Her jewelry box was next. The items were small—all of them fit into her palm—but some of them were of the highest importance to her. Then, the closet. She took only her best clothes, leaving most of the older things that made her feel slovenly and poor. Thankfully, her camera was still there, securely packed in its factory box.

Stacey-Lynn's naked form went up and down the hallway. She never noticed, but she stood up straight and flattened her gut as she did it. Her actions were smooth and brimming with determination as she stuffed her life into her purse, her pockets, and her mind. The groceries were still there on the kitchen countertop. She rifled through the bags, taking what was hers and leaving the food she had bought for Fitz. She even put it in the fridge for him.

A trunkful of groceries wasn't the only thing that had been left in the kitchen. What Fitz had referred to as A-Bombs, homemade blunts laced with heroin, were undone there on the dinner table. Her hand went to reach for the stash but smartly relented. In her mind, she saw the beef gravy granules spiraling down the toilet, a waste of epic proportions. Instead, she reached for her pair of Playtex kitchen gloves and the keys to Fitz's car—for now, the bag of illicit brown powder would be safe under the passenger side floor mat.

She closed the door to Fitz's car and turned to size up her own, making a rough mental estimation of how much she was going to be able to take.

Within minutes, the trunk stood open for the last time that night, the force of the storm making it bounce softly inside the wind tunnel of the carport. Even with the backseat mostly filled, it all looked so disappointingly meager as she stood there staring at it. Somehow, Stacey-Lynn found a curious freedom in the feeling. After, a rush of pride came in at the realization that she could so quickly let go of the material mindset she and Fitz had fed for so many years.

The curtains on the bedroom window were still open. A clunk from the transmission set the car in reverse, and it began to slip away from the house. As the wipers cleared her sight, Stacey-Lynn saw Fitz through her tears and the foggy, sopping panes. He just lied there in their bed, quiet and euphoric. Never thinking of life, its struggles, or its inhabitants. Just a warm yellow glow. The same kind that came from the headlights as they cut through the broad needles of rain, fading slowly from reality, and disappearing into the shadows of the highway.

Ernesto had been talking to his mother for a while. A long while. The ring from his phone angered him at first, as her incoming call knocked him offline in the middle of downloading Cameo's Greatest Hits off Napster. In case something was wrong, he caved in to his guilt and answered. Now, it was going on 9 o'clock (midnight his mother's time) and Ernesto still hadn't eaten dinner, taken a shower, or anything else for that matter.

"I know, mom. Yeah, she just can't keep the weight off, I know."

As his mother rambled on about Oprah's nutritional woes, Ernesto's eyes fell on the softly-folded lump on the bathroom counter. His hands began to brush away the tissue paper and dry-cleaning plastic. The smell of the material began to waft up at him.

"Stedman just needs to hide the silverware, that's all," Ernesto suggested.

His mom didn't think that was funny.

"I'm not saying it to be mean!" he defended.

Disapproving maternal squiggles chastised Ernesto's ear as he took out the kufi from his costume. He stuck the hat on his head, checking his reflection in the mirror. It was more than a tad ridiculous, but there was something stately about it, at least, there would have been if he hadn't been wearing the sweatpants and Bob Marley t-shirt he liked to sleep in. Ernesto loved to use his 'pyjammin' joke around others, but his mother had already heard it a hundred times before, and she wasn't exactly ready yet for another of his snide celebrity quips.

"Yes. Yes, she is thinner now than in 'Color Purple'. I just hope she can stay that way, that's all I'm saying! It's good she doesn't live with you, or you'd be makin' her eat those scalloped potatoes we used to have all the time."

Ernesto's defense didn't last too long. Out of his peripheral vision, he noticed a familiar shape pulling up into the parking lot. Heavy rain tumbled spryly down the slight grade of the driveway, cresting lowly against the tires of Stacey-Lynn's car as its brake lights went dark.

Something that probably alarmed Ernesto's mother more than the hide-Oprah's-silverware remark was how fast her son now got off the phone. It wasn't the notion that he was cutting her off, but that he sounded genuinely troubled as he stammered something about phoning her back this weekend before the line went dead. For all the times Ernesto had lied awake at night wondering if his mom was okay, there was certainly a bit of role reversal that evening as Ms. Taylor was the one to bed down with doubts. She eventually fell asleep to the notion that everything was probably just fine, and Ernesto would be a good boy and call back over the weekend, like he said he would.

But everything wasn't fine.

Ernesto, forgetting the kufi was still on his head, ran out the front door as Stacey-Lynn stepped out from the car, sobbing heavily, and pushing her absorbent bangs up out of her face. When he saw the glut of her belongings strewn over the backseats, the need to ask what happened dissipated with a sick rush. He held her tightly as she fell into his arms. The rain smacked their skin, and the sound clemently drowned out Stacey-Lynn's cries.

The next few hours were an anguished mélange of shouting, tears, apologies, and pledges. Finally, the quiet and fatigue of late night settled in. The heater was the only thing that made a sound as Stacey-Lynn finished off her cooling cup that had, just an hour earlier, been near-boil around a stray teabag found in Ernesto's cupboards.

The kufi was drying upside-down on the heater. Some of the darker colors had run into the lighter; though the result was pretty damn artistic, Ernesto wondered if Gubbins would get his tits in a wringer about it. His mind sprinted in wide, splintered paths, trying to juggle sympathy and plans for the future. The one thing of the utmost importance, though, was Stacey-Lynn's safety.

"He's gonna come lookin' for you."

"Don't worry," Stacey-Lynn said as her spoon gave a bell-like ting down inside the cup, "he doesn't know where you live."

Ernesto looked out the window at Stacey-Lynn's parked car. The midnight hour rain was lightening up just a bit. "Well, Beaver Lake ain't that big."

"I guess I'm leaving my job earlier than I thought." A soft sigh, perhaps one of relief, capped Stacey-Lynn's estimation as it rose from her simmering throat.

"What do you mean?"

"Fitz'll head straight there in the morning. I know the way he is, and whatever scene he makes there alone is sure enough to get me fired. I can't run the risk of him following me back here, either."

Ernesto shook his head, a little disappointed in himself for not thinking of that already. "You need to lay low tomorrow. All day. Don't even go for a walk, because someone who knows Fitz or from LeisureFace or whatever the hell is bound to see you." His eyes turned back out the window. "There's one thing we're gonna have to do before we get to bed."

Less than five minutes later, both of them were skittering across 101 to a used car dealership. Its parking lot was loud with crispy red and blue plastic flags that snapped in the wind, covering most of the noise they made.

Ernesto's criminal past fluttered briefly through his mind, slowing his steps as he made his way over to the body shop. He knew he'd seen them cover up nearby cars when they would paint or sandblast. Sure enough, a lone, dirty cover was rolled into a wet and crinkled ball by the locked-up paint compressor at the side of the building. Ernesto held Stacey-Lynn's hand as they ran back across the highway.

She took hold of the back elastic, and he took the front. Thirty seconds later, no one passing by would ever have guessed that Stacey-Lynn's car was under that unassuming, paint-smeared, gray sheet of polypropylene. By sheer luck, the winds died down by dawn, and the cover stayed on.

ACT OUT

[THAT NEW-FANGLED TELEPHONE AND THE TROUBLE IT KEEPS]

The front desk phone wouldn't stop ringing. Dorena was double-checking her morning QC sheets when Berta passed her in the entryway.

"Should we just answer it?" Dorena recommended.

"Where is she?" Berta craned her neck to take a look around the front side of the property. "I'm just glad Gubbins is gonna be late this morning. He called a few minutes ago—something about his wife heading out of town—but he didn't say anything about Stacey-Lynn."

"We're gonna be getting a shitload of check-outs in just a few minutes," Dorena advised. Her voice turned grim and sedate. "I got a bad feeling about her."

"Why?"

"If you knew her husband, you'd know why." Dorena felt like she'd just given away a secret of sorts but figured it was probably for the best.

Berta's eyes volleyed between the empty reception desk and the parking lot. "We've got to finish the StileCorp rooms."

Dorena gave a mischievous smile as she pushed up her brows. "You got your seaweed?"

Berta shushed her. "You got the Life Savers I gave ya?"

"I'm probably gonna need a wrench," Dorena confided. "The pliers aren't working too good."

"Junior's always got a few on the pegboards. They won't miss them."

Berta tossed off her solution before heading out to the elevators. "Come on."

At the mention of him, Dorena immediately noticed the absence of the Maintenance Manager. "And where the hell is Junior, anyway?" There was a part of her that wanted to tell him what she and Berta were up to.

Junior was on the other end of that ringing phone. He was on his fourth attempt in less than ten minutes to get hold of Stacey-Lynn. Berrick had his appointment card, his meds list, and a small stack of other paperwork ready for his doctor's appointment. Unfortunately, he was using it as a placemat for his bowl of Arizona Munch and two triangles of buttered toast.

"Where the hell is she, anyway?" Junior grumbled, hanging up.

"And what the hell is vitamin A palmitate?" Berrick questioned as he peered at the ingredients listing on the side panel of the cereal box.

"Stacey-Lynn's always there before I am. I don't get why no one's answering." Junior pulled on his LeisureFace jacket and began to round up his belongings. "We're gonna have to stop on the way. Hurry up and finish or we're gonna be really late."

"Can I bring my cereal?"

"No!"

"Okay, just my toast!"

Nuggetz sported a velour interior, so the yellow and brown toast crumbs stuck to the red passenger seat like Velcro as Berrick happily munched away. Junior had thrown some Hawaiian Christmas music into the cassette player, which helped level his mood as he pushed the limits of safe highway driving. They only had a little over a half-hour to get up to Newport, but thankfully the turnoff to LeisureFace was in sight.

Down the driveway the Firebird rolled, its engine throwing out a flattened growl as it slowed to a stop in front of the entranceway. The Hawaiian Christmas tunes kept going after the car was shut off, as the aftermarket stereo was easier to just hook up to the battery for the meantime. Junior was going to leave the keys in the ignition but reconsidered.

"Stay here. I'm just going to find Berta and see what's going on."

Berrick gave a little salute and behaved himself as Junior got out and met up with Ernesto in the Maintenance garage.

"Junebug, where you been, man?"

"Trying to get hold of the front desk. You seen Stacey-Lynn?"

Ernesto had to get creative with his answer. "Here? No." In a way, it wasn't a lie. "Still trying to figure it all out this morning." That statement certainly wasn't a lie, either.

Junior picked up the nuances of Ernesto's words, but didn't have the time to sort them out. "Alright, I gotta take my dad to the doctor's—"

"Is Berrick cool?" Ernesto's concern was genuine, as well. This was the first thing to get his mind away from the events of the past 12 hours.

"Yeah, yeah, it's just that I won't be back for a while, and no one's here to tell Gubbins. Berta around?"

Ernesto grabbed the walkie-talkie off this belt loop. "Ernesto to Berta."

At the same time, Dorena shuffled out of the elevator and out to the water heater room for her first official smoke break of the morning. The obscenely long and brilliant vermillion Firebird competed with the red curb of the fire lane. Dorena was never that impressed by cars, but the Polynesian sounds warmed her heart and lessened her nicotine craving.

Berrick looked over to her and smiled, hanging the crook of his arm out the window.

The guy was twice Dorena's age, so she figured was absolutely no harm in giving him a free hula. It would have been far more striking had she not been holding her lighter as she did it.

Dorena finally cracked up and ruined the effect, but Berrick gave a quick round of applause, anyhow.

"Thanks." Dorena's tobacco priority came back, so, without depriving herself any further, she burnt off the tip of her break-time cigarette. "Some nice Christmas cuts you got there."

Berrick couldn't help singing along, "Me-le Ka-li-ki-ma-ka is the

THING...to-say!" He looked like he wanted to continue but was a little too bashful. "They're my son's—he works here!"

"Ah! So, you're Berrick, eh?"

Berrick looked a little scared. "How do you know about me?"

It was easy for Dorena to laugh off the paranoia. An alleviating tone landed naturally in her phlegmy throat, placating any distrust coming from the other side of the Firebird's door. "Junior talks about you all the time."

Berrick had thirty years to make peace with his madness and the reputation that comes along with it, so there was no shame in his game. "Then I guess you know how eccentric I am!"

Dorena nodded, dragging long on her cigarette. "Mmm. That is, if it's true."

There was a challenge to her voice, a seductive calling that was deep and, as they said in Berrick's day, 'groovy'. At that moment, it hit him—this was the Dorena that Junior always talked about. Though he'd just scratched the surface, Berrick compared the likes of her to a sexy, chain-smoking Siren. No wonder his boy had taken a shine to her.

"Yeah, but what about the stuff I've heard about you?" he asked.

Half playful and half convinced, Dorena shook her head. "You haven't heard anything about me."

Berrick nodded. "Junior talks about you all the time—you're Dorena!"

Dorena was taken aback. Turns out she, too, had a reputation—all women eventually do, for whatever the reason—but she never expected it to reach the middle-aged father of a guy she worked with. He even pronounced her name right—dur-REN-ah, not dur-REE-na. She couldn't resist showing her appreciation, moving her cigarette back up to her mouth to offer a handshake.

"One and only. Nice to meetcha," Dorena's chewy words fell out sideways from behind the filter. "Where you headed today?"

"Doctor's appointment. See?" Berrick held up his appointment card, and that's when Dorena saw them.

The little red dots around his wrist.

Berrick rambled on about how he kept all of his appointment cards.

How they tell the story of his medical treatment. The reason he likes the gold foil ones the best. How they're useful for jimmying open the lock to the bathroom when Junior's been in there for too long. But Dorena didn't hear much of it. Her former job at the Golden Cedars hospice rushed back to her in a scary, dismal frenzy.

She took hold of Berrick's appointment card just so she could get a better look at the petechiae on his wrist, then trying to get a peek inside his collar and further up his sleeve. By now, everything she asked assumed the slightly formal intonation of a medical quiz.

"All this runnin' around at least makes you sleep good at night, I bet?"

Berrick squeezed out an ironic laugh. "Yeah, right. When I'm not still fighting the war in my head! Like to nap during the day—I get too hot at night."

"Yeah?" It was getting tougher for Dorena to not show concern. "What you picking up at the doctor's today?"

"Oh, just another round of scripts."

"Hey, pharmaceuticals make the world go round." Dorena let out a grump when reminded of her and Paco's need to step up their sales.

"As long as they keep me out of Golden Cedars, I'm happy!"

Dorena's blood ran cold. She took another drag off her smoke to help her forget.

"When was the last time you had a blood draw?"

"Just about a month ago."

"You write down on your card there to ask for another blood draw." Dorena was firm about it but just casual enough to bleed all the alarm out of the demand as it infused her smoky exhale. "They may even want to have a peek at your hip bone marrow."

Berrick sang, "The hip bone's connected to the...leg bone! The leg bone's connected to the...tail bone! Tail bone's connected to the..." Suddenly, Berrick's precise recollections of the human skeleton eluded him, so he opted for, "...dick bone!"

Dorena's eye tooth pushed gently on her lower lip as she smiled through the smoke. "Sounds like you got a whole new Hawaiian Christmas song goin' on there."

"Another blood draw? You sure?" Berrick's face soured, but he did as he was told. He took his pen out of the Firebird's console to jot down the suggestion.

"Mmm-hmm," she nodded without looking up at him. "Nurse Dorena wants to make sure you're okay." She decided to lighten it up a bit in making an effort to cap off the conversation, figuring Berta would be waiting for her by now. "You coming to the Christmas party tomorrow night?"

Berrick blushed and his eyes turned soulful. "Naw. Junebug wanted me to, but I told him I didn't want to cramp his style."

"Nuh-uh," Dorena's long, chocolate curls shook around her head as she heaved another lungful of ozone killer into the air. "That's bullshit. This is the jam of the year."

"Mmm, what kind of jam?" Berrick was confused.

Just then Junior came back to the car. "Alright, let's haul ass—" In his haste, it took him a second to notice Dorena. The fact she was talking to his dad didn't help his expression, either.

Dorena sounded resolute, keeping on point with Berrick. "You're the goods." She looked up to Junior, giving him a smile. "You gotta come. Junior needs to show you off."

"Okay!" This was, undoubtedly, the most fun Berrick had outside the house in weeks.

Junior dropped his forehead, giving Dorena back a slow, eye-rolling irony that made it obvious he was now trapped into having his dad in tow with him tomorrow night.

Dorena crushed the cherry of her cigarette into the damp, knobby tread of her shoes and tossed the butt into the bushes. Her gloating wink came Junior's way. "See you guys later."

As Junior got in and the Firechicken flew off, Berta popped out of Housekeeping, finishing off a cigarette of her own. A small but sturdy plumber's wrench was in her opposite hand.

"You got gloves?" Berta's voice pinged around the empty parking lot.

Dorena pushed her chin in the direction of the third floor. "Up in my bucket."

"Come on," Berta dropped her tone as she closed the main door to Housekeeping. "Let's get this done before Gubbins shows up."

The two giggled maliciously as they headed back to the elevators.

Gubbins squirmed on the couch, the cocoa-shaded leather burping and chittering under the small of his back. With all the zippers he heard sliding around upstairs ten minutes ago, he figured she would've been down by now.

He leafed through a narrow but very well-appointed brochure for a stunning resort on the northern coast of California. "*Crescent Treasures – Spa & Resort*" the cover promised in dreamy calligraphy, fronting a rocky shore at sunset that was dotted gently by windswept cypress trees. It seemed perfect—active yet relaxing, engaging, and peacefully romantic. Even if you have a lot of money, there's always something better out there than what you're used to. Always. And for Gubbins, the sleek photos of cedar saunas, hot stone therapy, and flawless, raked sand traps along the greenest fairways he'd ever seen were his idea of utopia.

He was shaken out of his dream by the clop of his wife's flats on the stairway. She was weighed down by the bulky, soft-sided suitcase in her right hand. Its leather tag bounced as she struggled, countering her balance by using the railing on her left side.

"Andy, could please help me?"

The couch gave up one last fart as Gubbins thoughtfully folded the brochure and got to his feet, taking the handle from his wife's grip. Within seconds, a boxy taxi drove up the circular driveway.

"Good timing," Gubbins commended.

Geraldine noticed her wallet and plane ticket sticking up from her purse. Her fingers moved quickly to stuff them inside and secure the clasp. She heaved a sad, bitter sigh as she flicked up the ends of her gray-blonde hair to reposition her silky neck scarf.

"I'll be lucky to make it there in time."

Gubbins was afraid to ask but did so anyway. "What's the latest word—four more days?"

"I wish you were coming with me," she said under a veil of self-pity.

"I would have," Gubbins assured her, "but it's just... This is our ticket to retirement, and it's got to come off perfectly."

There was something in Geraldine Gubbins' rouged face that told her husband she didn't believe him.

"She really wanted to see the both of us."

"I really wanted you with me this weekend." Gubbins countered. He didn't say it to be combative, but there's no way it couldn't be perceived as such.

"Andy, I've been here every weekend. You're out on the course, you're at work, you're up and down the coast the entire year now." As if exhausted at the thought, Geraldine trailed off for a trifling, tart pause. "It's tough to have a relationship with someone who's never around."

"Just us. I promise, after you're back, let's do something. I've been looking at some fantastic places! We can finally take a break and just spend some time together." His guarantee seemed to warm her a bit, and though he didn't particularly feel like asking again, he did so, anyway. "How long does she have—four more days?"

Outside, the taxi's horn gave a beep.

"Doctors say maybe a week." Geraldine refused to cry anymore. If for no other reason than she didn't have the time to do so at the moment. The driver opened his door and began to head up the long path of steppingstones to the front stoop.

Gubbins took her hand. "Let's both do the things that need doing...so we can go away for a while and forget about them." He couldn't help giving his wife a misty-eyed smile. "Okay?"

As the driver rang the doorbell, the two told each other 'I love you' and meant it. Gubbins made a cute little joke to the driver about taking care of his girl and getting her to the airport safely. And, as you may have guessed, Geraldine, still trying not to cry, gave a little wave to her husband through the window as he raised his hand in goodbye.

What you wouldn't have guessed was how fast Gubbins ran to the phone and flicked off its ringer as he grabbed the buckle of his belt.

"Ringer off! Pants down!"

Leaving his Pierre Cardin dress slacks behind, he bolted up the stairs to the master bathroom. The thought of what waited for him was enough to start making Gubbins' pisshole nice and juicy. His striped boxers were already down around his ankles before he could pull the folder out from its hiding place under the sink.

The tab on the plain manila folder was printed with "MORRIS, CASEY". Atop the employee file paperwork was a headshot everyone at LeisureFace had taken on their first day of work. Her blue eyes and enchanting smile were easily discernible, even buried in the murk of a Polaroid.

His hard-on jiggled and bounced as Gubbins shuffled his way to the nightstand to grab the cordless telephone handset. Not even men of his financial stature could have the luxury of cell phones—rumors of a decent reception tower were only starting to be bandied about Beaver Lake. He pushed Casey's headshot gingerly to the side, scanning the paperwork for the entry denoting 'home phone'. He began to stroke with the off hand as his fingers finished punching in the digits.

"Oh, I want it. I wanna fill your tight little pussy," Gubbins murmured as quickly as possible when the rings started to stack up, filling his ear.

A leotard-clad Casey didn't feel like answering, but she'd had enough of exercising and was looking for any excuse to bail out. She also knew damn well that Paco, who currently had gardening gloves up to his elbows in attempting to load a stainless-steel hash press, wasn't going to drop his work and run for the phone.

"Hello?"

It sounded like someone was being strangled. Casey held out the phone so Paco could hear it, too.

"HMM. HMMPH. URR...URRRGG!"

"The fuck?" Paco grimaced.

It was too grotesque to be an obscene call, so Casey listened closer. Subtle alarm rubbed up and down her spine. "Hello?"

A click popped and the call went dead. Gubbins would've stayed on the line had he not shot his load all over the Polaroid by accident.

Casey was spared a lot of ungentlemanly words as her unknown caller rounded up all the bathroom hand towels to reverse the damage. After a few moments, the worry that still knocked at the back of her head made her hit the switch hook and press down '*-6-9' on the keypad.

Gubbins' phone began to ring. He screamed as the paperwork up-ended all over the bathroom floor.

"That little bitch star-sixty-nined me!"

Every ring seemed to be louder and longer for Gubbins. The only thing more pressing for him than cleaning off the picture was that the gorgeous girl in it would hang up before he got to the phone. The manic, panting CEO only had six rings until the answering machine switched on.

"Hello!" Gubbins' salutation was phlegmy and bizarre, but at least he'd caught his breath in time.

"Hello?" Casey had no idea who it was.

"Casey!"

"Yes, this is Casey."

He could practically hear her expression sinking. "This is Cles Gubbins. I'm having some problem with my cordless. Can you hear me? Thank you so much for calling me back!"

"No worries." After a beat, Casey felt impelled to fill in the silence. "Are you okay?"

By now, Paco was totally confused.

"Just fine. I need to get some new batteries for these handsets, that's all." Now that Gubbins had recovered, there was no stopping him. "I wanted to give you a little courtesy call to make sure that everything was okay and that Dorena was still giving you a ride to the party."

Casey nestled the receiver into her shoulder and looked up to Paco. "You and Dorrie still going to the Christmas party together?"

Resolute, Paco's eyes lit up. "Barbecue? Hell, yes! I'm going with or without her!"

"Yeah, Mr. Gubbins, it sounds like everything's a go." As soon as

Casey said it, Paco finally realized what was going on. Coyly, she turned away so she wouldn't have to see his sneer.

"Great, great. You take it easy, and I'll see you at the party!"

"Will do. Bye-bye."

Gubbins heaved out a sigh as he hung up. His hand went south again. He couldn't help himself.

Casey stared at the receiver, scrunching up her face before slowly letting the handset fall into its cradle. That's when she turned to see Paco wearing *that* smile. The one guys always had when they thought their glorious penis wisdom could solve all your womanly problems.

"Look, I know your sister usually gives you some girl-type guidance on stuff like this," Paco's preamble began, "but since she ain't here right now..."

Casey knew it was coming, so she figured she'd just indulge him. "Yeah?"

"I say you let that geezer do whatever he wants," Paco said, the twinkle perfectly seated in is eye. "Go for the *di-ner-oooo!*"

"Paco?"

He was still nodding and smiling proudly. His lone word had such a swagger to it. "Yeah?"

"Why don't you shove your hash press up your ass sideways?" Casey recommended. "That way, you might be able to get your head up there even further."

Paco was shocked his sage advice wasn't taken to heart as Casey walked out of the room.

"Damn," Paco cowered back on the sofa, giving a tug on his outsized gardening gloves. He shouted back the hallway, "See if I ever give you any more valuable relationship counseling! I could charge big money for this stuff, you know!"

With her hand on the front doorknob, Stacey-Lynn steeled herself and walked outside. It was then she realized that she couldn't lock the door behind her—Ernesto hadn't left her the key—but she was only planning to be gone for a few minutes.

She made her way to the parking lot. The elastic cover popped off the back fender of her car as she rolled it up just enough to get in through the driver's side door. Not having much change on her, Stacey-Lynn rummaged through the ashtray until she uncovered a dusty quarter and a small stack of nickels. Hopefully, it was enough to make two phone calls.

Circle K was just down the highway, no more than a fourth of a mile. Praying that Fitz was awake by now, she made her way down to the telephone booth. No one saw her, and if they did, they didn't talk to her. Being ignored never felt so good. By now, she could start to make out the Pacific Bell logo.

The dial tone was music to her ears as she dropped in a quarter and five nickels, leaving her with only 15 cents. If she absolutely had to, the next call could be a free call to 9-1-1. It was tough to remember her home number, but her fingers pressed the correct sequence.

She waited. Finally, he answered.

"Yeah?" Fitz said, low and lean through the dead space in the lines.

"Fitz? You awake?" Stacey-Lynn's mouth went dry as the phone clicked and deposited her money.

"You. Goddamn bitch." He said it so calmly, almost resigned. Nothing else was offered.

"Fitz? We need to talk."

"I'm gonna come for you," Fitz promised, just as calmly. "You can't run away from me, little girl. Stupid little girl."

"I'm not coming back home, Fitz. I think—"

"Where you at?"

Somehow, Stacey-Lynn felt indestructible. All she had to do was finish the calls and go back. Past her covered car. Through Ernesto's door. She could be safe from Fitz, LeisureFace, the police, and anything else in this town.

"I think we've gone as far as we can go, Fitz."

"Where. The FUCK. Are you at?"

She couldn't help but smile. "I'm here at work, Fitz. But you can't come down here right now, okay?"

The phone went dead.

Her finger lifted and pulled down the silver flap inside the cradle. She made her second call, as planned.

Three minutes later, Stacey-Lynn walked back to Ernesto's with those same three nickels in her pocket.

It may have taken 50 cents to make a phone call, but for half that, you could get yourself a brand spanking new tampon or maxi pad from the wall-mounted machine in the ladies' room of the LeisureFace rec center.

At the moment, Berta and Dorena just happened to be emptying all the not-so-fresh ones from the sanitary napkin disposal next to it. Both of their hands groaned and squeaked from the latex gloves they wore.

"Dude, this is so fucking nasty," Dorena asserted, half-disbelieving she volunteered to do this. "How many do we have?"

"Way more than enough," Berta said with a grinding confidence. "The cleaning crew never empties these things."

"I'm totally burning these gloves as soon as we're done." Dorena realized she had said this out loud and couldn't help but snicker.

"Hey, the only reason we're doing this is because I didn't have the stomach to save used toilet paper!" The adhesive on a blocking maxi pad broke way and a series of springy, bloodied cotton pads dislodged from the disposal container.

"Gaaaah!" Dorena exclaimed as the bounty bounced to the ground like a bunch of wounded white rabbits. "How are you gonna sew up all the pillows again?"

"I brought in my sewing machine—it's on my desk! It'll take me less than ten minutes to do them all."

To Dorena, Berta seemed to be enjoying this way too much, but she had to admire her boss's sense of vengeance. "Yeah, but can you make them look new again? Finished edges and shit?"

For now, the bunnies were safely inside a clear trash bag. Berta snapped off her gloves and slapped her hands together. "4-H Sewing Club, 1962!"

Dorena wanted to follow Berta's lead and take off her gloves, as well —the tightness was already making her hands sweat—but the ick-factor of the past 60 seconds was enough to keep them in place. "You certainly know how to have a fun time. Who knew you were such a role model?"

"Yeah. Guess I'm glad I never had kids, for obvious reasons," Berta began her narration without ever having to look up to get her point across—the three little letters that bound the two women's pasts didn't need a roadmap to find its anguished destination.

Dorena tossed out the thought of her ex as soon as it came in. She was getting good at it by now.

The pause Berta had wedged into her explanation gave just enough of a window for her words to shine through. "But all my nieces and nephews just love their Auntie Berta."

For Dorena and Berta, the proud moment allowed them some relief, as if it was okay to pat one another on the back for making it this far down similar footpaths through their own private hells. At least, it would have been.

But that's when they heard the first crash.

Both of the ladies cowered behind the door as they cracked it open. Berta knew from the sound—the glass liner shattering inside a coffee carafe—that it came from Reception.

"Where the fuck are you??" Fitz's voice was too hoarse for them to know who it was until he screamed out a name. "STACEY-LYNN!"

Berta backed away from the door.

"Shit." Dorena recognized her and Paco's competition. She turned back to Berta, who appeared a bit rattled. "It's Fitz."

Finding out who the culprit was didn't melt away Berta's anxiety as her focus set on Stacey-Lynn. "Oh no," she muttered, her voice breathy and charged. "What's happened to her?"

Another sharp crash ricocheted back from the cathedral ceilings of the entranceway. The etched glass mirror featuring the LeisureFace logo dropped in large chunks to the tiled floor, smashing apart with rough gobs of staccato sound.

"You can't hide, little girl!" Fitz's voice was high and shrill as he strained. His syllables faded into obscure anger. Both women could hear him begin to argue with some of the guests. That's when Berta's nerve bricked itself up and she pushed back the door, running for Reception.

"Berta!" Dorena called after her, to no avail. She ripped the walkie-talkie from the back of her waistband. "Dorena to Ernesto!"

An older couple and their young granddaughter stood far away from Fitz, the grandmother shielding the frightened little girl with her arm. Another silver-haired retiree in a Speedo stood on the other side of the doors leading to the pool. He had pushed the trash can from aside the Jacuzzi in between the door and the wall to keep Fitz trapped inside.

"Fitz!" Berta yelled in the cavernous, breezy entranceway. He locked eyes with her, but she turned from his gaze to reassure the couple. The little girl began to cry. "It's okay, don't be scared."

Berta couldn't stop shaking. "What's happened to Stacey-Lynn?" Her question was quiet, but steely in its insistence. Berta saw Ernesto and Dorena heading for the entranceway, and it gave her the impetus to dig a bit deeper. "Just talk to us. We're worried about her." More guests started gathering around.

Dorena, and then Ernesto, caught Fitz's eye as they hurried up the entranceway. "You think you can hide her," Fitz smiled. A diseased, toothy gash of a smile that spread farther across his mouth than it should have. He looked right at Ernesto. "But you can't."

It was just an unhappy coincidence, but Ernesto nearly shit his pants, nonetheless.

Berta resumed her calming approach. "Do you know where she is?"

"She said she was here!" Fitz's teeth disappeared under a scowl, and he flicked his finger back and forth between himself and everyone present. "But we...we all know she's just a little liar, isn't she?" He gave a firm kick to the busted carafe. The lid unhinged and sprayed out decaf, showering the blond paneling under the check-in counter.

Ernesto saw a police car pull up and felt an emotional taffy pull of fear and relief. It wasn't just because he didn't want to face Fitz, let alone the cops, but his genuine concern for the guests impelled Ernesto to begin ushering them away from Reception and back out toward the elevator.

By now, numerous LeisureFace guests were standing outside their open doors in various stages of undress and annoyance. Dorena flagged down the cop as soon as he looked her way. What was probably the ride-along rookie, a young woman with her hair stuffed under her spotless hat, rode shotgun.

The cop was typically stern as he approached Dorena. "We're looking for a Mr. Fitzgerald."

At that same moment, Gubbins' Mercedes was turning off 101 and heading down LeisureFace's main driveway. In his heart, he felt optimistic and prideful, positive that the precisely manicured branches, shining greenery, and shouting rainbows of flowers adorning it all would make a great first impression on the arriving folks from StileCorp.

One thing that knocked the stately atmosphere down a peg was the drug dealer getting slammed against a state patrol car and cuffed just outside of Reception...as dozens of guests looked on in astonishment.

"Jesus Christ!" Gubbins roared as the car came to an abrupt stop at the side of the rounded driveway. He jumped from the driver's seat but was immediately blocked by the rookie policewoman patrolling the scene.

"I'm sorry, sir, please back away from this area," she said with mechanical resistance.

"What are talking about? I'm Androcles Gubbins, I'm the goddamned owner!" Gubbins barked. He saw Berta with Ernesto in the background as Fitz was roughly transferred to the back of the squad car. "You tell me what's happening here!"

"For your own safety, sir—"

Gubbins bent down the policewoman's arm and brusquely made his way past her. Broken mirror shards were everywhere. Berta held up her hand to the female cop, who relented and allowed the piping-mad CEO inside. He was immediately met by the staunch male officer.

"Mr. Gubbins?"

Gubbins saw the *Your Leisure Is Our Business—Be Back Momentarily!* sign on the countertop of the front desk. A few sharply uneven cubes of mirror glass were sprinkled around it. "Where's Stacey-Lynn?"

"Sir, could we talk to you in your office for a moment?"

Gubbins fumed, motioning to the corridor off the breezeway. He turned back to Dorena, Ernesto, and Berta. "You three, don't move from this room."

Dorena threw back her head with an impertinent roll of her eyes.

All three did as told and Berta knew they'd get their collective asses chewed off as soon as Gubbins got updated on the reason his Reception area was such a mess.

After reaching the door, Gubbins realized that he didn't have his keys, as he'd bounded so quickly out of his car that they were still in the ignition.

"Berta, if you would!" He stood a step back, pointing at the door with his open hand.

Berta carefully took out her keyring and walked down the hallway, swiftly unlocking the knob.

Gubbins ushered in the two officers and promptly slammed the door in her face. Her feet crunched through the glass as she walked back to Dorena and Ernesto.

They could hear Gubbins raving all the way down the hall.

"God, I hope she's alright." Berta finally offered as the guests seemed to lose interest and began to return to their rooms.

"She is," Ernesto said, vaguely decisive. "Stacey-Lynn's smart. She wouldn't allow herself to get this deep."

Dorena's eyes darted between her two co-workers. "I don't know, man, Fitz is certifiable. I'm no angel and no one in my circle is, but even I never thought he was a *tecato*."

Ernesto was a lightweight when it came to anything much harder than yeast and hops. "*Tecato?*"

Dorena assured them, "Yeah, I know needle drugs when I see them. Look, this place is gonna turn into a madhouse in a few minutes, what do we do?"

"Come on, let's go ahead and get it cleaned up," Ernesto tendered, turning to Dorena. "Can you get me the push broom from the water heater room?"

"Yeah, I could use a fuckin' smoke right about now, anyway," Dorena confided.

"Dorena!" Berta admonished, trying not to laugh.

Dorena seemed offended at first, but noticed Berta's smiling eyes and relented. "It was a joke! A joke, okay?"

"I'm gonna unscrew the rest of the mirror and go grab the Shop Vac." Ernesto had a plan, and it was all coming together. "It's cool. If we all pitch in, we'll get this done in no time."

But Gubbins had a different plan, and he looked none too pleased as his office door opened. Preceding him were the two officers, who gave the waiting three a bid of good day on their way out.

The toe of Gubbins' expensive loafer pushed some overturned paper cups from the coffee bar out of the way as he achingly made his way to his employees. There was no hiding his anger.

"Any of you heard from Stacey-Lynn?"

Berta and Dorena shook their heads. Ernesto stayed suitably mute, making sure not to lock eyes with anyone and risk giving anything away.

"No," Berta said quietly, "she never showed."

"She didn't call you this morning?" Dorena asked the owner, cavalier in her assumption.

"No, she didn't. That's why I'm asking." Gubbins' tone was cutting and unfair.

"Sorry. It's just you're the one with the seniority." There was something rotten at the end of Dorena's statement. "I figured…" She trailed off, trying to keep her insolence safely capped.

"You'd figured right, but when I'm not here, Berta's the one with the seniority," Gubbins reasoned in his haughty tone of empty corporate logic.

"And she did a damn good job," Ernesto piped up. "No one got hurt—"

"This *business* got hurt." Gubbins seethed. "All those guests who saw this got hurt."

"Come on, Mr. Gubbins." Ernesto was casual, but his tone telegraphed that he couldn't exactly take stock in Gubbins' stance. "The guy was clearly out of control, and Berta talked him down till the police showed up."

"And if Berta had exercised her seniority and kept a better eye on the property, we may not have the mess we do now."

"You're blaming me for this?" Berta kept her tears at bay for as long as she could. "For the love of God, I can't believe what I'm hearing."

Gubbins chipped away at his head of Housekeeping just a little more. "Given your bad judgment this morning, your disbelief doesn't surprise me."

"Uhh, fuck me." Under her breath, it was low and grumbly, but there was no mistaking what Dorena said.

"Miss Morris, you need to nix the opinions and get behind the check-in desk!"

Dorena, still needing a smoke and not particularly looking forward to dealing with about fifty confused and irate guests, balked at the suggestion. "You're looking at a goddamn lawsuit if anyone gets hurt here," motioning to the massive Reception mess, "so we need to help Ernesto clean this up—"

"Ernesto can manage that just fine by himself. I want you behind that counter now." Gubbins then turned his bitter stare to Berta. "And I want you to finish those StileCorp deep cleans. We have them starting to arrive in less than eight hours, and they had better be finished on time and perfect, understand?"

If StileCorp was arriving in less than eight hours, then Berta knew she was late taking her meds. And the price of those meds was the only thing that kept her from quitting that very second. But keeping your mouth shut doesn't necessarily go hand in hand with going out quietly.

As she headed into the hall, Berta's hand ripped at the thin, shattered corner of the LeisureFace mirror, the bulk of the remainder that had precariously stayed hanging on the wall came down with an almost supersonic smash.

"Aww, shit," Ernesto groaned.

Gubbins turned back to the other two. His eyes stayed shut for a long pause as he tried to keep his temperature from rising any further. "Where's Junior?" he finally asked.

"Took his dad to a doctor's appointment," Dorena said. "He even came in to tell Berta on the way."

Though Junior never knew, the way Dorena explained his absence got him off the hook. Any medical excuse is usually a safe one, but the fact she added that he made a specific effort, en route, to let a supervisor know cleared him from any potential reprimand.

"Alright, get to work," Gubbins groused. The only consolation for Ernesto and Dorena was that he slipped on some broken glass as he made for his office.

That afternoon, Gubbins maintained a stiff upper lip and screwed on his best salesman faceplate as, one by one, each of the StileCorp upper echelon arrived.

Brody Teague, a young, Black entrepreneur who had risen from travel agent to CEO of StileCorp in less than a decade, was the self-sufficient, congenial type Gubbins didn't have to concern himself about. However, his dapper whims were just executive enough to make him worry about Ernesto coming through with his tailor-made, African-themed performance.

Brody's finicky demands were mere child's play compared to others on his payroll. Overall, the Pain in the Ass Award of the Year had to go to the StileCorp CFO, a nervous Asian named Ken Tusumura, who dragged along his pedantic wife, Elaine, as if they were a donkey and apple cart clamped together at the waist. Two people whose superstitious hokum and fastidious bellyaching would've sent even the stoutest Buddhist monk in search of a loaded sidearm.

Nothing was good enough. Fast enough. Easy enough for them. They second-guessed the sturdiness of the lock on their top-floor balcony slider, because you never can tell when someone will climb 30 feet up in 80-mile-per-hour winter gusts to get into someone's room. Elaine requested five—not four, and not six—extra little shampoo bottles because she promised all five of her grandkids a present from the trip. And before the two sandy vaginas could barely make it over the threshold of their suite, they were making use of the television's parental control to block channel 4, as the number is closely associated with death in Japanese culture. Therefore, the Tusumuras had to make do without the TV Guide Channel.

The rest of the StileCorp crew was a bunch of faceless non-runners, tagging along simply to snag a free oceanfront suite for the weekend. Wholly understandable, but not exactly desirable.

Gubbins finally sat down to dinner—along with five glasses of scotch (not four, not six)—at 10:47 that night.

The rest of the day wasn't much fun for anyone else, either.

Berta finally took her meds but first made her way back to grab the bag she'd left in the ladies' room of the rec center. If you got close enough to Housekeeping that next hour, you would have been able to smell the smoke coming off her sewing machine. The edges of each StileCorp guest pillow were compromised and overcast-stitched back up impeccably, suitable for the perfect condition Gubbins instructed the rooms to be in by early that afternoon. She spent the rest of the evening trimming buds for the party.

Junior never did make it back to work that day. The backup at the doctor's office was mighty, and the fact that his dad kept harping on about Nurse Dorena ordering another blood draw didn't help expedite anything, either. Oddly enough, the doctor agreed, as he, too, took an interest in those little red spots on Berrick's arms.

Nurse Dorena herself was in a sour mood by the time she got home that evening. Her back hurt, and she chose to take it out on her sister, who had quit days earlier and surely would've gotten check-out duty had she still been there. Meanwhile, Casey was edgy due to having second thoughts about Gubbins and the party. Thankfully, Paco broke out his inaugural hash ball and everyone settled down a bit.

Stacey-Lynn second-guessed her husband's rage to a tee, but it still didn't prepare her for the emotional impact when Ernesto told her about it that night. She knew anything she left behind at the trailer was probably destroyed, but still had an unshakable need to go back home one last time. Ernesto talked her out of it, at least for the evening. Instead, they made plans and began to load up each of their cars with belongings. Though there wasn't a chance in hell of Fitz making bail, there wasn't any time to waste.

And Fitz? Quite fittingly, he spent the evening in the same town most of his drugs came from. John Everett Fitzgerald was booked into the Lane County Corrections Division in Eugene for Aggravated Assault, Possession with Intent to Distribute, Disturbing the Peace, and Vandalism. No, he wasn't sodomized. At least not that night.

The next morning, there was something that made Stacey-Lynn itchy about getting back to the house. As she drove up to it, she found out why.

Not even halfway down the driveway, she saw the pile blocking the entrance to the carport, obviously heaved out the partially broken-out bedroom window directly above it. She recognized all of it—her magazines, a Raggedy Ann doll from when she was a kid, the clothes she had left behind, her stand mixer. All of it drenched and waiting for her. It was heart-wrenching, but she felt oddly vindicated and blessed that she'd already filled up her car the night she'd left.

She and Ernesto made their way inside. The front door was unlocked.

It wasn't the traces of raging fallout Fitz had left, but there was just something about the way things were shuffled around that gave her the immediate impression that the cops had been here. Stacey-Lynn didn't indulge in the mental semantics and, then and there, began her long assignment of erasing Fitz from her life.

"Don't take anything more from here. You don't need it." There was a bit of sentry in Ernesto's warning. A big part of him wished he hadn't let her come here again.

But Stacey-Lynn didn't feel the need to lament the heap of her belongings out in the rain, or even swear to hate Fitz's guts for the rest of her natural-born life. She just wanted to start over. The only thing she really needed at the moment was her man. And some money.

And that's when she found a note by the phone in Fitz's jagged hand-writing. A 1-800 number and BANK OF AMERICA scratched into it so hard, he'd ripped the paper in two spots.

"Oh God," she whispered, turning to look straight into Ernesto's blank, ashen face. "We gotta get to the bank."

And that's where they were headed next. But not before Stacey-Lynn pulled Raggedy Ann and her stand mixer from the pile on their way out.

The Bank of America was all the way uptown. Both of them felt each agonizing mile as they got closer, with Stacey-Lynn petrified of what Fitz had surely done to her.

Finally arriving, Stacey-Lynn flew up to the ATM and pushed in her debit card. It was promptly swallowed whole by the machine after she'd entered her PIN.

Fitz had reported her copy of his bank card as stolen.

The account was solely in his name, leaving Stacey-Lynn worth the sum of $18.52, all of it currently stuffed under the snaps of her pocket-book. Actually, the total was $18.67 if you counted the three nickels that still glided around the murk at the bottom of her ashtray.

Ernesto held Stacey-Lynn as she cried for the first time that day. Upon first learning of Fitz's instability, he had warned her about get-ting her own bank account. She continued putting blind trust in him, and that's why Ernesto felt a bit angry, but now wasn't the time for I-told-you-so's.

"Don't worry, baby. We're going to be alright. Gubbins owes me. At least, he will."

By saying that aloud, Ernesto knew he was going to have to deliver at the StileCorp presentation that night. He walked Stacey-Lynn back to the car, which started and merged its way into the southbound traffic as they headed home to refine their plans some more.

Neither of them ever noticed Gubbins' Mercedes parked three spots away.

Seconds later, its owner strolled out of the bank with a determined look on his face. His key fob unlocked the driver's side, and soon he was safely back inside before he started to count out his money—all $1,200 worth in cash.

"It's true," Gubbins admitted to himself. "Once a cheater, always a cheater." The human blood in his veins made him register a baseline of regret, but in the case of men like Androcles J. Gubbins, that feeling never lasts long. "But the good cheaters don't leave a credit card trail," he prided himself in adding.

Gubbins pulled out his billfold and the small stack of hundreds slid inside. Over on the passenger seat, a slip of paper was clipped to the Crescent Treasures brochure he'd settled on right before his wife had left. His reservation number, check-in time, and some golfing details were printed legibly across the sheet. Inside the brochure was Casey's Polaroid. He closed the leaflet as fast as he opened it, as if to keep from tempting himself.

Gubbins headed home to get some preliminaries ready for the evening soirée. Single-mindedly, he made his way into the front door and up the stairs to the master bathroom, never seeing the multitude of blinking message lights on the answering machine.

He was too busy fretting in the mirror to notice. Too pale. Too wrinkly. Too gray. Honestly, he didn't have enough hair to worry about being too gray. After slipping into half of his Christmas-green suit and standing there looking at his reflection, Gubbins was suddenly very glum, and he knew he had to do something about it. He'd found a very old bottle of 'sunless tanning lotion', but neither that nor the "Just for Men" hair coloring he'd recently picked up at Safeway right before heading to the bank seemed the right answer. He even pulled back the skin of his forehead to rid himself of a couple of decades.

"Sixty. Forty! Sixty. Forty!"

Coming to terms with the fact that he was fighting a losing battle, his taut skin eventually was let go and sagged back down, landing firmly back inside the realm of late-middle-age.

That's when the other part of the mirror's reflection caught his eye.

A dark green that perfectly matched his suit hung off the bedside valet. He dashed back and whipped it off the hook. It went straight onto his head without Gubbins once more looking at his odious scalp. Suddenly, all was right. The golf cap made the rest of the outfit look smart and finished.

Feeling much better about his age, Gubbins did up his Santa-red velvet tie. He turned his attention to the overnight bag he'd begun to fill up earlier that morning before making the trip to the bank. Assorted sundries and two changes of clothes were fastidiously compartmentalized on top of the bedspread.

Gubbins' fingers flicked through some of the smaller items and found another purchase from the recent Safeway trip: a three-pack of Trojan 'Shared Sensation' condoms that promised a special wang-friendly shape for him, and a unique, vag-vibrating texture for her. Everyone goes home happy.

He looked at the little tear-open package and tried to remember the last time he had to use one. 1956? A part of Gubbins—and not just his penis—hoped they were a little thinner than they used to be. Fucking when he was younger required you to wear something on your erection that was approximately the same thickness as a Michelin tire.

Ultimately, Gubbins was only banking love-gloves in case his virginal ingénue turned out to be less innocent than he originally estimated. He didn't want that 'shared sensation' to be a V.D. burn or, even worse, that HIV virus, like Berta was rumored to have.

Gubbins bounced back down to the first floor with his packed overnight bag in hand. The chrome wall tiles at the bottom of the stairway served as a makeshift mirror for him to check his debonair reflection.

They were also what tipped him off to the series of blinks from the red light on the answering machine.

His conscience got rattled just a bit—there were a lot of messages on there—but even if his wife left him a ton of grieving, weepy messages about the passing of his cunt-in-law, the brimming confidence he had would allow him to deal with it just fine.

But the calls weren't from his wife.

Gubbins pushed down on the white plastic PLAY button.

Beep!

"*Hello, Mr. Gubbins. This is Steve, the night auditor.*" Though he never saw him much, Steve was fine fellow, and the reason for Gubbins' gilded opinion of him was evident in his voice, which was very even and skilled. "*I think we might have a problem with the StileCorp guest suites. A couple of guests have complained, and rightfully so, that the little flap on the refrigerator for the water and ice was...zip-tied down and slowly flooding the rooms.*"

The first of Gubbins' many brow furrows over the next couple of minutes rumbled along the shore of his forehead.

"*I sliced them off with some scissors here at the desk and cleaned up the mess. One of them wanted moved to a new room, so I did, but it's not a suite. Since the employees have booked rooms for the party this weekend, I don't have anything to offer.*" Steve's voice fell a bit, discouraged but not broken. "*Also, the pool will be totally out of towels in the morning since I had to use the remainder of them to clean up the rooms—*"

Steve's collected attitude was just professional enough to begin boring Gubbins. His finger dropped again on the button.

Beep!

"*Mr. Gubbins? This is Steve again.*"

Gubbins shifted from bored to annoyed at the sound of the same voice.

"*Uh... A few of the StileCorp people are complaining that there's a seafood or...seaweed kinda smell coming from somewhere in their rooms.*"

Gubbins' annoyance made him start talking to the recording. "Well, have 'em open up a damn window then, Steve!"

"*I gave them some deionizers and had them open the windows for a bit.*"

"Thank you!" Gubbins roared at the answering machine.

"I think we're finally okay—just wanted to give you a call since this was pretty out of the ordinary, and I wanted to keep—"

Another brow furrow pocked Gubbins' nose, and his finger slapped down the button again.

Beep!

"Mr. Gubbins, I just had the wife of one of the StileCorp guests down here...." Steve's hoarse, thickening voice paused, sighing. *"She's threatening to sue us if we don't pay for her dress."*

Sue? Steve officially had Gubbins' attention.

"Someone taped crayons onto the dryer drum and her clothes are now covered in wax. She wasn't happy talking to me, so I told her to give you a call in the morning."

Gubbins was bewildered enough to keep his mouth shut and stop talking back to the tape. He tilted his head closer to the machine to make sure he was hearing all this correctly.

"Meanwhile, three rooms have called to demand different pillows in just the past few minutes! It's like something got spilled on them or in them or something. They brought one down and it smells positively awful! Look, I'm sorry for how late these calls are, but get back to me as soon as you get this—"

Gubbins' panicked finger pushed down so hard, the PLAY button cracked.

Beep!

"Gubbins, I don't know what's going on here, but four—count 'em—four StileCorp people have told me that there's something wrong with the showers now. It's like mint or chicken soup or I don't know!!"

By now, the professionalism in Steve's voice was gone.

"I have no idea who booby-trapped your rooms tonight, but I've got one spooked Asian guy running around with nothing on but a shower cap, screaming about how the building is cursed by ghosts, so now I have the cops down here—and they said this is the second time today they've been here!"

Desperate, Gubbins began scanning the area for his keys before realizing they were already in his pocket.

"Listen, I don't know where the FUCK you are right now, but you've got

some really unhappy people here, and I'm one of them! You need to get down here RIGHT NOW."

Beep!

It was a good thing Gubbins lived on the LeisureFace property. Within seconds, the Mercedes' speedometer was blur and gravel popped and slung onto the long driveway leading to the awning outside the main entryway.

As if he was waiting for him, StileCorp CEO, Brody Teague, was out there in front of the main entrance. He had a doubting look on his face as he took a drag off a cigarette. The whiteness of the stick showed perfectly against the backdrop of Brody's warm, brown skin.

Gubbins pumped the brakes gently and threw the Mercedes into park. Before he could open his mouth, Brody started his gazette with an ominous bit of irony.

"You missed quite a show."

Gubbins motioned for Brody to follow him, and soon they were through the door bearing the CEO's nameplate.

"You know," Brody began with a dangerous smile, "you promised us quite a weekend. I don't know if what it's been so far is exactly what any of us anticipated."

Though he hadn't heard a single specific from Brody yet, Gubbins felt the need to begin with an apology, based on the series of answering machine messages he'd heard less than five minutes ago.

"Mr. Brody, I deeply apologize for anything that may have happened this past evening to you, the Tusumuras, or any of the StileCorp—"

"Ah yes, the Tusumuras." Brody's smile evened out again. "Let's just say the Tusumuras have checked out for the weekend, and we'll leave it at that."

Gubbins' lips parted but nothing came out for a second. Finally, his curiosity took over. "Are they alright?"

"Mr. Gubbins, as you may already know, the Japanese are a proud and resolute people. Proud of their customs, which include a little superstition, but they're resolute enough to get over a criminal charge of indecent exposure."

"Indecent exposure?" Though Steve had alluded to it on the answering machine messages, it was so bizarre to hear it confirmed.

"After dealing with a mysterious burning shower, some really foul pillows, and a hot dryer full of wax crayons—by the way," Brody pointed to the front desk, "Mrs. Tusumura left a bill for the damage to the dress she was going to wear tonight—my somewhat high-strung Chief Financial Officer took to the hallways, naked, to warn all your guests of a curse on the building."

Gubbins wanted to laugh—the thought of Mr. Tusumura's tiny tush bouncing around the exterior corridors as he made like some kind of Japanese Henny Penny was certainly something to snicker at, but he couldn't do it. The notion of never being able to retire made everything remarkably staid at the moment.

"I don't know what to say," Gubbins said quietly.

"Hell, I wouldn't, either!" Brody laughed, allowing the mortified LeisureFace patriarch a chance to have his sense of humor live vicariously through him for a short, splendid second. He looked around Gubbins' office, the shortening butt heating his fingers. "You got an ashtray around here?"

Gubbins looked around and, subserviently, dumped out his pens onto the desktop, allowing Brody to commandeer his pencil cup.

"Thank you," Brody remarked as the cigarette's last gasp of smoke whispered up to the ceiling. His hand went immediately into the pocket of his blazer. He pulled out a small white ring. "There's a reason for everything, Mr. Gubbins, and Ken Tusumura's burning shower was nothing more than this."

"What is it?" Gubbins asked, narrowing his eyes at the half-melted object.

"It's a Life Saver. Peppermint. Someone put it in the showerhead, I take it. Just like someone taped crayons to the inside of your dryer drum. And the pillows?"

Gubbins was almost afraid to ask. "Yeah?"

"The night auditor sliced one open. They were full of tampons and sanitary napkins. Used tampons and sanitary napkins."

Both of Gubbins' hands raised over his face. "Oh my God," he grumbled, wanting to simply disappear from sight. A thought of Casey and his forthcoming night with her was the solitary thing keeping his head above water, and so his brain grabbed onto it like, well, like a lifesaver ring.

Brody clapped his hand on Gubbins' back. "Have a seat, Mr. Gubbins." There was a lot of understanding in the cheery, professional imperative, so Gubbins did as told, his old knees sinking him into his desk chair. Brody continued, "Like I said, there's a reason for everything, and I think the explanation we have here is that you haven't yet told your workers about the StileCorp team taking over at the first of the year, I take it?"

"No, I haven't." Gubbins felt a weight of sorts lifting off him as he admitted it, but the air he heaved, in turn, was foggy and restricting. "I'm still trying to figure out how they all could already know."

"Come now, Mr. Gubbins," Brody chastised, "you're not that naïve, are you? You can only keep a lid on a piece of information like that for so long before it crawls out the jar! This acquisition ain't my first rodeo, and I've seen this kind of thing before, believe me. So, here's what I'm gonna do: I'm gonna round up all my folks and take them out for a nice lunch while you get to work finding us some new guest rooms here."

"New guest rooms?" Gubbins parroted.

"That's right. I'm sure you have some—first rule of the hospitality industry, Mr. Gubbins, is to set aside some rooms during a busy time so, if something unexpected happens, you don't disappoint anyone." Brody's voice hardened, almost imperceptibly. "And I know, I know you're the kind of man who won't disappoint StileCorp."

Gubbins' mind was already beginning to race for ways to save his ass before it had the opportunity to rise out of the chair.

"Absolutely."

"Alright then!" Brody's teeth shone, and he looked quite satisfied. "I'm going up to let everyone know lunch is on me and to ready their bags. And oh," Brody pulled a piece of paper out of his back pocket as he opened the door, "I told Steve, your night auditor, that I would give you this." He turned back to Gubbins at the main entranceway. "Is two o'clock good for you?"

"Yes!" Gubbins nodded his weary head. "That will be just fine."

"Right on! Then the StileCorp gang is off in search of some local smoked salmon! See you later, Mr. Gubbins."

Gubbins waived as merrily as he could before opening the folded paper from his night auditor.

LICK ME WHERE I SHIT, GUBBINS! SEND ME MY FINAL PAY-CHECK!!

And, just in case there was any doubt regarding how Steve felt, underneath the bolded adieu was the charming drawing of a hand with its middle finger raised.

The soles of Gubbins' shoes gave a harsh clap on the tile floor as he zoomed back into his office, wrenching up the receiver to the phone. His Rolodex spun and blurred until it rested on "MANCARI, BERTA – HOUSEKEEPING LEAD".

Berta was happily readying her party supplies for that evening when the phone started to ring. For a second, she debated whether or not to answer. For some reason, she had an inkling that she didn't want to talk to whoever was on the other end of the line.

She should've gone with her gut, especially since the answering machine beat her to it.

"*Hi, this is Berta!*" the jaunty recording announced. "*Please leave a message and I'll get back to you soon...*"

Berta's hands raked up the receiver just as the shrill *beeeeep!* kicked in. "Hello, Mancari residence, this is Roberta."

Gubbins' black voice flew out of the receiver. "I know it was you."

"Who is this?" Berta was pretty sure who it was, but there was a smidgen of doubt in her mind whether or not it was really Gubbins. His voice sounded so...weird, underlining just how irate he was.

"You know who this is, now you listen to me. Because of your little stunt, I'm canceling your room for the party so I can move some of our poor StileCorp executives that you inconvenienced with your asinine little tricks!"

Berta was busted cold but put up a great act. "What are you talking about?"

"The zip ties on the refrigerators. Peppermints in the shower. Crayons in the dryer! The goddamn maxi pads in the pillows!"

Despite underestimating how frightening Gubbins' rage could be, Berta's smile was hard to hide.

"You're out of your mind," she snapped back, flatly. "I paid for that room a month ago—we all did! I'm not giving it up because of your lack of foresight to block out some rooms during one of the busiest times of the year."

"Lack of foresight? Lack of foresight?! I know you and your classless little shit of a flunky, Dorena, set this up, and I'll be writing up her termination first thing Monday morning, in case you were wondering."

"First of all, I still have no idea what you're talking about." Berta paused to pop a Pep-O-Mint Life Saver in her mouth. She crunched it as she talked, reveling in the thought of sparks flying out of her mouth and through the phone, zapping Gubbins at will. "And, even if I did, you have no proof whatsoever of any wrongdoing from anybody!"

Berta was starting to sound like a paralegal, and that was probably a good thing. She was surprising herself by how well she was handling this. The four joints she smoked late that morning probably helped.

"Playing stupid isn't helping, and for wasting my time, I'm going to keep your $50 for damages to the room! But you're lucky, Berta, you're a really lucky lady," Gubbins teased. "You wanna know why?"

"Sure. Tell me," Berta groaned.

"Our company Christmas party has got me in the holiday spirit so much, Miss Mancari, that I'm not going to fire you...because I know how much you need medical coverage." Gubbins paused as long as he could, as if the more silence he pushed into the breach could make the next sentence hurt even more. "That, and because I'll always need a woman to wash all the shit stains out of my guests' towels. That's really why I'm keeping you."

It worked. Berta exploded.

"You're not keeping anyone! Everyone knows you're selling to

StileCorp this weekend—that's why you're having this party!" Berta's toes mashed into the carpeting, and the phone cord whipped and rattled against the kitchen paneling as she paced. "You don't give a shit about your people and you never did! So stop acting like you're doing any of us a fucking favor, because we've known the whole time what you've been up to!"

"Well, Berta, after tonight, that all changes for every single one of you slobs on my payroll." Gubbins was nothing if not smug as he bid his farewell.

He just wasn't suspecting Berta to get the last word.

"Bet your ass it does, Mr. Gubbins."

Berta crashed the receiver back into its cradle and cried, hating herself for letting the pettiness of Cles Gubbins get to her this badly. All of her set up was for nothing. She decided she wasn't going to the party.

Sitting down at the computer, the harangue from the back of the tower scratched her ears as the dial-up made its connection. Her hand navigated the cursor around until she could resume the research she'd begun a few days back: consulting with a headhunter in Portland. Berta detested the idea of moving back to the city, but finding a new job with her level of medical benefits in Beaver Lake before summer, which is when her exorbitantly-priced COBRA extension would expire, was going to be next to impossible.

The proposals from Hal, the happy headhunter, seemed out of reach. For at least the hundredth time in the past week, Berta's eyes scanned down the list of jobs he was considering for her. Cushy, decent-paying bed and breakfast work in Lake Oswego. Housekeeping Supervisor at a new lodge out by the foothills in Sandy. A 'fun staff' and 'good bennies' with a Westin resort in Oregon City. Maybe one or two things on the coast, but to hell and back from Beaver Lake. Long shots. All of them. It seemed like any path she chose led to the same expensive inertia she faced now.

Which is exactly why she changed her mind.

Berta stood up and wound her way to the bedroom, headed straight for the top drawer of her dresser. Inside is where she kept all her work supplies out of sight when she wasn't on the job. On the far right of the jumble was her Housekeeping keyring. The flat card marked "MASTER" taunted her from the shallow depths.

She snatched it and slammed shut the drawer again, off to the kitchen to begin rounding up her supplies for the party.

ACT NOW

[SERVING SACRED COWS FOR SUPPER]

Just like Berta, party supplies were also the main priority for Paco at the moment.

The man was a force to be reckoned with in the kitchen. Impressively seasoned hamburger patties and sausages were being stacked up on the counter among a variety of open-mouthed spice jars. The expansive prep area may have been a general mess, with cumin and cayenne sprinkled positively everywhere, but the bright white wax paper stacks were the work of a professional. The only thing the man took more seriously than drugs was barbecue, and Paco was determined to get compliments all around.

When they had first gotten together, Dorena used to watch her human meat-grinder of a boyfriend with awe as he'd ready the goods for a cookout. That was long ago, though, and she had other things to deal with at the moment. Casey was being quiet and withdrawn, and Dorena knew it had to do with the prospect of going out on a date tonight with her ex-boss. To her big sister, Casey seemed to be taking the whole thing too far—she'd become all introverted and moody the past couple of days. With the party starting in just a few hours, Dorena was too busy rounding up bags of snacks and buns to worry much about Casey, who had sequestered herself in her bedroom.

Paco nodded his head as he surveyed all the meats he was, somehow, going to have to fit in a modestly-sized Igloo cooler. He loved what he saw.

"Hell, yes. Dorrie, this is gonna be the bomb."

"You got my extra oregano?"

"Shit, who you think you're talkin' to?" Paco feigned being insulted, but his joy was just too much to contain. A slick smile materialized sooner than he intended.

"Speaking of green," Dorena warned, "you better bring some extra smoke in case Berta forgets hers."

Paco was pumped and didn't want to waste time on nagging. "I'm on it, baby, get the chips ready! Let's go! Let's go! Let's do this, chica, come onnnn!"

"Case!" Dorena called back the hallway.

There was no answer, so she headed back towards Casey's bedroom. There was a strange, gurgling hum as she got closer to the door.

"Pac's getting the cooler ready," Dorena said, pushing back the door as she walked in, "can you help with—*holyJesusfuckingChrist!*"

"Dorena!!" Casey screamed as she prematurely cut off her orgasm. The vibrator, a shiny metal purple one, burred on and on inside of her as she scrambled desperately for the duvet to cover herself.

"Okay, you, like, totally have to start closing your door the whole way," Dorena chided, turning away.

"Get out!"

Dorena closed the door behind her but couldn't resist posing the favor she came in to ask of her sister. "When you're done, could you give me a hand with the snacks?"

Inside the room, Casey fumed in a ball on the bed. "I am done," she huffed under her breath. Her last tarot reading sure hadn't warned her anything about this. Indignant, she reached beneath the covers to twist the end of the vibrator, and the curious, even hum choked out.

Paco was drawn back the hallway to the commotion. Dorena was quick to stop him, though.

"Don't go in there, she's gettin' dressed."

"Oh!" Paco made a mock smooth of his hair and continued his lothario intent before Dorena pushed him hard against the wall just outside Casey's door.

"No, seriously," Dorena said, never cracking a smile.

Paco wisely turned toe and headed back to the kitchen to play with his meat some more.

It was already starting to get dark. It wasn't just from the December tilt of the Earth's axis, but a rich bolster of storm clouds jogging in from off the water.

Stacey-Lynn's backseat was bloated with both her and Ernesto's belongings, and she was doing her damnedest to cushion the box of her camera in between a Trailblazers throw blanket and the backside padding of her driver's seat. She locked up and headed back to the apartment. Before she could even get inside, she felt two raindrops plunk down through her poofy blonde hairdo.

Ernesto was still getting dressed. Blurs of orange and black and green and gold flitted around the bedroom as he got himself ready for the party.

"Anything else you want?" Stacey-Lynn called into the bathroom.

"Just you, baby," Ernesto pledged.

"Well, I know that," Stacey-Lynn giggled, excited to see what Ernesto looked like in his costume, that is, if he ever would come out of the bathroom. "But are you sure it's okay to leave the rest?"

A confident voice rushed out through the bedroom. "Yeah. The super said he'll take the entertainment center, and the rest he'll just round up for his next donation run. Alright," Ernesto vamped, "you ready for this shit?"

"Yes, yes!" squealed Stacey-Lynn, overripe with anticipation. "Get on with it already!"

Ernesto stepped out into the bedroom. His closet had sliding mirrored doors and, with the way he was standing, Stacey-Lynn got a 360-degree view of the costume. It was unbelievably resplendent—a long rust and gold dashiki with flecks of green and black trim. The proportions were very flattering, even down to the hat, which took on a more realistic feel after bleeding out part of its colors in the rain. It looked like it had been tailor-made for him.

"Wow," Stacey-Lynn said quietly, "that's not bad at all, hon." For the past 25 minutes, she had been getting ready to bust his balls, but the outfit was, quite simply, a cascade of fucking awesomeness.

A natural smile jumped, for just a second, across Ernesto's mouth. "I threw away the damn feathers."

The ends of Stacey-Lynn's eyes turned up and her white teeth shone their support. "Good move!" Still, there was something intrinsically wrong with the whole thing, though, and she could read it on Ernesto's face. "I can't believe you're really doing this."

Ernesto removed his hat, as if doing so could remove some of his shame, too. "It's money we really, really need right now," he countered with a reasonable amount of credibility.

"A lot?"

The shame rose a bit more. "He never said." Ernesto's fine, rust-wrapped shoulders squared as he turned back to her. "But any amount an old, rich white dude has in mind is a lot to us."

With less than twenty dollars to her name, Stacey-Lynn couldn't help but nod her agreement. "You ready?"

Ernesto took his next-to-last look around his home. "Yeah, almost."

"Okay," she patted his arm. "I'm gonna be out in the car."

Ernesto leaned over and kissed her quick. It was a subtle attempt to keep any more of his anxiety from being too easily read. He felt a great need to be strong for her now. "Cool, baby. I'll be right there." He seated the kufi back atop his head as Stacey-Lynn walked out of his place for the last time.

It was then Ernesto comprehended that, five minutes from now, he would be homeless. There was a certain terror on his dry lips, but the beating of freedom, love, and joy in his heart overrode the societal norms we sometimes take for granted.

At that moment, Ernesto Taylor was faced with having no safety net and no friends to help delay the inevitable consequences. The woman he loved had even less than he did, and they both were on the run from someone who'd certainly have whoop-ass in mind if and when he ever got out of the Lane County Adult Corrections Facility.

And he couldn't have been more thankful.

He had his health, he had a clean slate in front of him, and he had the liberty of being able to follow his heart, which belonged to the woman down there in the parking lot, and who was probably wondering what was taking him so long.

The keys clinked on the kitchen counter, leaving them just where he'd promised the super. This is when Ernesto took the last look at his home. He had to remind himself that it was no longer a 'home', though. Just a gutted box he used to live in.

The black Saturn revved up, its wipers pushing away the sluggish raindrops to clear Ernesto's path. Both the cars sloshed out onto 101, headed for one last stop before being able to leave everything else in Beaver Lake behind.

"Come on, what's taking you so long?" Junior called up the town-house stairwell. He could hear his father's footsteps scramble along the bulk of the living room ceiling.

"I'm coming, I'm coming! Keep your shirt on," Berrick griped from above.

"I'll keep mine on if you finally get yours on! I thought we were going to be early, and now we're almost late!" Junior headed over to the table where he finished readying his overnight bag and a load of Full Sail Amber big enough to lay flat any alcoholic in town.

As he'd started to get everything in place, Junior had cracked open the patio screen door a bit earlier, and you better believe the local raccoons were already taking notice.

"No!" Junior scolded at a little furry guy with a short tail before having to slide everything shut again for a while.

Berrick clomped down the steps quite proudly, his arms struck out so his son could survey his outfit for the evening.

It was a tuxedo.

"What are you wearing that for?" Junior's mouth scrunched up so much, you could see some of his molars.

"Oh, come on," Berrick protested. "I haven't gotten to wear this since your mom's wake!"

"It's a Christmas party, not a prom." Junior had no idea why he was even making the effort to argue. He knew his dad wouldn't change his mind, let alone his clothes. He took solace in the probability that perhaps, just maybe, this would be the most embarrassing thing his dad did the whole night. "I don't know why you even still have it."

"So I don't look stupid when I go to parties!"

Junior made good on his promise to not argue the point any longer, as it was starting to get late. "You got a bag? This is probably going to be an overnight stay. That's why I got the room for the night!"

"Just like the rabbi once said..." Berrick pointed out the shape of the cross on his front side as he continued with the punchline. "Spectacles! Testicles! Wallet! And watch!"

"You got your pills?"

"That's part of testicles!" Berrick rattled his pocket to show it was full of meds.

"Just making sure." Junior zipped close his overnight bag. "Ready?"

A dark and heavy air fell around Berrick all of the sudden. "I know now why I don't go to these kinda things anymore."

Junior was just curious enough to indulge his father, noticing the sullen change in his mood almost immediately. "Why?"

"Since your mom's not around anymore, I feel like such an idiot going stag to everything. When you don't have a date, I don't know, everything just feels wrong." For just a second there was a disagreeable, shaky tone to Berrick's voice. A bitterness of being left behind.

It didn't last long, though.

"If things don't work out with Dorena, can I have her?"

Junior didn't know whether to hug or punch his father. "Get in the car!"

"Oh good!" Berrick jumped up and down, genuinely pleased. "We need to stop off on the way for some rubbers, though."

"Make yourself useful and grab some of the beer!" The patio was raccoon-free for the moment, and Junior pushed back the sliding door to utilize the shortest path to the car.

"Yes! Yes! Good idea," Berrick commended his son as they both headed out. "I'll get her nice and drunk first. That'll make it easier!"

"You're in for such a knuckle sandwich," Junior murmured as he locked up for the night.

Just as Berrick and Junior were loading up Nuggetz's hatchback, Paco was carefully pulling all the barbecue-bound meats from his trunk. Dorena rounded up a handful of sundries from the backseat as Casey was stuffing some makeup back in her purse. She had to put on her face as they rode to the party, and with the suspension on Paco's car not being what it used to, she had a few last-minute mistakes to correct.

"Alright beautiful, go find your date," Dorena joked, secretly still interested in the possibility that her little sister could pull off a big coup against her former boss.

Casey threw a disapproving look her sister's way, which only served to make Dorena sputter a mean, elfish giggle in return.

"Baby, you're gonna have to open the door first and then I can bring all this up," Paco safely estimated. "They got any luggage carts and shit? I don't wanna fuck this up."

"No, but the elevator's over there," Dorena pointed past the Reception area. She turned to Casey. "You comin' up to check out the room?"

"Uh, I'll come up later," Casey said shiftily, breaking eye contact with her sister a bit too soon to persuade her she was totally up for this. "Here, can you take my purse up to the room? I don't want to carry it around all night."

"I'm surprised you didn't bring a suitcase," Dorena muttered just loudly enough to be heard as she looped the narrow strap of her sister's bag up over her shoulder. Paco smiled.

"It's a date, not an overnighter," Casey objected, quite rightfully. Inside her head, though, she wasn't thoroughly convinced.

"Mmm-hmm," Dorena mocked back like a shot.

"What?!" Casey was starting to get mad. At herself, especially.

"I didn't say anything!" Dorena said sweetly.

"I've got this," Casey assured, confident enough to match her sister's eyes once again. Though the party hadn't even started yet and she was already in too deep, there was a calm intelligence that radiated from her. Somehow, she still could end up being the dark horse to win the evening. "I'm going to the bathroom before I hit the rec center. I'll come up and check out the room in a bit."

"Remember—stick out your tongue," Dorena advised in a surreptitious half-whisper as she locked up the car. "You can get it down your throat further."

Paco started to laugh.

"Whatever. Smell you guys later." Casey did her best to not let it get to her as she headed up the hill to the rec center. Her heels were already digging into her Achilles tendon, and she wished she'd worn something else.

"Come on, just bring it," Dorena instructed her beau, motioning to the cooler. She breezed her way toward the elevator, key card in hand.

"With all this fuckin' ice?" Paco cried. "It's heavy!"

"Quit doggin' it, Mr. Muscles. Let's go." Dorena's pace slowed for only a second before it was back in full effect. She was starting to get curiously eager to see what the night held in store.

Paco let out a string of Spanish, most certainly derogatory, as he hoisted the ice chest and carefully made his way to the elevator. The ride was swift and brought them just a few feet away from their door. Dorena slid the key card through, but the handle didn't give.

"Come on." Dorena coaxed. Technology is a wonderful thing, but only when it works right.

Another pass of the key card. And another. The little red light ridiculed her each time, refusing to roll over green.

Paco's arms were pulling out of their sockets. "What the fuck, Dorrie? Open it!"

"Don't bother with your key," a familiar voice advised from around the corner.

Paco and Dorena shot up a look and saw Berta standing there, a glass of wine in one hand and a plump joint in the other, the cool ocean winds pushing its smoke back to the parking lot.

"It won't work," Berta apprised. "Gubbins moved people into your and my rooms and redid the key cards."

"You gotta be shitting me." Dorena spat out harshly.

Berta shook her head. "He called me. He knows it was us who pranked the rooms."

"That's fantastic. That's just fuckin' fantastic." Dorena's words shaved off her tongue, defeated and sour.

"You sayin' there's no rooms left after we paid for it?" a furious Paco grunted from under the weight of the ice chest as he let it drop with a stuffy *whap!* on the hallway floor. "No way, fuck that shit! We're getting in here, one way or another."

"Stop, Pac." Dorena interrupted.

"Get out of the way, man. I can do it!" Paco was lit and hell-bent for barbecue, ready to kick in the door.

"You can't do it!" Dorena shouted.

Paco fumed, flushing at his lady's demand. "Who the fuck cares? You're getting fired, anyway!"

"No!" Dorena insisted.

"Why, man?" Paco shouted, taking umbrage.

"Cause if you do it, it's technically breaking and entering." Dorena's exasperated words flew by at high speed. "Security cameras already have us coming into the parking lot. You want that shit on your record, too?"

"Hold it, hold it. You don't need any of that," Berta promised.

"Wait a minute," Dorena said calmly, considering the parameters as she looked at Berta. "How the hell did you get in here then?"

Berta held up her Housekeeping keyring. The card marked "MASTER" dangled in front of everyone's nose.

Within seconds, the three of them were headed to one of the abandoned rooms that they had booby-trapped over the past couple of days. It was only a few doors down from another of their compromised suites that Berta had already claimed for the night.

Since the room was originally intended for the StileCorp folks, it was on the top floor, had the best view, and was way bigger than Dorena and Paco needed or expected. There were just a few things they'd have to contend with first...

The stench of seaweed clobbered them over the head as they stepped inside.

"Aww dude, that shit is rank!" Paco exclaimed, the stink nearly enough to make him drop his cooler again.

"Wow," Dorena threw praise in Berta's direction, "you really over-achieved, didn't ya?"

Unaware of her own pranking powers, even Berta's face twisted at the smell. The windows were soon thrown open a bit more, despite the chill that rode around on the sea breezes. She manhandled a settee and stood up on it to reach the curtain rod over the balcony doors.

"Give me a hand with this, will you?"

Everyone's expression got worse as they lowered the rod down, with the stench harshening as it got closer to all their noses.

Berta opened the balcony door, and a tough gust nearly knocked her off-balance. The winds had blown away any rain in the area, but a huge sheet of charcoal sky was beginning to writhe out on the horizon. After sizing up how far it was to the beach, Berta was finally able to take enough cover from the gust and enjoy another hit off her joint. "Either of you ever thrown a javelin?"

Dorena tilted her head Paco's direction. "No, but he did shot put in high school."

It was only meant as a joke, but Berta's eyebrows went up, hopeful. "No shit?"

"First place!" Paco delivered, still amped up from wanting to kick in the door. Catching a glimpse of the gas barbecue on the balcony made him even more hyper. Up went the pinky and index fingers on both his hands. "Beaver Lake High, ninety-four! WHOOOOO!"

Berta began to make a straight path to the open patio door, sliding the settee out of the way and pulling up the throw rug in front of the door. "Well, unless you want to smell that all night, I suggest you go for the gold again right now."

"You serious?" Paco double-checked, eyes afire.

"Do it," Dorena nagged. "I'm not sleeping with that shit in here tonight."

The possibility of Dorena being agitated at bedtime was the final confirmation Paco needed. He took hold of the curtain rod, counted off his steps, and heaved that fucker as hard as he could, nearly harpooning two hard-luck seagulls in the process. His hand smacked smartly on the balcony railing as he regained his footing so that he could see the end result. It sailed impressively over the rocks, getting lost under the crash of the slate-gray surf.

"Good arm!" Berta nodded, handing her joint to him.

"Bullshit, you got lucky," Dorena joked, barely able to keep from smiling.

Paco had to defend himself before he got the chance to take a celebratory toke. "Hey, man, that was good! It made it, didn't it?"

Dorena couldn't help needling her boyfriend just a little more. "Wind totally caught it. I've seen you do better."

"Damn!" Paco yelled, pretending to be insulted. He knew it had been an impressive performance. He took a small hit and then, to make sure, a much longer one, delighting in a level of quality he wasn't expecting. "*¡Bomboncita, qué linda!* That's a smooth burn! Where you getting this from?"

Berta smiled. "My guest bedroom."

Paco turned to Dorena, who busied herself with removing all the booby-traps from their room. "Dorrie, we gotta get in business with this one!"

"Whattaya say?" Dorena's smile beamed the proposition to Berta. Her hand disappeared inside the dryer, tearing off the tape that held two crayons to the drum.

Berta laughed off the suggestion but couldn't help being flattered. "Nah, I was never good with logistics."

"Hey," Dorena reminded her as she moved to the bathroom to begin unscrewing the showerhead, "you got a good enough product, the people come to you, not the other way around." Dorena tapped out two chicken bouillon cubes from behind the filter screen. "This was one of our chicken soup rooms."

"Ewwww," Paco interjected, half-impressed by the ladies' sick ingenuity.

Berta gave up another laugh as she motioned to the bed. "You better check the pillows!" she said, exhaling another round of rich pot smoke. "And where's Casey?"

"Looking for Gubbins," Paco said, tacking on a smile that was a tad confounding to Berta.

"Yeah?" Berta mused, sipping a bit of wine through the side of her mouth. "Well, if she's thinking of getting in line to punch him, she's going to have to take a number."

With the showerhead back in position, Dorena emerged from the bathroom, wiping her hands on one of the washcloths. "She's his date."

"What?!" The sharp end of the word tugged and gashed the back of Berta's throat.

"Low self-esteem is a bitch, man." Paco shook his head as his bewildering smile got a little bigger.

Dorena began to rattle off her words, mostly out of defense. "I made her do it as a goof, but I think she's taking it..." She trailed off as she pulled down the bedspread.

"A bit too seriously?" Paco raised his brows as he finished his girlfriend's thought.

"That's the understatement of the week," mused the disappointed big sister.

"But Gubbins has got to be at least forty years older than her. And he's married!" Berta blurted out, rather inelegantly.

Dorena grabbed the closest of the bed pillows. "Yeah, like that means something these days."

"If she was smart," Berta mumbled, "she'd just butter him up and take every dollar she can get outta him."

Both Dorena and Paco agreed in unison: "That's what I said!"

Dorena took a big whiff of the pillow and nearly puked.

Despite how smart his suit looked, Gubbins caught his reflection in the driver's side window and quickly regretted his choice of outfit for the evening. Sure, the forest green with red trim was wonderfully evocative of the holiday season, but he couldn't help thinking he ended up just looking like an oversized, aging leprechaun.

According to his warped reflection, nothing seemed too out of place, though, and with him having already ushered in most of the StileCorp folk, he tried to relax a bit before the next heart-stopping moment tonight: his speech. Gubbins humanly retained a few jitters, considering all the stock he'd put into this party—Casey, his company, his retirement, damn near everything.

Brody strolled up in a fine tweed suit. He looked like something out of a catalog, and it made Gubbins feel very old all of the sudden.

"There's the master of ceremonies himself!" Brody smoothly complimented, shaking Gubbins' sweaty hand. "Now, not to freak you out or nothing, but I'm going to be sitting in the front so that I can control all the video cameras filming your speech, alright?"

Gubbins' expression fell flat, terrified. "Huh, what?"

Brody gave an impressive laugh. "I'm just messing you with, Mr. Gubbins, come on, don't be nervous, don't be nervous." He kneaded one of Gubbins' forest green shoulder blades to help loosen him up. "Tell you what, just remember S. P. E. A. K."

"Speak?" a jumbled Gubbins asked.

"That's right. It's my way of handling this type of thing. First, you got your S—that's Smile! Right? That's putting your best foot forward, you got it? Then Project! Because if no one can hear you, nothing you say matters."

"Project and smile, mmm-hmm." Gubbins was so intimidated at this point, he forgot about Casey for a second. His brain swam laps from one side of his skull to the other until he swore it was leaking out of his ears.

"E and A are Engage and Analyze," Brody went on. "You know—talk about what your audience came to hear and gauge their responses."

Gubbins nodded. "And analyze and smile!"

"Finally K—that's Key Topics. So, go back and summarize all the shit you just said in case anyone went to get a beer or something, you know what I'm talking about?" Brody whooped an empathizing sort of laugh, the kind that only can be done by successful businessmen.

"Sure do!" Gubbins offered a handshake as he beamed a confident smile.

"Hey, there's your S, right there!" Brody congratulated. "I'm heading in!" He turned around at the door. "S-P...E-A-K! S-P...E-A-K!" he chanted back to Gubbins, disappearing inside.

Gubbins noticed the commotion from the rec center was getting louder, and he tried as hard as he could to push out all the night's distracting factors and just enjoy himself. He checked his coat to make sure the small, wrapped present was still there not far from his heart, both literally and figuratively. He was bursting at the seams to give it to Casey, who still hadn't shown up yet. Another layer of doubt piled onto Gubbins' drowning brain.

At least Ernesto drove up just then to divert him for a little bit.

Gubbins was so overcome by how good his Minority Trump Card looked, he didn't notice the second car pulling up a few moments later and Stacey-Lynn getting out.

"It's splendid!" Gubbins beamed to Ernesto as he came closer. "You're going to do great."

"Thanks, Mr. G. I'm looking forward to it," Ernesto said, basking in the attention. "So, when do I go on?"

"You have your song ready and everything?"

"Yeah," Ernesto shrugged and pointed to his temple, "it's all up here."

"Good, good! You'll go on right after my speech." Gubbins let a little of his anxiety slip as he added, "I'll try not to make it too long."

That's when Gubbins turned to see the new arrival, the one missing in action from the Reception desk for days now.

"Hi, Mr. Gubbins!"

Gubbins was flabbergasted, and so much so, he could hardly speak. "Stacey-Lynn! Where have you been? We've been so worried!"

"Oh, you don't need to worry about me," she said, nearly blushing.

Gubbins dropped his tone, confused for so many reasons, not the least of which was when Stacey-Lynn put her arm around Ernesto. The thick cotton appliqués of his dashiki gave up a scratching sound as she did so. "So, where is your husband?"

"Jail, and thank you for asking!" Gubbins' befuddlement wasn't getting any better. "And how is your wife doing?"

"Oh! She's visiting family. Unfortunately, her mother is in a lot of pain and ready to pass." The end of Gubbins' statement was curled with discomfort.

"Pass gas?"

Gubbins' eyelids rose from a weird kind of droll umbrage. "No. Pass away!"

"Oh my God, I'm so sorry!" Stacey-Lynn warbled as she took aim again. "Well, the best thing I can say is that you won't have to worry about any more mother-in-law jokes, if you know what I mean."

Gubbins should have been highly offended. That is, if he didn't hate the woman so goddamn much. "I do!" he said through two pursed lips.

"You give Geraldine my best when she gets back."

Gubbins took notice of the clue. "Well, aren't you coming back soon?"

"No." Stacey-Lynn's word was quiet. "You know what they say, Mr. Gubbins. Sometimes you have to be the one who makes the change, rather than having it made for you."

Gubbins kept a stone countenance. That bitch Berta was right after all—everyone knew what he'd been up to. "I understand," he offered plainly. "I'm sure Ernesto will make us all real proud tonight."

"Thank you," Ernesto said, and the two of them slipped out of sight through the double doors.

The chunky, expensive watch at Gubbins' wrist read two minutes till seven. One last thought of possibly being stood up rang in his head before looking up to see Casey standing there on the curb of the rec center parking lot.

She was, quite frankly, a bit underdressed in a simple spaghetti strap top, a long, chill-busting cable-knit scarf, and some crisp black jeans, but, to Gubbins, no one in the tri-state region could have been wearing it as sublimely as she was right now. There was no second-guessing that Casey's painful pumps weren't appreciated—gratitude washed all over the CEO's face as he absorbed her form, from pillar to post.

"You afraid I wasn't gonna show?" were her first words, semi-shouted due to the short distance they were away from one another.

Gubbins shook his head before answering... "Yes."

Playing innocent, Casey joked, "You have to be fashionably late!"

The crook of Gubbins' green arm was offered to his date. "No, no, darling, don't say that. You're right on time."

It was tough to know exactly whom to feel sorriest for when they walked into the party, but each of them felt like a million bucks as they did. Gubbins had the edge, though: the only thing better than making a party entrance for the first time in your life is doing it with a girl who's a third your age.

The stragglers began to pool for another minute or two. From across the parking lot, Dorena and Paco argued as they hurried toward the rec center.

"No!"

"If I stay in the room," Paco whined, "I can get the coals started and have barbecue ready by the time your boss has his speech done!"

"Nice try, shit for brains, the barbecues are gas!" Dorena's impatient tone nipped at her boyfriend, turning angry as she continued. "We gotta check on Casey, anyway. And my boss is behind us—that fuck Gubbins isn't anything to me!"

Berta was following behind the arguing couple. The steady mix of wine 'n' weed since late this morning was starting to affect Berta's footing, and she swooned just enough to the right to catch herself before she fell. Maybe it was just because her purse was heavier than usual. Or maybe it was nerves, as she knew Gubbins wasn't the only one who was going to give a speech this evening.

And that's when the final two attendees arrived.

Seconds after Paco, Dorena, and Berta filed into the rec center, Nuggetz and its flip-up headlights bore down the LeisureFace entrance-way, winding its bloated wheelbase into a parking spot.

"Alright!" Berrick cheered before checking his cuffs. "Let's get to the room and then feed the seagulls off the balcony!"

"It's dark, the gulls are asleep, dad! Come on, we gotta go to the opening first," Junior said, jumping out from behind the wheel.

"Man, the coons would love all this shrubbery!" Berrick hailed, taking in the finely trimmed hedges that led to the rec center.

"We're late!"

"Well, if these new pills you made me get hadn't given me the shits this afternoon, maybe we wouldn't have this problem!" Berrick dissented.

"Come on!"

The two of them entered the building in a flash and with only seconds to spare. Inside, the decorations were kept to a dispiriting minimum. There were no centerpieces on any of the round tables everyone sat at, and only small smatterings were strategically placed, almost hidden, along the sides of the room and up on the stage. One of the VCRs that Ernesto had resurrected ushered a loop of snowy, seasonal landscapes onto a television pushed into a far corner.

"They could've at least sprung for a tree," muttered Junior, his rebuking aside just loud enough to be heard by Stacey-Lynn, who had her camera out and was giddy from snapping her first photos of the night.

"Hey, come on over!" she said as emphatically as she could without causing too much of a stir. She seemed really glad to see Junior again, not to mention Berrick, who always made a lasting impression on everyone he's bumped into over the past fifty years.

As Junior pulled out a seat for his dad, he didn't know what to do or feel when seeing Stacey-Lynn and Ernesto in public for the first time together. He clapped his hand into Ernesto's, his friend's African attire quickly jogging his memory. Despite this, and the fact that Gubbins was approaching a red and white candy cane-wrapped podium on the stage,

Junior immediately opted to direct his only question to Stacey-Lynn, asking "How are you doing?"

Stacey-Lynn could tell that he was genuinely interested in hearing what she had been going through, but only gave a thumbs-up as everyone started to applaud the CEO when he stepped behind the mic.

"Aw, thank you!" Gubbins said with all the sincerity of an insurance salesman. "You're making my holiday season even brighter, each and every one of you." He was a mess on the inside, but, unless you looked closely, you couldn't tell. Casey, having the catbird seat at Gubbins' table right next to the stage, looked impressed. At least, so far.

"I do want to thank you for coming to LeisureFace's big holiday shindig this year," Gubbins added. "The only thing better than looking back at our past twelve months together is looking ahead at our next twelve."

Selected folks around the room rolled their eyes. Not coincidentally, all of them were LeisureFace employees who would soon be looking for a new means of income. A certain one of these employees was stone-faced. Sure, the Olympian amounts of wine she had already soaked into her system helped give her a whimsical, unaffected stare, but the details of what Berta had planned required careful consideration, even under the spell of chardonnay.

Gubbins began to eye Ernesto—it was easy to spot his bright colors in the darkened back rows—as he kept his speech moving at a good clip, trimming the fat on the fly and striving to maintain interest. "One thing I'm very proud of is our diversity in the workplace. Single mothers, people of color, those with serious health impairments, and..." Gubbins motioned to himself, "even one or two elderly employees..." Like clockwork, he stopped for the laugh. It came. Gubbins beamed. Everyone moved on. "We stand side by side in making LeisureFace the face of leisure, and the top of its industry."

Stacey-Lynn squeezed Ernesto's hand, not just as a way of showing her support, but to ready him for what she knew was coming. Ernesto squeezed back, a smile on his lips for so many reasons. He had practiced this performance in his mind since coming across his inspiration in the kitchen of his apartment a few nights back. The apartment he no longer had. A surreal, detached anxiety hit him, making him fully aware of the strange circumstances he was living out. Ernesto turned to Stacey-Lynn. He was so appreciative of her care, her strength, her love, and it was his intent to thank her at that very moment, but stardom calls, and he found himself being politely cheered up to the bright, baking lights of the stage.

Though the lights rolled a cooler amber, and Ernesto could feel the audience's fortifying endorsement, the glare was still too bright to make out many of the faces that wished him well. He swallowed hard to make sure his throat wasn't dry and unleashed a tenor that filled every empty glass, every divot in the soil of each potted plant, and high up in the top reaches of the ceiling as Ernesto put out his arms and fed his shadow with a soul-freeing song.

"Nohshojees, nohshojees, Darhee...Towwwwws."

The pitch was perfect, and the notes carried as if they came directly from the mountaintop. Stunning! It was like Ernesto had swallowed an angel on his way up to the stage. People instantly wanted to chat with their table partners about the sound they were hearing but couldn't do it. They just sat there. It was motherfucking sublime.

"Torhah! Torhah! Teehahsheeeeeps. Harta! Harta! Feeshalee! Flava-ha! Flava-ha!"

All surprised eyes were on Ernesto as he gave them everything in his heart. Eyes closed, he swam his arms and legs through the waves of inspiration, the glut spilling out over the stage and soaking his audience with a fervor they never could have anticipated.

"Asupa Bee-grabah! Tree! Treepon Tree Onsbag!"

Brody Teague wiped away his tears without shame. People around him, people who weren't even his color, felt the exact way he did right now. It was the most profound artistic statement he'd ever witnessed. Regardless of anyone's background, Ernesto made them all understand the motherland and its enduring message to humankind.

No one felt this more than Stacey-Lynn. As her eyes welled up and she made for the door, every attendee thought they could empathize with her emotions.

But they were wrong.

Stacey-Lynn couldn't hold back her laughter anymore and had to get out of the rec center as quickly as possible before she'd blow the whole thing. What the audience didn't know was that the words to Ernesto's African spiritual were nothing more than the entire front side on a snack-sized bag of Doritos.

She made it just in time. The door closed right as a peal of uncontrollable laughter sprang from her lungs, which ached and swelled with a desperate air. Inside, Ernesto's celestial holiday carol closed with a solemn and beautiful dignity.

"Honlee…Nohn-tee-nohn. Sennnnnnds."

Ernesto bowed his head behind a pair of clasped hands. Through his cracked eyelids, he saw the garish white of the stage lights rise again as the crowd went positively apeshit. He had never felt acceptance like this before, and, just in case he never would again, took the time to bow graciously and offer a few humble waves to the crowd.

Judging from the look on the Gubbins' face, Ernesto bet he was duly impressed.

The CEO returned to the stage. "Thank you, all, and to all a good night!"

The thoughts of his payment jingled in Ernesto's head, but his main priority was finding Stacey-Lynn. He made his way back to the table, with Berrick immediately pointing to the door through which his other half had disappeared.

Outside, Stacey-Lynn threw her arms around him and washed him in a cascade of giggles. "That was great, sugar! They totally fell for it!"

"You see that shit, baby girl?! You see that? I even saw a brother tearin' up!" Ernesto looked around, his mind back on money, and his face carved with serious intent. He tore the kufi from his head. "We gotta go back in and find Gubbins, though. We get paid, and then we can get on the road."

"And if we get on the road…" Stacey-Lynn stopped, a mix of joy and regret filling her eyes as she took refuge in the front of Ernesto's dashiki.

"No, no, baby. Come on, don't cry. We gonna do this. Together!"

The promise of a new start with her man at her side stopped Stacey-Lynn's troubled tears. Unbending, she nodded. "Together."

"Come on."

They both headed back inside towards the table as some Christmas music began to get people out of their seats for a slow dance. Ernesto's eyes tore through the bouncing crowd, but finally opted for some assistance.

"Junebug!" Ernesto called, with Junior turning back to him. "You see where Gubbins went?"

Junior shook his head, his expression a puzzle as he, too, scanned the crowd without finding any trace of their boss.

Stacey-Lynn pulled on Ernesto's clammy palm. "Let's go, he's gotta be here somewhere." They headed out the rec center entranceway.

There was only one person who knew Gubbins had a habit of ducking out the back exit, which is exactly where he and Casey were headed.

Outside, the area emptied into a garden of sorts, replete with tall green shrubs that followed a long walkway leading back to Reception at the main building. Gubbins' hand was already in his inside coat pocket before his and Casey's feet started to crunch the rounded shale under them. His gift, bow and all, was still in there.

"Oh, I'm so glad that's over!" Gubbins gasped. Half of him did it with the slyest melodramatics, while the other part seemed truly happy to be done with this year's party introduction.

"Why were you so nervous?" Casey pressed, her voice firm in its assumption. "You did fine. I never knew Ernesto could sing like that!"

"Neither did I!" Gubbins chuckled, imbued with a fortunate giddiness. "We just made a quick agreement when my original plans crapped out. Oh, man! He did amazing, didn't he?" Right then, Gubbins should have remembered that he owed Ernesto for stand-in services rendered, but every one of his thoughts flew away every time Casey opened her mouth.

"Beautiful. Absolutely beautiful." Casey was genuinely rapt, or at least enough to forget about her too-tight shoes.

"Speaking of beautiful." From his pocket, Gubbins produced a flat envelope wrapped in a gauzy bow of gold trimmed in green and red.

"What?" Casey half-coughed, taking hold of the present. "You want me to open it now?"

"Yes!" Gubbins could barely contain himself. His heart raced behind his Santa-red tie, and his corona started to swell like a little pufferfish back behind his zipper. He thrust a hand into his pocket to stay his excitement as Casey's fine fingers began to undo the wrapping.

Out of the heavy cardstock envelope slid a pair of three-day admission passes to the Crescent Treasures Spa & Resort. Though Casey periodically reminded herself not to take the beauty of Beaver Lake for granted, Crescent Treasures made her hometown look like Beirut by comparison. Cypress trees! Hot stone therapy! Two-hour facials! Flat beaches that weren't cold enough to turn your nipples into thimbles!

As she looked up to Gubbins, there was a bit of disbelief on Casey's youthful expression, as if she privately wondered if there was an even greater price to be paid than the cost of the tickets in her hand.

That's because anyone older than Casey's nineteen naïve years would, with no doubt whatsoever, swear on a stack of bibles that there would be a tremendous price to pay. Exhibit A: Gubbins, who was still standing there pushing his boner into the uppermost crook of his thigh, and had a very different kind of facial in mind.

His words were tempting and calculated. "Three days, all-inclusive. Golf. Sand. Sun. Dining. Massage. All of it."

Casey opened her mouth. "Wow..."

Gubbins naturally figured she was going to decline, so he jumped in straight away to cushion the blow and allow her time to reconsider. "Don't answer now! I figured we could just stay here with everyone else and enjoy the evening, so go ahead and think about it for tonight."

"Okay, I definitely will!" Gratitude pushed up her lips a bit farther to show off Casey's pleasing, milky teeth. "Uh, can you hold on to these for me for now, though?" she said, passing back the glossy tickets. "I gave my purse to my sister, and I don't want to lose them."

"Oh, sure, sure, sure." Gubbins' nervous hands bumped the passes back into their gussied-up envelope. "And just so you know, I even got two queen beds, so please don't think I'm trying to pressure you into anything."

Casey, clearly flattered, nevertheless still had confusion rimming her eyes. "Why are you doing this for me?" she said with an egoless curiosity.

In order to keep his sinking heart afloat, Gubbins ardently stammered out more details. Most all of them were pure, unadulterated bullshit.

"I just..." his voice cracked on command, and he dragged out the pause for maximum manipulation, "Miss Morris, I always felt badly that you left the way you did. You were obviously unhappy with your position, and I wish there could have been something that Berta or I could have done to make things better for you."

"Well," an intrusive, groggy voice began from behind the tall green columns of shrubbery, "some people are destined for better things in life than changing sheets."

Berta stepped out from behind the bushes. The diction may have been slurred, and the wine bottle she held wasn't the same one as she started with at Paco and Dorena's room, but her words were sincere, all the same. Casey beamed at the sight of her former boss for the first time in what seemed like forever.

"Hey there." Berta smiled at her former crew member, all at once motherly and brokenhearted.

"Hey!" Casey whispered from behind the lump in her throat. She couldn't resist reaching out and hugging Berta, whose wine bottle poked her petite ribs as she did so.

"Evening, Berta." Gubbins was steely and aloof, barely summoning enough tolerance to make it through the two simple words. If you listened closely, you could actually hear his erection deflating.

For the moment, Berta ignored the CEO and turned her attention to Casey. "How you been?"

With a short glance to Gubbins, Casey answered quite nervously. "Good."

In an attempt to not make things any more awkward than they already were, Berta chimed in, leveraging a professional and quietly confidential approach. "Look," she asked of Casey, side-nodding her head Gubbins' way, "can I borrow your date for just a second?"

"Yeah, sure." Casey and her pretty grin backed away so that Berta and Gubbins could walk a few private strides down the shale path.

"Mr. Gubbins." Berta halted, almost hating herself for what she had to do. At least the alcohol was making it easier than she anticipated.

"What is it, Berta?" Gubbins asked in a brittle tone.

"I just want to apologize for what I said to you tonight. It was unfair of me to talk to you that way after all you've done for me and my workers. I appreciate you, and I really value the belief you've had in the crew all these years."

Berta already knew she was off the hook before Gubbins even opened his mouth.

"Berta, I forgive you. I know this change is going to be difficult for everyone—even me." Gubbins smiled in spite of himself, his cheeks softening. "But we need to remember that moving on is part of life."

Berta nodded and sighed. She was just a few more seconds from being home-free. "Hey, why don't you two just get out of here and have fun?"

"I'm trying!" Gubbins offered softly with a sly raise of his eyebrows.

"Tell ya what," Berta bartered, "why don't you let me go in there and man the music controls?"

"Well, our night auditor was originally going to do it." There was a sheepishness in Gubbins' reply, probably because he was reminded of yet another final paycheck he'd soon be cutting.

"Oh yeah, poor Steve," Berta's glazy words came out with an extra dollop of irony she wasn't expecting. "He quit before he even had the chance to be fired."

"Well, I—" Gubbins stammered around, "I just went and pre-programmed all of the music for the evening."

"Bah!" Berta scoffed with a burp. "We can do better than that! Come on, let me make it up to you. I used to do this kind of thing all the time when I was in college."

"Okay!" Gubbins grabbed Berta's bait, if nothing else to get back to the beautiful young thing waiting for him a dozen steps back there at the top of the shale path.

"Yeah, I knew it," Berta said. She turned back to Casey, "You keep an eye on this guy tonight, and make sure nothing happens to him."

"Yes, ma'am," Casey joked.

"He's gotta be back at work on Monday, so don't let him drink too much." Berta joshed as the couple started to head down the path. After they got a few steps away, Berta piped up one last time. "Hey!"

The happy duo turned back to her.

Even there in the darkness of the outdoor sodium lighting, you could see Berta's eyes start to shimmer as they filled. "Merry Christmas, you guys."

Peering back at her lonesome ex-boss there at the top of the walk-way, Casey looked like she wanted to cry. Instead, she offered her best smile, because that's what Berta deserved.

"You too, Berta!" Casey called. Gubbins gave a wave of his hand before they started crunching their way down the extensive length of the path.

Berta stood there swigging wine and watching their every step until they were out of sight. After that, she wound between the shady breezes and pushed through the back exit until she came to the foot of the stage steps.

Looking out at the StileCorp crowd, she couldn't help but stifle a heartburn-fueled laugh. All of them were languidly slow dancing to a playlist of Christmas carols. It was pathetic, and so much so that she felt it was her civic duty to do something about it.

Berta took to the steps, nearly falling as one of them reached up and grabbed her miscalculating foot. Knowing she would need it later, she stowed her purse under the podium for safekeeping.

A worried look crossed Berta's face as she gazed upon the music set-up. Though she really had done this kind of thing in college, it had been thirty long years ago. Vinyl and a PA system had been replaced by a patched-up, computerized thingamajig that shit RCA plugs out its backside like they, too, were going out of style.

For all its intimidating looks, Berta soon found that it worked much like a Windows Media Player, quickly tamed by fluttering a mouse around on a monitor to load each song. Click by click, Frosty, Santa, Rudolph, and the grandmother that got run over by him were deleted from existence. Even with the playlist empty, the lugubrious Christmas fluff continued. Berta's nerves broke and she tore out the side plug.

"*TEEUUUARRRRRRREEEEEER*" the feedback screamed as most of the StileCorp folks grabbed for their ears.

"Alright, fuck that Jack Frost shit," Berta mumbled to herself as she paged through the rest of the song catalog, not knowing the microphone was broadcasting her voice to the dance floor. She looked up and saw everyone had slowed their feet to a complete stop. Berta didn't know much about modern music, so she just went with the first thing she recognized from her college days: a group that called itself MC5.

Berta had to cover for the silence and quickly leaned over the microphone. "Now. Who wants to up the ante a little?" she asked, clicking the mouse and quickly shoving the side plug back in. A DJ star was born.

"*Kick out the jams, motherfuckers!*" sprung open the party gate by a band that sounded as if the rhythm section was playing their instruments with their foreheads. Immediately, the faces out in Berta's audience became a sampler platter of human emotion. Hate, fear, adulation, and wild abandon divided and conquered the crowd. She flipped through the song list some more, punching in every single thing she knew had more than fifty beats-per-minute. Jefferson Airplane. The Emotions. Led Zeppelin. The Doors. Alice Cooper. The Who.

"There. That should hold them for a bit," Berta said to no one in particular who could have heard her. She was going to give these people a night to remember, or die trying.

"Let's go, it's time for B-B-Q!" Berrick insisted, tired of listening to his stomach growl for the past hour. His hands held a six-pack of Full Sail at each side of his cummerbunded waist.

Junior was taking a few things out of his overnight bag and putting them by the bathroom sink. "Okay, okay! Get some beers to take over."

"Way ahead of ya. Come on, Junebug, the smell of the stuff is killing me!"

"I had to unpack some things first," Junior said, defensively, on his way around the hallway corner.

Berrick threw a rakish, fatherly barb his son's way. "Do you want to go be social with Dorena or not?"

Junior's jumpy anxiety made him groan. "Yeah, but I'm not looking forward to being social with her boyfriend." One of the reasons he was stalling was to get his courage out of reserve.

"Well, that's why we have beer!" Berrick suggested, gleefully. "*Ándale!*"

Considering Paco was Latino, Junior wondered if his dad was just fucking with him a bit more in light of the little Spanish interjection he'd suddenly chosen. He quickly opted to drop the prejudice and wrangled his dad out the door. Bottles clinked the whole way down the hallway to Dorena and Paco's door, which was already open. The smell that punched them in the nose as they walked in was nothing short of tantalizing.

Junior's heart sank a bit when the first thing he saw was Paco manning the barbecue. Winds whipped at his t-shirt, clinging to a physique just impressive enough to make Junior want to vomit. Suddenly the scrumptious smells weren't as enticing to him anymore.

Berrick raised his beers. "Hey! Who's had enough of reality this week?"

Dorena, who'd been off to the side on a loveseat firing up a brass pipe, applauded sharply and waved her hands toward herself. "Bring it!" she yelled from behind a blast of hash smoke.

Paco smiled at the sight of the beer but quickly went back on watch. "Buns are toasting! Who likes 'em rare?"

"Me!" Berrick shot back like he'd been waiting hours to say it.

Paco gave a quick wave of barbecue tongs to acknowledge the order and gulped from a red tumbler perched aside the grill. He was keeping a keen eye on his finely seasoned handiwork. Nevertheless, Dorena pulled Junior by the arm over through the open slider.

"Pac, this is the guy I'm always telling you about. This is Junior."

"You talk to him about me?" Junior quizzed Dorena, terrified to think that the woman he'd been admiring from the shadows for ages was talking about him—and to her boyfriend, no less!

"He's the big cheese in Maintenance. And that's his dad, Berrick," Dorena went on.

Paco refused to look up. "Fuck. Cheese!" he mumbled over his girlfriend, remembering just late enough into the grilling to sour his face. "Gotta put on the parmesan."

A new voice bounded into the room. It was wrapped in an exquisite rush of air as a bottle of Full Sail lost its cap. "Hey, you leave your door open and some no-good nigga like me is gonna kipe your beers!"

Dorena screamed and ran over to Ernesto, who, unknowingly, was saving the day once again. Junior gave a wave to his best friend and Stacey-Lynn, who smiled just as big as she always did. There were congratulations for him and concern for her. Both of them seemed happy together, if somewhat in a rush, as Dorena and Berrick got lost in conversations with the two of them.

That left Junior standing there with Paco.

Junior knew one of the best ways to combat waves of doubt and fear was to simply jump headlong into the waters. He tried his best to make eye contact with Paco but didn't quite pull it off.

"Uh, so how long have you and Dorena been together?" Junior

instantly cursed himself for putting so much emphasis on their relationship, which is the one thing he didn't want to know more about.

"Long enough."

The sizzle of the burgers was drowned out in the speed of the wind. For just a second, Junior honestly wondered how the gas was staying lit, let alone keeping the heat even enough to cook anything. "Looking good there. You more into mesquite or hickory?"

"Look," Paco said, turning his chin up slowly, his glance dark and direct, "you need to go tell your pops that his burger's ready to roll, *comprende?*"

The two endured a stare-down that went on for longer than either young man intended. Junior could hear his dad finishing up with Ernesto and Stacey-Lynn, and, just about as he thought he might get his ass kicked right then and there, Berrick arrived with a fresh beer in hand to keep the peace.

"One rare to go, please!"

"Hey," Paco nodded, sliding the work of art onto a plate, "you may go, but you'll be back for seconds, man. Guaranteed."

Junior slinked away as his dad took the first bite of Paco's cow magic.

"Mmm-MMM! Good man! You even did a final broil to get the char just right on the outside. It helps keep the juiciness in!" Berrick stated, eyes wide. He offered his latest beer to Paco. "Here, brand new! My lips never touched it! I swear!"

Paco wasn't usually so trusting, but when his ego gauged the satisfying way the old guy tore into his burger, he surrendered.

"Right on, man." Paco nodded his gratitude and took a swig, sliding the rest of the patties around to get them away from the main flame areas.

"So, tell me," Berrick dropped his voice casually, "you got some star anise in here, don't ya? I can taste it!"

Paco clammed up in an instant. "Shhhhh, don't tell everyone, holmes!" A guilty, mischievous smile browned his rounded cheeks. "That's one of my secret weapons!"

Junior was making himself feel better back in the company of

Dorena, but his main focus was on Ernesto and Stacey-Lynn. They both seemed as if they were trying to have fun but, for some reason, couldn't. Finally, Ernesto gave some insight.

"Any of you seen Gubbins?" There was a tinge of desperation in Ernesto's voice.

"I should have never left that fucker alone with my little sister." Dorena was now lamenting the frivolous choice she'd made in Safeway that night.

"What do you mean?" Stacey-Lynn queried with a worried frown.

Dorena sighed, fluffing up the back of her hair with a self-loathing impatience. "Gubbins asked her to the party, and I told her to do it."

Ernesto found solace somewhere in the ass-backward logic. "So that's why she was with him tonight." He turned to Stacey-Lynn. "I wondered what the hell they were doing together!"

Stacey-Lynn's mouth went crooked. "They were probably wondering the same thing about us." Ernesto tapped her on the arm with a smile. Stacey-Lynn saw that Junior was grinning, too. The cumbersome weight lifted from them now that their secret was quickly becoming common knowledge.

"Well, I told her to do it as a joke, but she's kinda fallen under the spell," Dorena lamented.

"Gubbins has a spell?!" Stacey-Lynn joked.

"Hey, we're just as surprised as you are," Junior admitted with a laugh.

Even Dorena couldn't help but slip a pitying smirk into the mix. She shrugged, "She's nineteen. She's not used to anyone paying her any serious attention yet."

"Well, the dude owes me some money from my little Star Search shit tonight," Ernesto came clean, "so if you all see him, can you point his upper-middle-class wallet in my direction, please?"

"We couldn't find them, either," Dorena's quick words chipped off. "And now Berta's gone, to boot."

"Ah, they're probably just bullshitting together down at the beach, or something." Though it wasn't entirely right, Junior's supposition sounded just likely enough to keep them from worrying any further.

The reality was that Berta was still whipping up the crowd at the rec center and nowhere near the likes of Casey and Gubbins, who had, indeed, walked the whole shale path and continued down to the poolside lookout. The winds were caressing folds into their clothing as they stood there gazing out on the void of a forceful, smashing surf. The shoreline was crisp, white, and bubbly, but any farther out was nothing but an unsure blackness, lost in the symphony of waves. For both of them, it was dangerous and romantic, but for altogether different reasons.

Though it seemed so vain and foolish, Gubbins was hoping his perfectly-matching green golf cap wouldn't blow off his head. He tugged on the brim a bit. Since it seemed well-seated on his crown, it gave him the iota of confidence he needed to begin explaining his situation.

"My mother-in-law is dying. Right now."

Though she thought it was a strange topic to jump-start a conversation, Casey couldn't help but feel the pins and needles of regret. "I'm sorry," she mustered, quite heartfelt. "As long as she loved while she was with us, she won't be forgotten."

Gubbins was impressed with the summation, but pity wasn't exactly what he was after. "Actually, she's a shrew who's always hated me, but that's not really the point I was trying to make."

Casey let flow a short giggle, and it wasn't just to make Gubbins feel more at ease about whatever was on his mind.

"Despite the bickering and bad tidings, I'm learning a lesson from this," Gubbins admitted. Casey looked directly at him, the wind blowing shaded blonde strands into her eyelashes before she could bat them away for a few seconds. "Don't take your youth for granted," he continued, adopting an embarrassed glance down at his shoes right after saying it. "I know I probably sound like someone at your high school graduation, but it's true. Even for us who had our graduations over forty years ago."

Gubbins was only digging his hole deeper. He winced as he brought up the one thing he promised himself not to—their age difference, since it was already something painfully evident, at least to him. His bald scalp began to chill there underneath the green cap that hid it, but he continued on as eloquently as he could.

"My mother-in-law isn't the only death I'm mourning."

Intrigued, and a little concerned by the revelation, Casey fine-tuned her attention as Gubbins' confessional lingered on.

"My marriage died long ago. I'm just realizing that now." Gubbins looked down at his shoes again. His rounded toe kicked a piece of beauty bark into the blackened grass. "When two people constantly misinterpret what one another do as an excuse not to care anymore, it's tough to stay in love."

Casey was dumbfounded by the candor. Though she had mentally prepared herself for this—based, of course, on what the last two day's tarot layouts told her—she wasn't quite ready to be put in the position of marriage counselor. But she couldn't quite shake the feeling of responsibility to Gubbins. The sap just stood there, unaware of how many people hated him for his money and power, staring out at the sea and wishing he could go back and fix where it all went wrong for him.

Looking at his pensive, weathered profile, Casey found that he wasn't a boss or a friend or a lover or even a date. He was a karmic investment—someone to whom you simply show some graciousness as you make your way down the path of life. She always believed that kind of thing was what truly made people into better, happier souls.

"Mr. Gubbins," Casey started.

"Oh no, no!" he withered, his hand rising up to stop her. "Please, just Cles."

"You need to be happy. But only you know what makes you happy." Casey's intellect, though perfectly fine for nineteen years of experience, failed her. She squinted her eyes shut and tried her best to impart the wisdom she wanted so much to share. "It's just," she sighed, ashamed, "I know you can be happy, so don't let anyone, not even yourself, keep you from finding it." She opened her eyes—blue, rapturous, and wide once more—humbled for the first time by the life experience of someone almost the same age as her grandfather.

"I believe you're helping me find that happiness again," Gubbins said so gratefully. He took Casey's cool, fragile hand in his as excitement purged all the doubt in his soul. "Come with me. I want to show you something special."

Stacey-Lynn stepped out on the balcony of Dorena and Paco's room to get some air. She didn't want to seem anti-social, but the beer Junior had offered had gone right to her head, and the stuffy humidity back in the room was starting to get to her. Though she figured she'd only need a few moments to recover, she ended up staying out there for untold minutes, staring at the dark seascape, so hypnotic and wild. It was a rush to her senses, which cleared quickly out in the biting breezes. Eventually, Ernesto came looking for her.

"Hey," he started slowly, "you alright out here?"

"Oh yeah," an awed Stacey-Lynn assured. "It's just, I was always stuck down there in Reception and never got to see everything from this viewpoint. Even here in the dark, it's spectacular!"

Ernesto offered up a bottle. "Want another beer?"

Stacey-Lynn laughed, covering her face. "No, I just got the first one out of my system!"

"Come on, one more!" Ernesto knowingly grinned.

"Noooo!" she giggled, embarrassed. "I gotta get back inside, though. I don't want them to think I'm being a party-poop or anything."

"Yeah, I feel ya, but we need to find Gubbins," Ernesto stated with a keen sense of urgency, twisting the top off his latest bottle. "I gotta go talk to Junebug, though."

"You really want anyone to know?" Though she adored Junior, there was an understandable trepidation in Stacey-Lynn's voice. Both her and Ernesto's thoughts ran to Fitz for just a second.

"We can trust him." Mist ringed Ernesto's eyes. "If nothing else, I just gotta say goodbye."

Stacey-Lynn nodded her tousled head.

Ernesto hugged onto her, making sure his new beer didn't spill all over her. "Shouldn't take long, okay, baby?"

"It's all good," Stacey-Lynn admitted with an agreeable conscience. "I'll be in soon."

Ernesto found his way back inside, and it looked as if Dorena, Paco, and Berrick, had been chewing the fat in a circle on the floor. Serendipitously, Junior stepped out from the bathroom at the same time. Ernesto tipped the neck of his beer, pointing to the front door with a serious look. Junior caught the gravity in his friend's glance and nodded as he killed the lights above the bathroom's vanity mirror.

Junior called over his shoulder as Ernesto crossed the room, slapping Berrick five along the way. "Be right back."

"Where you going?" Berrick huffed.

"And don't drink my beer, dad." Junior scowled.

Dorena pulled the beer her direction to keep it away from Berrick, who started to whine.

As soon as the front door shut, Paco plucked it away and handed it over. Berrick shrugged and took a swig. "He's got more in the car, anyway."

Outside, all the beer was starting to get to Ernesto. He felt fine, but hung there over the third-floor railing looking at his and Stacey-Lynn's cars. Both were crammed with everything they had to their names, other than the love they had for one another.

"You heading out soon?" Junior figured.

"Uh, yeah." Ernesto was surprised by the open interpretation afforded him. For a second, he considered not confiding in Junior the secret he would have just ten seconds ago. "I mean, we gotta find Gubbins, and then we'll be going."

"Well, you tell your mom hi for me when you get there."

Ernesto went agape, and it wasn't just because he was about to raise his bottle to his mouth. "How'd you know, man?"

Junior shrugged. At first, he didn't have an answer. Then, after a second or two to reflect, it all made a lot more sense. "So many reasons really. Not the least of which is Fitz. I mean, hell, you saw what he did to the lobby. I don't think anyone could imagine what he'd do to you guys when he gets out."

"If he gets out," Ernesto corrected, agitated and unsure. As a concession, he added. "You're right, though, and I don't want to imagine it, let alone find out."

"You guys got the funds?" a doubting Junior queried.

Ernesto shook his head, smiling despite his situation. "That's why we're lookin' for Gubbins."

"I wish I could help in some way." Junior's frustration was all over his face, but he always held a certain blind faith in his friend, one that made everything seem better, more focused.

"Nigga, you can. By not telling anyone. Ever."

"You got it." Junior offered his hand, which Ernesto grabbed onto, pulling in his friend for a tight and despairing embrace. "You have me and dad's number. Keep us updated, alright?"

"I will." Ernesto's pledging, ambitious tone belied the swipes he made across each of his tearing eyes.

"And be sure to list me as a reference," Junior added in earnest. "You know I'd be more than happy to jump-start something for you, wherever you end up. Just do me one favor in return."

"What's that?"

"Hang around just a little longer tonight, okay?" Junior ordered with a slightly hesitant smile. "I know you need to get your money and split, but everyone's keyed up from your little performance tonight. You surprised a lot of people and made them feel good. And, if you stay a few more minutes, you won't have to regret that you didn't once you two are alone out there on the road."

Ernesto's aura of gratitude shone all around him. The two headed back inside.

Gubbins turned the lock to the pool maintenance room. It clicked open with a crude *thunk* as he and Casey's entry jostled one of the pool skimmers. Casey caught it as it fell towards them.

"Watch your heels," Gubbins warned his date, motioning to the drain almost dead-center in front of Casey's path. She sidestepped it as they made their way to the back corner of the room.

A rubber-coated utility tray was screwed to a dirty door. The brass fitting around its bolt lock was rusted slightly and looked like it hadn't been open in years. But that was just part of the camouflage Gubbins kept up so no one would suspect what was behind it. Another key was introduced and soon the secret passageway was a secret no more.

Gubbins looked back to make sure no one was watching. "Come on in," he smiled.

Casey walked into the narrow but fully kitted-out efficiency apartment. The kitchenette had a little humming fridge, the living room was fitted with a very comfortable-looking loveseat and fleecy woven rug, and the whole place smelled positively delicious from the many scented vanilla candles that held sway at the entrance to a back bedroom. The aroma suddenly made Casey remember that she hadn't had anything to eat yet this evening, and, for a second, wished she was up with her sister eating Paco's star anise burgers.

"It's the old groundskeeper's apartment. I had it converted years ago. I come here when I want to escape the rest of the world," Gubbins proudly confided.

"It's awesome!" Casey admired softly, as if raising her voice could sully the cozy ambiance Gubbins had put a lot of thought into over the years. From the tiny television to the little ice bucket seemingly too narrow for the champagne bottle that stuck up out of it, everything seemed to properly wedge itself into the kind of luxurious underground-bunker mood any cockeyed romantic would adore.

"With the pool room being on the other side, I only have to worry about noise from the corner suite above. And if things get too loud," Gubbins paused, pulling back a set of heavy drapes, "I can just drown them out with the sound of the waves."

A heavy glass door opened, and the sound of the Pacific Ocean sloshed around their ears. Here at the end of the world, Gubbins even had his own first-floor deck. Like the rest of the room that led to it, it was barely big enough to contain one person, let alone two, but maintained that undeniable dollhouse charm, nonetheless.

Casey began to feel a strange kind of divisive inner turmoil. All at once, she found herself not only getting used to Gubbins' kind of seven-figure indulgence but out of place in it. Her feminine DNA moaned deep inside, determined to be pampered, despite how empty and shamefully trivial it seemed. The whole thing was making her palms sweat. She found the key to her Pandora's box slipping from her fingers and into Gubbins' hands.

Thankfully, Gubbins found an errand to run at the very same moment.

"Oh damn," he grumbled, "I need to run to Reception for just a moment and get some ice." He removed the chunky champagne bottle from its ice bucket. "Please, please, make yourself comfortable! I'll be back in just a second."

"That's okay," Casey smiled with genuine relief. An ice run at least gave her time to get her thoughts together. Very quickly, she was letting the onslaught of her emotions and girlish cravings for creature comforts cloud her judgment. That nagging between her legs wasn't exactly abiding by common sense at the moment, either. Remembering the last tarot layout she did—just minutes before Dorena had walked in on her in a rather compromising position—Casey now knew that she had to corral her conscience and do it fast.

Fearing the possibility of fumbling the bucket on his way back in, Gubbins elected to leave the door open as he heeded a string of careful footsteps out to the pool. Wasting no time, he was soon approaching the circular, chattering hum of the ice machine. Gubbins sank the entire bucket into the cubes. The freeze on his hands was surprisingly refreshing. Though it was a breezy December night, it was more humid than usual, even for the coast. He stole back out to the pool area without being seen.

Gubbins took one more look over his shoulder as he disappeared from Reception and walked straight into Brody just a few feet from the pool maintenance room.

"Ooph!" The melting cubes in his glass rattled for a second as Brody gasped, the wind half-knocked out of his drunken chest. "Hey,

Mr. Gubbins, you have got to come check out what your lady is laying down."

Thinking Brody was referring to Casey, Gubbins' mind was immediately affronted. "What?!"

"Berta!" Brody cheered, some of his drink swinging around the rim and toppling over the edge of his glass. "Your girl droppin' joints on the dance floor that are taking me back to when I was just a little nigga!"

"Oh, really?" Gubbins smiled. Though he hadn't used any slang since before groovy was mod and hadn't the foggiest idea what Brody was talking about, he was appreciative of the diversion Berta was supplying all the StileCorp people. He assumed most of them, like Brody, were three sheets to the wind by this point.

"Yeah. I mean, I told her to play some Commodores, but she couldn't find anything other than 'Easy' and 'Still', and you can't dance to that shit, you know what I'm saying?" Brody's question morphed into a loud, tart belch. "Pardon me, pardon me!"

"It's great to hear all of you are having such a fun time with Berta. She's a good woman!" The ice was starting to give Gubbins' chest an uncomfortable chill.

"Come on! Let's go back up," Brody insisted. "The two of us. Shake that thang, come on!"

"No, no, I can't. I mean, I'll be up in a little while," Gubbins stammered, his eyes reassuring him that he was only about 30 feet from heaven. Mercifully, Brody has his back to the dark open doorway to the pool maintenance room.

"Ah, I see." Brody's glazed eyes narrowed above a knowing smile. "You got it all goin' on with that young thing I saw at your table earlier."

Gubbins' expression gave him away.

"Ah—see! I know a snatch hound when I see one!" Brody looked straight into Gubbins' wide eyes. "So whatcha got in store for her, player? Hmm?"

Though he figured he shouldn't tell, there was something inside of Gubbins that couldn't take it anymore. He wanted to confide his passion, his lust, and unbelievable good fortune. Male DNA can only go so long without turning its owner into a loose-lipped braggart. "I'm taking her to a resort in the morning."

"Solid! Which one?"

"Crescent Treasures!" Gubbins said as his smile and eyes flashed in unison. "Down near Eureka."

"Dang, I almost bought that place, too!" Brody laughed. "Great people down there. A-1. And the best golf north of Pebble Beach! I'm tellin' ya something here!" More of Brody's drink went AWOL over the top of his glass as he pointed a finger at Gubbins. "You get your dick wet and hit some links? Now, that is a Merry Christmas, my friend."

"I know! That's why I'm going!" Gubbins confirmed. "I don't care if she likes it, I just want to have some fun."

"With your nine-iron!" The back of Brody's hand knocked Gubbins in his forest green crotch, and both men burst out laughing in a fit of sports-related misogyny. "Amen! Santa Claus is bringing us all something good this year!" he hailed, throwing back a quick swig. "Right, I'm outtie. You come join us when your golf bag's empty, you hear?"

Gubbins' face tightened, knowing he just had a few more seconds to go. He nodded, somewhat overenthusiastically, to compensate. "Don't you worry! I will!"

Brody gurgled away through Reception, heading towards the rec center. His rendition of "Lady, You Bring Me Up", complete with both lead and background parts, rang off the angular LeisureFace eaves until he was far enough up the shale path to be out of earshot. By that time, though, Gubbins was already back inside the secret room.

"Oh, I'm sorry that took so long!" Gubbins apologized. He turned the bolt lock and then settled the champagne down into its cool bucket once more.

"No worries!" Casey urged. She had taken the interim to lounge out onto the loveseat, paging through the tide charts she found inside the latest Central Oregon Coast telephone book. "I'm just enjoying the quiet."

Gubbins thought it a peculiar thing to say. "Really?"

"Yeah!" Casey explained with an amenable look, "When you live with your sister, your sister's boyfriend, sometimes your little nephew, lots of people coming by...you tend to forget about peace and quiet."

Convinced, Gubbins pushed up his eyebrows. "Imagine so! You ever think about getting your own place?"

"All the time." The phrase came out of Casey as if it was mortifying her to say so. "Don't get me wrong, I love my family."

"Of course!" Gubbins agreed.

"And I have a weird need to help protect them."

"Any decent person would!"

"It's just...I have needs, too." Casey sat up, conscientiously pushing her knees together. "I need to spread my wings and start doing the things I've dreamed about. You know what I mean?"

It's a good thing that Gubbins didn't need to speak in order to reply to Casey's interrogative. He nodded his numb head, hoping the meager gesture would suffice.

"You have dreams, too," Casey cooed. "I can tell."

Another mute nod came from her date.

"You can tell me anything. I won't tell a soul," Casey intoned with a sexy kind of solemnity. "What are your dreams?"

The heaviness of the moment found its way into Gubbins' brain. All his wishes curved and morphed as he struggled to recollect them in a nutshell. A string of unintended honesty came out of his drying throat.

"To retire. To stay healthy in this old body as long as I can. To be happy."

"No," Casey interjected, her shaded, cornflower gaze never breaking. "Something tangible. Something that can be done right now. What do you need in this life?"

"When I first saw you in the grocery store," Gubbins started, dropping his head to evade the young stare.

"Yeah?" There was so much support in Casey's one word.

"You had quit and said that you wouldn't be back at LeisureFace without being dragged and handcuffed. But...you're here." Gubbins' features went lax, smiling without a prompt.

A shifty glance countered across from Gubbins, though. It was unsure and a bit scared. "Do you want to handcuff me?" Casey said in a challenging, victimized whisper.

"No. Me!" Gubbins' hand pulled at his red Santa tie. "That's what I need in this life. My wife...she'd never do that. She can't." It was almost as if Gubbins was about to cry under the frustrating memories of the past forty years. "I can't blame her, she's just not that kind! One of the reasons I fell in love with her was because she was so gentle and kind and shy!" After a minute of finding every reason to look away from the scrutiny of his date, Gubbins finally was able to match Casey's gaze once again, and the reason came from pure defiance. He reached into his back pocket. "But she can't give me what I really need in this life."

A pair of handcuffs slid forward in his palm.

Gubbins surveilled Casey's face for a sign of repulsion, misunderstanding, or simply I-don't-do-kinky-shit-get-away-from-me. But it couldn't be found. The same provision was there—the same regard, the same position she sat in on the loveseat, the same precocious sympathy. Everything remained the same, and Gubbins knew then what he felt wasn't just infatuation. It was a bond.

For a moment, Casey turned away, intent on the waves. Gubbins gave in to his insecurity, wondering if he was about to censured for his vulnerability. Cast off because of his honesty, like his wife liked to do.

After a moment of contemplation, Casey finally conceded, "I've always dreamt that my first time would be at the seaside."

Ashamed and helpless, Gubbins' dick began to slide and dance inside of his boxer shorts. He tried not to think about it, but doing so also meant blocking out Casey's words, which meant the world to him right now.

"Why don't we let the champagne chill for just a few more minutes, and then we can go down to the beach?" she said, looking one more time at the dark Pacific. "I think there's a way we can help each other."

ACT YOUR AGE

[HOW TO BE SOCIAL WITHOUT BUSTING YOUR HYMEN…IF YOU HAVE ONE, THAT IS]

The bass got so heavy, Brody could feel it rubbing up against his aorta as he got close to the rec center. Every single table at the StileCorp Christmas party had been issued a bottle of wine, and, as the wine had disappeared, the music had gotten louder.

Some people, like Brody, had brought a secret stash of their own libations, but mostly it was the crazy grapes that were responsible for the fun pulsating at all four of the rec center's walls. It was like having a band playing live in your own stomach, a glorious Mach 1 on steroids.

Brody's glass was empty—even the ice was gone—so if he was to continue gliding high, there was only one place he was going to be able to do it.

The entrance door opened up, providing an escape hatch for Disco Tex and the Sex-O-Lettes. Funky cat scatting, double entrendres, and chunky piano from 25 years earlier ran roughshod over Brody as he stepped back inside. Napkins and some less-hardy decorations were out on the dance floor as heels and respectable, shiny Oxfords stepped all over them in an attempt to keep the beat.

Up in front of the whole splendid mess was their queen.

"I see you people in the back!" she scolded through the foam grate of the microphone. "You know, if you'd pull that stick out of your ass, maybe you'd dance a little better. Let's go!"

You could barely see Berta through all the smoke coming out of her.

Her cigarette ashes had begun to pool in an upended, metallic rendering of Frosty the Snowman anchored atop the sound system. A totally different wine bottle than any of the others she'd had so far that night sat perilously close to the electronics board as Berta jived out of her mind and into everyone else's soul.

Her purse, and inside it the reason she had done all this, was still there under the podium.

It was getting difficult for Berta to breathe. The booze, the smoke, and the stone-cold grooves were slowly deflating her, as if she was one of the red and green balloons already starting to lose their helium on the slow nosedive to the stage. Needless to say, the evening's festivities had blown her regimen to hell. It was already past her bedtime, and all her medications for the second half of the day were still back in her LeisureFace guest room, perfectly ordered in the dark and waiting for her. She took a look at her purse, squashed down there out of sight, and decided the next song would be her last.

Even in her undermined condition, swaying at the podium with a sprig of poinsettia behind her ear, Brody found Berta to wield a profound control. For validation, all he had to do was look at everyone there on the dance floor. Some of them were so godawfully off-beat, he could only grin at the whole spectacle. Not one person in the room cared that they sucked—they were dedicating themselves to a collective blindness to anything that set them free. It was kind of beautiful in a way, especially if you were getting a refill on your drink, as Brody was now. With a topped-off glass and ego-fueled confidence to match, he headed toward the stage.

But the record ended too soon, and Berta began her intended swan song before Brody could even get close. The opening to "Last Dance" started to sparkle through the dense, black speakers. "Listen up, all you choice babes and shining knights, even the most righteous have to sleep sometime, so, with this last song, I wish a Merry Christmas to all, and to all a good night!"

Before she even got done, the crowd started to boo. Some of them didn't even stop dancing to do it. Words of encouragement, some of them particularly angry and smelling of merlot, rose up with a vengeance from the mob. They insisted Berta not only give up the funk, but to tear the roof off the sucker, too.

"No!" Brody contended with a stinging breath. "Drop the needle, foxy lady! Come on!" The crowd hitched up their wagon to Brody's love train as his mode changed from come-on to cheerleader. "Berta! Berta! Berta! BERTA!"

The crowd screamed and chewed on the word like one-cent Bazooka. Berta couldn't believe it. She looked down at her purse, finding something about the adulation that scared her. She gave in, holding up her hands to all those people out there under the lights. "Alright, alright! Just a few more, just a few more!"

Both Berta and Donna Summer were given their reprieve as a double-barrel of cheers unloaded from inside the rec center.

Paco had been waiting to show off his handiwork all week.

"Give me your cig," he ordered to Dorena as the rest waited with varying degrees of impatience. Paco then threw a disapproving look Junior's way. "You really gonna let your pop smoke this shit?"

"Are you kidding?" Berrick beamed. "This is one of the only things that got me through 'Nam! I hope it's not too oily."

"Yeah, I know." Paco's tone sounded less than confident. "Fucker bubbles up and you got a mess." In all honesty, every party-goer was already drunk enough to lack the competency to judge Paco's debut pressing.

When the cherry was hot, a small hash nugget was dotted right below the edge of the paper. With due haste, Paco pushed it quickly through the small hole he'd made at the bottom of a plastic Coke bottle. It was fashioned just big enough to get the cigarette in, but with a small vertical slit, which gave it tight elasticity. That way, you didn't have to worry about holding onto everything as your brain started baking.

Dorena chuckled and said to Junior, "Man, I could never do this with my parents. You're the shit." She put up her hand and Junior was only too happy to slap it.

Already, the two layers of smoke drifted up enough to tease the cap. Paco carefully handed off the bottle to Stacey-Lynn.

"Why do I have to go first?" Stacey-Lynn exclaimed as the others egged her on. "Do I just take the cap off?"

"Yeah, and then pass it over, baby. It don't last forever!" Ernesto directed.

"Okay, okay!" Stacey-Lynn screeched before pulling off the cap. She wrapped her lips around the inaugural hit. And it was a monster one.

"Hold it!" Berrick instructed, clamping off his own air to lead by example.

Stacey-Lynn finally coughed out her wall of smoke. The rest cheered while Paco decided to cut off a few more of the sticky dots to go around. The cigarette was reloaded, and Ernesto was up to bat.

"Were those lyrics you sang tonight really Swahili, or whatever?" Junior asked Ernesto as he was holding in his hit.

Ernesto handed the bottle back to Paco for another top-up as he blew out noticeably less smoke than Stacey-Lynn had. "Junebug, I gotta tell ya." He paused, noticing the effects within seconds. "Nigga, that was the straight-up literary works of Frito-Lay."

"What?" Paco asked, smiling as he finished readying the next shot.

Sleepy-eyed and all cool, Ernesto answered, "It was the words on a Doritos bag."

"He's all that and a bag of chips!" Loud, uninhibited, and as funny as the joke itself, Stacey-Lynn's stoned laugh was infectious, to say the least. Everyone else in the room couldn't help but take her cue.

Ernesto shrugged with a simple grin that he couldn't have gotten rid of if you paid him. "It was just layin' there in the kitchen." He meant to go into a big story about why he did it, and how much he wanted to screw over the StileCorp folks, but he didn't get the chance. Or maybe he did? Fuck it.

Paco sorta accidentally on purpose made the next hit a little bigger. He handed it off to Junior, who sucked it up like a pro.

As he couldn't help but be a little impressed at Junior's beginner's luck, Paco advised, "Go easy, homey. Damn!"

Junior began to turn his head about five degrees every few seconds, as if his neck had become some kind of sluggish stopwatch. "My cheeks feel like they're huge." Everyone joined in on the communal laugh that made its way round the sloppy circle of guests fronting the couch. "Do my cheeks look big? Do they?"

No one had an answer for Junior, which was good because his dad busted in yelling "My turn!" as Paco stuck another hash bit on the cigarette.

"Drum roll, please," Dorena asked. Stacey-Lynn squawked as Ernesto began to tickle one of her thighs.

Berrick was patient and waited for the hazy goodness to climb both sides of the bottle before tearing off the lid and going at it.

"So weird watching your dad get high!" Junior told the crowd.

Ernesto nodded his drowsy head. "That is definitely some ill shit."

Berrick blew out his cloud bank like a dragon. "There's nothing wrong with this!" he choked.

Junior bent his neck to confess to the others. "This coming from a man who thinks that 'Gonna Let Her In' song by John Travolta is about a guy taking from a girl with a strap-on."

"Hel-fuckin'-lo!?" Ernesto gasped as the ladies of the room both surrendered to a mix of disgust and giggles.

"You young folks may not know the classics from the seventies, but listen to those lyrics!" Berrick defended, sending the bottle home to Paco, who prepped Dorena's hit.

"This is it, ladies and gentlemen," Junior said with a sweep of his hand. "This is the kind of thing my father talks about when we watch reruns of 'American Bandstand' on VH-1."

"I gotta tell ya," Dorena deadpanned as she sucked back the dense white fog, "I've never heard that interpretation on any of John Travolta's 'Entertainment Tonight' interviews. That's for sure."

Berrick didn't budge an inch. "I get back from eight years of running for my life through the jungles of Southeast Asia, and this is what I gotta listen to on the radio! You go and listen to that song. That's what it's about!"

"Man," Paco marveled, almost to himself, as his lady pushed out a lungful, "that is gay."

"He said it's about a woman with a strap-on, not a guy," Dorena censured her boyfriend.

Paco paid no attention. "I mean that's like 'first-I-was-afraid-I-was-petrified' kind of gay."

Dorena rolled her eyes as she turned to Junior. She tilted her head quizzically. "I think your cheeks are getting big."

Junior's hands slapped his cheeks to check.

"You look like the 'Home Alone' kid!" Stacey-Lynn screamed, quickly digging for her camera to capture the moment. Just in time, the flash ricocheted off the white walls.

"Hey Ernesto," Berrick piped up. "You watch 'Entertainment Tonight', don't ya?"

"Not as much as you, Berrick," Ernesto dropped back, sliding his tongue over his teeth.

"So, who'd you think would win in a fight between Biggie and Suge Knight?"

Stacey-Lynn scoffed, "Ah, this one's easy!" She checked her camera's screen and was satisfied with her picture of Junior.

"With or without TEC-9's?" Ernesto pushed, his voice cracking with suspicion.

"Biggie!" Junior bet. "Always go with the weight, man."

Stacey-Lynn shook her head. "Nuh-uh."

"You think Suge?" Ernesto asked with disbelief.

"Yeah—Biggie's dead!" Stacey-Lynn lost it and the kookiness was catching. Before you knew it, everyone was roaring in a wavy unison. Finally, she collected herself enough to talk through her gasps. "Alright, I don't wanna hear any fat jokes, though, okay?" she said, wiping away tears of laughter.

"Preach, sister, preach," Dorena approved.

"You ain't fat, baby, you just know how to use a fork, and there ain't nothing wrong with that. Jesus H. Christ, you've gotta start loving you as much as I do." There was something sweetly supportive in Ernesto's words that made the underdog in each of them smile, if only for a second.

"Whiiiite girrrls! Mmm!" Paco purred.

"Mmm-hmm!" Ernesto volleyed.

"White girls will do anything!" Paco agreed.

Dorena and Stacey-Lynn both shouted in unison, "We will not!", which made Berrick laugh so hard, he hit his head on the coffee table. By now, he felt no pain, so he didn't waste a moment reveling in the hilarity.

Ernesto threw up his hands. "Hear me out, now hear me out! Black girls got merit, too." You could almost hear the two ladies of the party brace for the hit. "The lips!"

"Hey!" Stacey-Lynn smacked her paramour in the arm.

"It's true," Junior decided, twisting the top off of his fourth or fifth (but definitely no more than seventh) beer of the evening.

"Sensuality!" Paco exploded.

Berrick couldn't resist. "And that coarser hair, so you can get your nuts scratched as you bang 'em!"

"Dad!!" Junior spilled his beer as he laid into his father.

"Aww, dang!" Paco fell backward, hiding his face as his morals were punctured for the first time all evening. Maybe all year.

"Aw yeah, that's it!" Ernesto was united immediately. He got on his knees to slide closer to Berrick, holding out his fist. "Big up, baby, right here!"

Berrick fist-bumped him as the guys celebrated and the girls went on an estrogen revolt full of defensive groans.

"Okay, I'm going outside to throw up now," Dorena said, gathering up Paco's lighter.

Junior wasn't buying it for a second. "Oh, don't give us that! You're not offended!"

"You're right." And with that, Dorena earned herself the award for Sexiest Smile of the Holiday Season as she looked at Junior.

As Paco stood up, he stretched his arms as far as he could, coming within a half-foot of the ceiling. "I gotta get some air."

Dorena swung her head to the balcony. "Come with. I gotta have a smoke." She noticed her boyfriend wrapping his hands around his midsection. "What is it?"

"Ah, it's my stomach, man."

"It's all that goddamn beef!" Dorena surmised.

They stepped out into the winds that hustled in and around the cold steel railing. Dorena pulled her jacket up, whipped back her head, and threw herself into the corner, trying to keep her flapping curls from igniting with the end of the cigarette. The lighter crapped out a few times but ultimately lasted just long enough to catch the flimsy paper. She turned and faced the sea breeze, her smoke cracking and breaking all over her face as she exhaled. "Oh yeah, that feels good. It's so hot in there."

Paco, seemingly lost in thought, still buzzing or maybe even hiding something, grunted his agreement. He leaned into the wind, both hands gripping the railing. The muscles of his biceps stretched and dented, his skin becoming darker in the contrast of the faint light.

"God, I hope Case is okay," Dorena thought aloud.

"She's fine, Dorrie, alright?" Paco's tone and stance were somewhat uncaring, but the lack of concern was strangely soothing to Dorena's ragged worry. "You gotta stop treating her like a little kid."

Another dirty exhale came from Dorena. This one was full of shame. "Yeah, I know."

"And the only way she's gonna grow up is for you to cut the strings. Let. Her. Go, man. We all gotta find our way."

Dorena, guilty as charged, decided to change the subject. Not just because she shivered at the thought of finally turning her naïve little sister loose on the world, but because something else was bothering her.

"So, where the hell is Berta, anyway?" she wondered. "Can't believe how long she's been gone, and something tells me none of those StileCorp jerkoffs are that good of a conversationalist."

It was the perfect in for Paco. He seized the moment.

"Yo, I was serious about getting her in on the business."

"Berta?"

"That was some of the best shit I've had in months," Paco admitted, painfully. "I've been trying to find quality that good for years, and she probably has an entire room of it."

Dorena sighed before bringing the cigarette up to her mouth. "She's not interested."

"Well, talk to her!"

"You talk to her!" Dorena snapped, casting off her ashes to the gale. "I'm not turnin' the screws on someone to jump hip-deep into dealing during a motherfucking Christmas party, alright?"

"You know she knows other growers," Paco assumed with a tantalizing curl at the end of his words. "They could get on board, too."

"Pac, do you have any idea how hot the flames of hell are?" Dorena said with a straight face. "Because that's exactly what's gonna burn your ass for all eternity if you start trying to wrangle HIV patients to fill our orders. Besides, with Fitz out of the picture, at least for the moment, we're fine. We don't need the extra muscle right now."

"Right now is when we build a wall!" Paco shouted, his incensed features cemented into place by a mix of defiance and greed. "We make it strong, keep new people out, keep steppin' up our shit, make our money, and leave. That's the only way we're going to get to the big time."

Paco wasn't even done when his other half stepped all over his plan of attack. "Wait, I'm not leaving here. I'm not leaving Petey."

"Think of the money, Dorrie."

"I'm thinking of my child! I'm not going to Eugene or Boise or Portland or fucking Seattle where I never get to be in my son's life, okay?"

"He's not my responsibility," Paco shook her off, coldly.

"No, he's mine," Dorena asserted. "Even though I don't have him right now, he's part of my life, and if you want me, he's part of the package deal."

"Fuck this shit," Paco muttered. He ripped a cigarette from his girlfriend's pack and hurled the slider door aside hard enough to nearly jostle it off its white aluminum track.

As Stacey-Lynn was getting Junior and Ernesto framed just right in her camera's viewfinder, Paco crashed into the living room. Grabbing a huge nug of hash, he manhandled his burnt-out Coke bottle from the coffee table and stormed back into the hallway. The wind from outside began to rattle all the window coverings and squeeze a quick chill into the room.

"*¡Perra egoísta!*" Paco yelled, throwing himself down on the master suite bed. Just as he was pressing a good fraction of his handiwork to the end of the cigarette, the sound of the toilet flushing smacked a queer expression onto his face.

In his perfect tux, Berrick stepped out of the bathroom and got an eyeful of a hit-in-progress. "Are we moving in here for round two?" he asked, excitedly straightening his cummerbund.

"Fuckin' A," Paco's apathetic pout offered from behind the filter. His thumb ground the wheel of the lighter, sparking it.

"Yay!" Berrick cheered as he jumped onto the bed.

Gubbins had thought of everything. He and Casey held champagne flutes as their shoes ground into the sand. The wind had a peculiar way of missing them since the stairway to the beach emptied out behind a stout envelope of sandy rock. Casey gripped the bottle, looking at the flapping ribbons of water breaking and popping not far from where they stood.

"We need to start dedicating ourselves to our fantasies," she said, just loud enough to be heard over the racket of the sea. "They're what make us happy."

The glass dropped from her hand, the foot of it disappearing into the fluffy grains of sand. She began to slowly and steadily shake the champagne bottle. Casey's sapphire stare was hypnotic to Gubbins, and it took him a heavy moment or two before he regained his concentration enough to realize the consequences of his date's actions.

"No! Stop!" Gubbins' smile was playful, but there was a realistic apprehension in the quaver of his voice.

Casey just shook her head as the bottle went up and down, refusing to give in to anything but her fantasy.

"It's going to explode everywhere!" Gubbins hooted. His last couple of syllables broke, imbued with a little laughter and a whole lot of horniness.

"I know." Casey stopped shaking the bottle long enough to contemplate the phallic, emerald neck with a dreamy reserve. "And when it does...I want you to put it inside me."

The swish of the liquor started up again as Casey resumed shaking the bottle, up and down. Up and down. Gubbins was losing his mind. As Casey stepped towards him, he found himself pinned against a huge, heavy chunk of driftwood.

To Gubbins, it seemed like the moment went on forever. Watching that bottle and all its potent liquid dance and spin made his mouth dry and his parched lips crack with desperate anticipation. After stripping the foil, Casey's fingers squeezed and untwisted the wire cage. All that remained was the cork.

"Grip it real tight." the high-pitched voice ordered as she rubbed the bottom of the bottle on Gubbins' tenting, forest-green crotch.

Gubbins did as told. Looking down, it seemed like some dreamlike extension of his own dick, which bent uncomfortably under the bottom of the green bottle. His date's instruction trumped his discomfort, though, and he held onto the smooth coldness with both hands.

Though Casey's ankles were killing her, being barefoot at night on the beach wasn't a stellar choice. She left her pumps on as she slid down her jeans, with the denim gliding off surprisingly fast. Giving a coy turn away as she stood in front of Gubbins, she slid down her panties. Straddling the neck of the bottle, which poked out just a bit between her legs, Casey pressed herself hard against Gubbins' abdomen, feeling the titillating coolness of the bottle as she rubbed along its length.

"Pop it. Ohh, I want it! Pop it, now!" she cried, frantic foam dotting her lips.

Gubbins' thumbs pressed firmly out and away from him, feeling the cork slide upward. Half-inch! Quarter-inch! An eighth! *BAMM!* The force sent the shot out from in between Casey's thighs, arching long into the surf. His wrists wrenched back and pushed as the bottle began to gush. Gubbins was, at first, worried that he didn't get it in. Then, a different kind of anxiety took him over as Casey began a savage screech of what appeared to be pain, but her words and shaking thighs told an entirely different story.

"Ohhh fuck, YES! Oh God—OHHH!" Froth spurted and thrust with weighty pressure, filling and satisfying Casey completely. Finally, it emptied out of her, slowly coating her legs with a rigid, but refreshing, stickiness. Champagne began to seep into the sand as the waves crept a little closer to the driftwood.

Gubbins could feel his own wetness close against him and knew it wasn't the champagne. Things like shame and doubt never registered, though—he was positive that he could last out here all night!

Dorena stared over the balcony with her eyes lost in the darkness, never imagining her little sister's dalliance was happening on the beach right underneath her. Her head emptied itself of everything as she just hung there over the railing, hitting the cigarette's soft filter to her lips every couple of minutes.

Junior stuck his head out the slider door left open by Paco's wrathful entrance back into the suite. "You okay out here?"

As the tide continued to come in, the winds had gotten worse. Dorena softly scratched the hair out of her eyes as she turned to Junior. "Did he leave?"

"Uh, no," Junior scrambled, ultimately opting for the truth. "I think he's doing more hash with my dad."

Neither of them could imagine the thought without laughing a bit. Junior's intensity tempered a bit at hearing Dorena's titter, regardless of how innocuous it seemed. "So, are you okay?"

"Yeah, thanks, it's cool," she added.

"You may want to tell that to Paco then," Junior joked a bit more, though his face registered a good measure of uncertainty as to whether or not Dorena's mood was ready for any more humor.

"I'm stuck."

"What do you mean?" Junior truly had no idea what she was referring to. "Stuck where?"

"Here. A place that won't allow me to get any further."

There was just enough give in Dorena's voice to encourage Junior to take his first step closer to her. "What makes you believe that?" he asked, sliding shut the patio door.

"I'm unable to keep my kid myself. So, I partner up a little side business that will give me the money to give my kid the life he should have. And then they take my kid because of the business and the background of my partner..." Dorena started to cry.

Junior was stunned. Dorena had always been such a relentless motherfucker. So independent, so outspoken, so strong. Dealing had given her what she wanted, that being a continuous stream of greenbacks and the security of having a man in her life. But it had taken the one thing Dorena needed, and that was a healthy, loving relationship with her little boy.

"I'm stuck, Junebug. I'm stuck in the loop, and I don't know how to get out." Dorena sent her butt over the railing and burst into tears. She clamped onto Junior, the only person who seemed to care enough to listen. Her sobs stopped as Dorena hesitated. If she only knew just how much Junior really did care, she would have put every shred of her trust into him at that moment.

And that's when Junior was dedicated to pushing his own agenda aside. She really did mean that much to him, and he struggled for the wisdom to put her mind at ease and give her the only other thing besides her son that she needed: hope.

"Everybody's got a loop. The one you got now? It's just temporary. Remember that." Junior meant to pause, but his mouth kept going. "Hawaiians have a saying about it. Pili nakekeke." Dorena mused at the funny-sounding syllables. Junior explained, "Means 'loosely-fastened'. Nothing's permanent, especially when you're miserable enough to decide to move on."

"Peely knock-a-knee-knee." The ironic smile flashed as Dorena garbled it. The slowing tears clinging to her brown eyes shimmered brightly in the limited light out on the balcony.

"Kee-kee," Junior corrected, bashfully.

"Kee-kee! Sorry," Dorena amended.

Just as Dorena was getting her diction together, the slider door opened again, with both Ernesto and Stacey-Lynn tentatively hovering over the track.

"We're not bustin' in on anything are we?" Ernesto asked with a timid slyness.

Both Junior and Dorena shook their heads. "No, what's up?" Junior replied.

"We just wanted to say goodbye!" Stacey-Lynn's voice started to quake as she hugged Dorena.

"Already? It's still early." Junior pressed.

Ernesto slapped his best friend's hand, squeezing the palm. "Yeah, we gotta get on the road."

Junior gave a strong hug to Ernesto and then moved to Stacey-Lynn as Dorena kissed Ernesto on his cheek.

"You guys let me know if you get stuck out there," Junior reminded them. "Seriously. Keep us updated, okay?"

"Yes, sir," Ernesto said, the words parting around each side of the lump in his throat.

Dorena could feel her tears coming back. "God bless, you guys. Have a Merry Christmas, okay?"

"You too, girlfriend," Ernesto said as Stacey-Lynn blew them a kiss. They closed up the slider from letting in any more of the chilly air.

By now, Paco was officially crazier than Berrick. Bloated on an unadulterated party mix of hash, Full Sail, and 93% ground beef, he was laughing uncontrollably at any cracked joke. He giggled maniacally at the plight of his worst business competitor as he relayed his history with Fitz. Berrick listened intently, propped against the headboard, and was surprisingly mellow since he was taking only a fraction of the hits Paco was.

"And now, that fucker's over in the Eugene pen, taking it up the butt as I'm taking all his customers!" Both he and Berrick continued their breathless guffawing. "And since that *culo apestoso* got inside," Paco concluded, raising the smoky Coke bottle, "my stash ain't never tasted so good!"

Though she tried not to listen, Paco was so loud in his mouthy drug-fuckery that Stacey-Lynn couldn't help recognizing Fitz's story as she made her way back the hall with Ernesto. She stuck every emotion that ganged up on her deep inside. Within the hour, she would be out of Beaver Lake forever. She was almost home-free, so now wasn't the time for sentimentality.

"Man, you guys are serious about gettin' flame-broiled and shit!" Ernesto said as he walked into the bedroom. Both Paco and Berrick immediately tried getting him and Stacey-Lynn onto the bed with them, erupting in an overlapping lump of come-hither gestures and crashing, slurred syllables.

Ernesto slapped a handshake on Paco (who misgauged his hand and nearly missed it) and gave a hug to Berrick.

"Merry Christmas, you guys!" Stacey-Lynn wished happily as she gave a hug to each of the two bleary-eyed fellows on the bed.

As the couple slipped out the front door, Paco threw a wave up to them as Berrick offered the final coda of, "And watch out for cops!"

"You too, Berrick!" Ernesto said with a great, white smile, and both Berrick and Paco were back to holding their stomachs and laughing for no reason again.

Paco sighed. "I can't believe you said that shit about Black women's pussies. Cuz, that was fucked-up." He stopped and grabbed his stomach harder—this time, it didn't have anything to do with hilarity.

"That was true!" Berrick insisted, his mind racing back to his military days. "After eight weeks of basic training and eight in AIT, you learn a few things." Berrick noticed Paco's groans and lost his train of thought. "What's wrong?"

"Gaaaah! Oh, shit!" Paco screamed, his feet tangling in the slippery bedspread. "Fire in the hole, fire in the fuckin' hole!"

Paco would've run on his kneecaps if he had to. The bathroom door slammed and a split second later, a huge series of blops and bfffts and farts and assorted anal merriment exploded inside the toilet bowl.

"OH! OH, MAN! *Awwwwwww.*"

It sounded as if all the air was being let out of Paco at once.

Berrick, safely on the other side of the bathroom door, couldn't help but smile. He stood off the bed, shouting through the door. "What's got ya by the tail, chief?"

"Uuuuhhhhhh," Paco grunted. "Ah man, this shit is intense!"

"I know what you mean!" Berrick empathized. "Got some new meds that made me do the exact same thing lately. You want me to bring you a beer?" He tried to keep a straight face but didn't quite pull it off.

"Nah, nah," Paco's guttural vocal smear pushed under the door. He gasped and gave another extended groan. "Ah man, I hope I don't shit myself in the car on the way home."

Berrick couldn't help but ask. "You got leather seats?"

"Uh...yeaaah." the stoned reply eked out.

"Don't worry then—just wipes off!" Berrick recommended, chirpily.

The grim voice from inside the bathroom continued. "I think this is gonna take a while."

"You work it out, buddy! I'll check on you in a bit, okay?"

Paco could only give a lulling fart in reply. Berrick left the room, his hand thrust into his pocket to rattle his pills, of which there were a few less than when he arrived at the party. He stopped and noticed the shadows of Junior and Dorena still out on the balcony. Their shapes talked and swayed in a friendly, casual way that made Berrick offer up his last, sweet smile of the evening.

He opened the front door and stepped out into the chill of the night, winding his way back past wrought iron railings and clean sodium lighting to his and Junior's room. He popped the top on a Full Sail that had been left behind in the kitchenette, using it to down the rest of his pocketed pills. Undressing before he could even get to the back half of the suite, Berrick folded his tux neatly onto the dresser top and opted for the left of the two queen beds. Only a minute later, he was asleep.

The steel links of the handcuffs tinkled then stretched taut as Casey let the one bracelet fall from her fingers. The chain swung back and forth as she studied the pockmarks in the tangled wall of drift-wood behind her and Gubbins. It didn't take her long to find two perfect spots.

"Now," Casey promised, "your fantasy."

Seductively, she slid her hands down Gubbins' arm, rubbing his pulse point with her thumb. The first of the two toothy chrome rings clicked shut around an elongated branch rising out of the left side of the log. Casey listened to her date's gasping becoming shorter, teetering on panic.

"It's everything I ever wanted." Gubbins stopped, trying to perfect his intent. "You're everything I ever wanted."

The second cuff threaded through a thickened, woody hole and clinked closed tightly around Gubbins' right wrist. "Then tell me you're not afraid," Casey instructed.

"I'm not," Gubbins panted, closing his eyes. "I'm not afraid."

Casey's poised, defiant stare could have cut diamonds. "Well...you should be."

For Cles Gubbins, the Earth's emergency brake suddenly got de-ployed. His head beat and swirled, trying to block out that moment in time when he realized that he'd finally been had. Casey Morris was going to be the one to see to it that his whole selfish, misogynis-tic, grandstanding, two-faced, racist, ugly-motherfucking-golf-pants-wearing world got dismantled, one iota, one dollar, and one little silver link at a time.

"Golf and pussy? 'I-don't-care-if-she-likes-it-as-long-as-I-have-fun'?" Casey mocked. "You know, if you're going to talk shit about your date, you might wanna think about at least closing the door behind you before you do it!"

Casey turned and straightened the spaghetti straps of her top before cranking the length of her scarf back around her neck. Next, she pulled her jeans up from their crinkled, denim ball and shook the sand off them.

To Gubbins, it appeared that she couldn't get dressed fast enough.

"What? What are you doing?" he bellowed into the wind.

"What someone should have done to you a long time ago!" was the sentence handed down from a kangaroo court of karma. "But they didn't, because they were too scared of getting fired, or being felt up, or sued, or losing their health insurance, or a hundred different other things assholes like you do to employees every single day!" Casey righted her stature as she fumbled her pumps back on.

"You! I'm going to see to it that you never get another job in this town for the rest of your white-trash life!" Gubbins' eyes were almost bulging out of their sockets. "I put a champagne bottle up your little twat, you bitch!!"

"Because your little dick wasn't ever going to get up in it, that's why!"

Gubbins didn't even hear her. "Don't you forget it! Ever!"

"Go ahead," Casey implored, "keep on screaming. As I was listening to you talk about my pussy and your nine-iron and all that stupid shit to your little takeover partner-in-arms, I had a look at the phone book tide charts in your trumped-up outhouse up there."

Gubbins shot a look out to the angry winter Pacific. It was no longer romantic and harmonious, but instead, it was stinging, sweeping, and coming straight for him. And it came an inch closer each time it reached out its fingers in his direction.

"You go get the key to these cuffs. It's on the bar by the ice bucket, and you do it NOW!"

Casey reasoned, "I'd say you have about two more hours." She dusted off the bottom of the champagne bottle, which thankfully still held about half its quietly-fizzing contents.

"You do it! They're going to lock you up forever, you crazy little whore!" Gubbins tried to collapse his thumbs and somehow Houdini his sorry ass out of this situation, but the cuffs were far too tight. "You have no idea. No idea how powerful of a man I am. You'll never work again. None of you will!"

Casey sacrificed a splash of the expensive champagne to Gubbins' face. "Unless you want fish shittin' in your mouth in two hours, you better start screaming!"

"HELLLP! HELP ME!!!"

At first, Gubbins' screaming seemed loud to Casey, but, as she started up the stairs, she found that, not more than 10 yards away, the ruckus got lost in the piercing wind.

Ernesto and Stacey-Lynn stopped in their tracks at the faint sound of a voice. It brushed past their ears on the way down the embankment past the swimming pool.

"Hear that?" Stacey-Lynn asked. Ernesto nodded, and they both turned westward.

Just then, Casey arrived at the top steps of the beach access.

Sandwiched in between the twisting layers of salty gales, they all could hear Gubbins raving on, "I'll kill you, you prick tease! You'll see! I'll get free and you'll see!"

Ernesto tilted his head, peering down the stairway. "That Gubbins?" he asked Casey, who took a swig from the big, green champagne bottle.

"He's all yours."

Her scarf caught the wind as she headed back to the LeisureFace building. Soon, she was in the windless safety of Gubbins' converted groundskeeper quarters. She pulled the slider door shut after her, but reconsidered, opening it just a crack. She could barely make out Gubbins' lunatic ravings as she kicked off her uncomfortable shoes and grabbed a new champagne flute from the bar. With her crisp glass of bubbly, she lied back on the loveseat, the small whistle from the crack in the slider door whipping up the aroma from the warm vanilla candles, lulling her racing mind to sleep.

Confused, but definitely intrigued, Ernesto and Stacey-Lynn trod on the sticks and sand that cluttered the bottom of the beach access stairs. There it was: A screaming Cles Gubbins handcuffed to a huge piece of driftwood, complete with flapping red Santa tie, treacly, champagne-sprayed face, and a small, drying stain leaking through his green suit pants. Stacey-Lynn tried hard not to react, but her gut finally punched a laugh up and out of her. Ernesto chose to go the social route.

"Well, hello there, Mr. Gubbins! Damn, it looks like you probably should have stayed home with the wife this evening!"

"You two! Get me out of here! That little shit of a Morris girl did this to me! It's all her fault!"

"I'd like to help you, Mr. Gubbins," the preamble began, with Ernesto knowing full well he was driving out of Beaver Lake tonight with every penny he was owed, "but first, I need to talk to you about some financial matters that need addressing."

"Are you nuts?" Gubbins cawed. "I'm not giving you a fucking thing until you get me off here!"

Stacey-Lynn picked up right where her beau left off. "Now, the way we see it, sir, is that you owe me for my last week of work—"

"Your drugged-up husband caused hundreds of dollars of damage to my Reception area!"

"And my final week of work," Ernesto jumped in, tugging the collar of his dashiki, "as well as this little Uncle Tom shit you talked me into so you could suck up the ones sewin' together your golden retirement parachute. So, this means you better break out some ends quick if you don't wanna get saltwater fuckin' up them nice shoes. You know what I'm saying?"

"You greedy bastard!" Gubbins barked. "When I get off this thing, so help me God, boy, I'm going to stick my finger up your Black ass and spin you like a basketball!"

"This nice shit ain't working," Ernesto deadpanned to his lady.

"Oh, Mr. Gubbins, don't get so worked up. Here," Stacey-Lynn took down Gubbins' green slacks and, even worse, his red and green boxer shorts.

"No! NO!!"

Even considering the staunch December wind chill coming off the Pacific, that penis was mighty small.

"Yeah, cool out, Mr. Gubbins." The CEO continued to rave incoherently as Ernesto motioned to his exposed crotch. "We'll be out of your hair before you know it!"

"As long as you have your pants off, let's have a look in the pockets!" Stacey-Lynn peered around Gubbins' hairy knees to begin raiding the back pants pockets. She gasped as she pulled out his wallet in no time at all. "Wow, Merry Christmas to you, too, Mr. Gubbins!"

Gubbins shook, head to toe, from both rage and the freezing whip of air on every inch of his skin below the waist. "Put that back this instant!!"

Stacey-Lynn's eyes grew wide as she slicked out each bill. "One hundred—"

"This! This is robbery!"

"Two hundred! Three hundred! Four hundred!"

"That money is not yours!"

The money just wouldn't stop, and so neither did Stacey-Lynn. "Five hundred! Six hundred! Seven hundred!"

"I'll find you both," Gubbins seethed, a bloodshot hatred tucked behind the corners of his sand-scrubbed eyelids. "Your asses are mine when I do!"

Ernesto started counting along. "Eight hundred! Nine hundred! A thousand! Eleven hundred! Twelve hundred!" Finally, the billfold was exhausted.

"Whoo!" Stacey-Lynn cheered as the dozen bills fluttered in the tight grasp of her fingers.

"Lord have mercy! Dude, you shouldn't ever carry that much cash!" Ernesto's warning continued, whistling into the briny air. "Don't you know there are thievin', small-town white girls that'll take your shit? And! They'll take your picture when you're naked, too!"

With that, Stacey-Lynn pulled out her beloved Nikon and took the last photo she'd ever snap in Beaver Lake. The fact that Gubbins was once again shouting, "Nooooo!" as the shutter tripped, made the final effect all the better. There, inside the little frame of the LCD screen, they checked to make sure Androcles J. Gubbins was preserved just the way they wanted to remember him.

"Well, now that we've received our costume deposit back," Ernesto said, slipping off his colorful dashiki to the sand, "me and Stacey-Lynn would like to wish you and yours, and you little bottle cap dick there, a happy Kwanzaa and a very humble New Year."

Gubbins' howls followed them up the stairs but were eaten by the churning output of the sea. The time had come when Ernesto and Stacey-Lynn not only couldn't wait to leave everything behind but could welcome the life that awaited them out on Highway 101. They began to run, hand in hand, to the parking lot.

They reached their cars, huffing and laughing. Ernesto wrapped his arm around his love's shoulder as they looked back at LeisureFace one last time.

"So, where you wanna go?" Ernesto's whisper cut through the night.

Stacey-Lynn looked down at the wad of hundreds in her hand. Staring straight ahead at all the lighted windows, she could only speak what was in her heart. "Somewhere with no bad memories."

Ernesto's face reflected the peace and opportunity of their newfound freedom. "Ya ever see the Carolinas?"

And so, pulling out of the rec center parking lot, that's exactly where they headed.

Ernesto and Stacey-Lynn, however, were too consumed by the possibilities of their new life together to notice the thumping, twisting bass that still rocked out the four corners of the rec center after three brain-melting, boogie-down hours.

Sure, there were a few people who crapped out, especially the ladies, since heels and dresses aren't very forgiving on the dance floor. But for the most part, the StileCorp crew were still at it. Several of them were still wearing the 'SIT ON MY LEISUREFACE' paper hats that Berta had handed out to them in the past hour, too. They weren't just drinking down the wine, they were absorbing every cosmic sensation Berta was giving to them.

It was about now, though, that Berta was regretting that she didn't stop when she intended. The crowd pushed her on, but that also made her open yet another bottle of wine. She'd seen so many labels this evening, she had no idea what tasted good, what was expensive, or what people recommended. She didn't care. Her seventh bottle of the night sat mostly empty by the console, its cork floating sideways in a sad, shallow puddle just above the punt.

Michael McDonald was into the chorus of "What A Fool Believes", selling the crowd the notion that what seems to be is always better than nothin'. But now, sprawled in a folding chair and barely breathing, with her skin giving off a bluish halo under the lights, it was clear that Berta had had enough of what seemed to be.

With her hand swiping through the air to pull herself to the podium, she twisted the strap of her purse around her hand. It raked across the floor to her feet. Thankfully, the answering machine fell part-way out. Berta was able to grab the attached cord of the AC adapter and feed it through her fingers until she reached the plug.

The Doobies were unceremoniously cut off as the auxiliary was pulled out. Berta took off her own 'SIT ON MY LEISUREFACE' hat and tore off its elastic band. She used it to fasten the microphone to the speaker of the answering machine as the crowd slowed to a confused halt.

"And now these messages." You could barely hear her introductory words as everything clicked on.

"*Hello, Mancari residence, this is Roberta,*" the recording began.

Gubbins' irate voice, through clenched teeth, sounded evil in the dark corner echoes of the nighttime rec hall. "*I know it was you.*"

The volume was loud and clear, with both Berta and Gubbins' voices banging off the walls, as well as every partygoer's skull. The effect was barren and shocking.

"*Who is this?*"

"*You know who this is. Now, you listen to me. Because of your little stunt, I'm canceling your room for the party so I can move some of our poor StileCorp executives that you inconvenienced with your asinine little tricks!*"

The crowd was already starting to ponder the reason for Michael McDonald suddenly getting the bum's rush from the playlist, but as soon as Gubbins threw out the word 'StileCorp', the answering machine had everyone's undivided attention.

"*What are you talking about?*"

"*The zip ties on the refrigerators. Peppermints in the shower. Crayons in the dryer! The goddamn maxi pads in the pillows!*"

That last sentence caused some concern for a few folks in the audience, but they all kept quiet as the tape went on.

"You're out of your mind. I paid for that room a month ago—we all did! I'm not giving it up because of your lack of foresight to block out some rooms during one of the busiest times of the year."

"Lack of foresight? Lack of foresight?! I know you and your classless little shit of a flunky, Dorena, set this up, and I'll be writing up her termination first thing Monday morning, in case you were wondering."

"First of all, I still have no idea what you're talking about." The crunch on the tape came from the Life Saver candy she had popped in her mouth. A woeful smile pulled up the corner of her mouth as Berta listened to herself. *"And, even if I did, you have no proof whatsoever of any wrongdoing from anybody!"*

"Playing stupid isn't helping, and for wasting my time, I'm going to keep your $50 for damages to the room! But you're lucky, Berta, you're a really lucky lady. You wanna know why?"

"Sure. Tell me."

"Our company Christmas party has got me in the holiday spirit so much, Miss Mancari, that I'm not going to fire you...because I know how much you need medication coverage. That, and because I'll always need a woman to wash all the shit stains out of my guests' towels. That's really why I'm keeping you."

Brody strode up to the side of the amp. He couldn't believe what he was hearing and, judging from the looks on the rest of his employee's faces, none of them wanted to, either.

"You're not keeping anyone! Everyone knows you're selling to StileCorp this weekend—that's why you're having this party! You don't give a shit about your people and you never did! So stop acting like you're doing any of us a fucking favor, because we've known the whole time what you've been up to!"

"Well, Berta, after tonight, that all changes for every single one of you slobs on my payroll."

"Bet your ass it does, Mr. Gubbins."

Berta's inebriated grasp couldn't get the buttons on the answering machine to work the way she wanted, so she simply ripped the plug out of the wall. It went zooming back through the air and skidded across the stage, leaving a weird, ambient silence in the rec center. There were dozens of people standing there, but if you shut your eyes and tried to pretend you were somewhere else, like Berta was doing right now, you would have sworn to God that everyone had already gone home.

"This is what Mr. Gubbins is like when he's not on stage," she finally said, with a dry and thickened tongue making it tough to get her words out. Her hands grappled alongside the podium as everything started to sway.

"I know that, for somebody with HIV—someone who needs their job and their insurance—this may seem like suicide to a lot of you. But I want you to know who you're dealing with, because just like me, you've all been fooled."

Berta wanted to cry but couldn't. She felt both her windpipe and sinuses revolt as everything began to glare and fade. Though she didn't realize it, the crowd did, and they began to rustle softly in the background.

"And if you go on with the takeover," Berta strained for her last words as she caught Brody's eye, "he wins."

A lump rose, blocking out the neat pathway to her lungs. Berta began to choke violently, gripping the sides of the console as a wide jet of tan vomit broke sloppily, splashing over the edge of the podium. Immediately, women screamed and men barked orders, but Berta never heard any of it. Falling straight back, her head smashed against the wood planks of the stage, a sickening thump filling space around the heavy curtains.

Within twelve minutes, two cop cars and an ambulance were on the scene, and LeisureFace's annual holiday party was officially over.

ACT OF FAITH

[YOUR LOOP...AND HOW TO BREAK IT]

For almost everyone, the two weeks before Christmas sucked reindeer dick.

Dorena spent the week following the party watching Paco pack up all his things. The hash press, his spices and cooler, and most of the furniture was going with him to Eugene at the first of the year in an effort to 'play in the big leagues', as Paco coined it. The only thing Dorena was starting to hate more than dumb baseball analogies was Paco, and maybe herself. She started making a mental tally of how much time she'd wasted away from her son because of Paco and his quest to build a life out of making other people forget theirs, one little baggie at a time. Ultimately, Dorena decided to stay in the apartment until the lease ran out in March. That way, it gave her the space to get her proverbial shit together and try to snag another job. That was, if there were any jobs to be had before March.

Mrs. Taylor welcomed Ernesto and his new girlfriend, Stacey-Lynn, at her little townhouse in Myrtle Beach. Needless to say, she made too many scalloped potatoes and liked to ask a lot of questions as she got to know what she hoped would be her future daughter-in-law. Everyone took it in stride as the young couple learned to stand on their own. With only about $400 left of Gubbins' money, Ernesto promised his well-meaning mama that they'd look for jobs right after Christmas was over. He and Stacey-Lynn were hoping to be able to afford a small place down near Murrells Inlet by the end of February. Until then, there was a lot of pavement to hit and a lot of standards to be lowered—as they pored over the want ads, their hearts sank when they found Myrtle Beach's wages were even worse than Beaver Lake's.

Though Stacey-Lynn never knew it, Fitz had tried writing her from jail. Their mailbox back at the trailer kept getting more and more crammed with mail, until finally Stacey-Lynn updated everything with the USPS. The letter came back to him around the time he was to have his day in court, which was slated for the third week of February. Though it was only a few paragraphs, Fitz hoped whole-heartedly that the note would reach his wife; if nothing else, because it contained a windblown Tampax paper he'd found on the perimeter of the yard one sunny day. Oregon State Inmate DC#397341 was, like most people on the inside, turning into a sentimental old fool.

And while we're on the topic of fools, Gubbins turned out to be a luckier son of a bitch than anyone ever estimated. Despite the debacle of the LeisureFace Christmas party, he was still able to sweet-talk Brody into going through with the takeover, affording him the picture-perfect retirement he had connived for months. Unlike all of his subordinates, and how it usually was for golden assholes like Gubbins, everything came up roses. There was only one thing left for him to do: gloat.

He gloated at the fact that now-former employee Berta Mancari's little answering machine stunt in the rec center didn't work. He gloated that he had enough cash and tourism pull to keep his driftwood rescue from the Lane County Highway Patrol under wraps from his wife and out of the newspapers, as well. But worst of all, he gloated that he was shooting down in flames with extreme prejudice every single work reference call he received in regards to Casey Morris.

And it was hitting Casey even harder than he could have ever hoped.

She had spent days in her room, the bottom sheet of her bed a rumpled mess of tarot layouts that told her everything she didn't want to know. With even Dorena choosing to ignore her, Casey's new best friend became the Nine of Swords. It came up now in almost every single reading. Doubt. Guilt. Refusal to acknowledge your efforts. It was all there. Not just inside of her, but right on top of the bed, time and time again. She tried to piece together some optimism as the cards of Judgement and the Queen of Cups flipped up from her hands, but it was no use. Her mind was too cluttered to see a light at the end of the tunnel, even if it really was there and not just a bout of wishful thinking.

Dorena brought in the mail for the day, wishing she'd put on a jacket to do so. The weather was typically dreadful, and so she ended up soaked from the shoulders up after a quick jaunt to the postbox. Two spots of holiday cheer that brightened up the melancholy Morris household were Christmas cards with a postmark from South Carolina. Casey's name was on one, so Dorena slipped open the flap on the other that was addressed to her. A jolly, if generic-looking, snowman wished her a Merry Christmas. Stacey-Lynn's handwriting boasted in thick, red ink on the inside of the card: *"Loving it over here! We miss you so much and want to wish you the warmest (and driest!) holiday season ever!"*

A genuine smile floated somewhere around Dorena's lips. She was able to catch it for the shortest of moments while looking at the signatures of her two now very faraway friends. She exhaled through her nose, not wanting to make the trek to her depressed sister's bedroom, but knew it was for the best.

A knock slid on the door, making Casey look up from her deck. "Come on in," she offered in a weak and unaffected voice.

With the mail in hand, Dorena sauntered in. "Hear anymore from the Super 8?"

Casey shook her head. "Four in the past week. Four fucking interviews and not a single offer." She stopped her self-pity just long enough to stare up at her sister. "Dorrie, I know I should've had at least one of those jobs."

Dorena fluffed her humidity-flattened curls as she sat on the edge of the bed. "You should've had 'em all." She paused with a bloated hesitancy before asking, "You think it's Gubbins, don't you?"

Casey motioned to the cards on the bed. "That's what they tell me."

"Oh, screw your stupid cards!" Dorena fumed, batting away the glower her little sister threw at her. "What?! I don't care what the cards say. What do YOU say? You've been using these things as a crutch since you were eleven. Locked in your goddamn bedroom, just like you are now, shufflin' your ass off and trying to figure out what's coming next in life instead of going out and living it!"

The wound was very deep. Never in her life had Casey been so insulted, but she just sat there, her stupor filing down the edges of how much it hurt. "You want me to leave when Paco does? Don't you?"

Dorena could feel her cheeks rouging over with shame and hopelessness. "No! No, I don't."

"Oh, spare me," Casey hissed. "I know you want this room for Petey!"

Dorena was so frustrated, she wanted to cry. "Yes, he'll need a room, but that doesn't mean I don't want you here."

Casey, in all of her funk and self-absorption, suddenly caught the wind of change in her sails. She stood up and eased her into her sister's arms. "I'm sorry," she repeated more than once.

"It's okay—" Dorena started.

"No, it's not."

"It will be." Strands were sticking to her moist eyelids, so Dorena shook her hair out of her face. The perseverance came back to her voice. "We'll find a way around Gubbins. You'll get a job. I'll get a job. Petey will be back. We'll move and everything will be cool beans again, okay?"

"Alright," Casey nodded with a laugh, wiping her eyes.

"Oh," Dorena flipped through the mail, pulling out an envelope for her sister, "we got cards from Ernesto and Stacey-Lynn."

"Sweet! They made it!" Casey's pale face beamed, a tinge of pink rising up her cheeks. She started to open the card but stopped as her sister turned back at the door.

"Since tomorrow's Christmas Eve, I don't feel like cooking tonight. You okay with Papa Murphy's?"

"What kind?"

Dorena thought for a second. "Maybe the Hawaiian. Pineapple-Canadian bacon?"

A breezy wheeze slipped out between Casey's teeth. "Hawaiian? You've been hanging out with Junior too much."

"Hey," Dorena reasoned with a raise of her eyebrow, "buy one, get one half-price!"

Casey quipped, "Two? We're gonna be eating them till Valentine's Day!"

As she pulled the door shut, Dorena came up with a solution. "Pac's taking half what's in the freezer, so at least we'll have room for leftovers."

Turning her attention back to the card, Casey slipped it out of its envelope and turned it over. There, in the middle of a holly-trimmed border, was a beautiful rendering of the birth of Jesus.

"Aww," Casey said as she took in the farm animals and kneeling wise men surrounding the Savior. Stuck to the inside of the card was a printed photograph of Cles Gubbins. He was slightly overexposed in his smart, forest-green suit and red Santa tie, handcuffed and screaming as his cute little button-sized dickhead was forever captured in all its photographic glory.

It was the best Christmas present Casey Morris would ever receive.

The same thick-tipped, red pen that Stacey-Lynn used to sign Dorena's card had scrawled a single, holy sentence of ten capitalized words underneath the picture:

FOR CHRIST'S SAKE, GO NAIL HIS ASS TO THE WALL!

Other than Casey's little come-to-Jesus Christmas card miracle, the only other positive thing that happened in the days before Christmas was Junior becoming the new Maintenance Division Manager of the Beaver Lake Comfort Inn. Sometimes in life, the smaller victories are the sweetest—especially for your bank account—and Junior rejoiced with a Don Ho cassette on the drive home through the Saturday afternoon darkness. As murky as it was at only a quarter after four, you never would have guessed that the days were starting to get longer.

At home, Berrick was having yet another look at the tiny card he'd received yesterday in the mail. But as soon as he heard Nuggetz's engine roll up, he quickly threw it under his bowl of Arizona Munch.

Junior ran in and beamed even brighter than the bubble lights and tinsel draped across the ridiculously robust Christmas tree dead center of the living room window. "I'm king of the maintenance world!" Junior bellowed with arms up.

Berrick bounded from his chair. "You get it?"

Junior nodded and his dad cheered, giving him a huge hug before they pulled apart in a shared, triumphant laugh.

Berrick offered, "Hey, it may not be the most glamorous gig in town—"

"You ain't lying," Junior cut in with a groan.

"But full-time with insurance and weekends off?"

"I know, I know!" Junior busted with an eagerness his dad had rarely seen. "Weekends off! Man, no one on the coast has that."

"So," Berrick queried as he sat back down in front of his cereal, "when you start?"

"Oh dad, what are you eating that for? I told you if I got this we'd go out to dinner! To celebrate! Come on!"

"What? I got hungry! I didn't know how long you were going to be!" Berrick complained under a mouthful of butterscotch nuggets and chocolate pickaxes.

Junior gave an annoyed but playful sigh as he plopped down at the dining room table. "Well, at least your stomach seems to have gotten used to the new meds."

Berrick gave a relieved grunt. "Finally! I mean, I know they said it would take a while, but I was repainting the walls up there for ten days straight!"

"Eww, dad!"

"Hey, I knew it was going to be a battle. Maybe not as bad as it was for Paco, you know, but..."

Berrick trailed off as his son studied his face for a hard moment. Immediately, he knew he'd said too much.

"What about Paco?" Junior's mouth formed the words without ever breaking his stare.

Berrick dropped his head. "Ah, pigshit." His dejected whisper seemed to try and hide under the dining room table.

"Are you...Are you telling me you gave some of your meds to Paco?"

"I was just trying to help!"

"Help?!" Junior bounded from his seat as if his ass was on fire. "Is that why he was in the bathroom the entire second half of the night?! Are you kidding me?"

"I! I...I!—"

"You! You! What?!" Junior yelled in disbelief. "What did you do to him?"

"I knew you wanted some time alone with Dorena, so..."

"So, you poisoned her boyfriend, yeah?"

"Oh, I just put a couple of my pills in his beer, that's all!"

"You can go to jail for that kind of thing, dad!"

Berrick gave a wheezing laugh. "Not going to jail for that! He spent a few hours on the can." The laugh got bigger. "You should've seen it."

Taking his seat again, Junior jibed, "I don't know if I care to." Sure, the thought was disgusting to him for numerous reasons, but there was something back there, deep behind his indignant tone and clamped lips, which bubbled with the same pleasure his dad was taking in all this.

"He almost shit himself because he caught his foot in the bedspread trying to run for the toilet!"

Finally, the smile started to come through Junior's face, piercing the edges of his shining eyes and tickling his nose.

Berrick continued, almost unable to speak from a grenade burst of laughter. "At first, every time he'd fart, he'd start singing, 'Mmm, ahh, ohhhh, Poppin' Fresh Dough!'" And with that, he blew a huge, wet raspberry to try and dupe Paco's little gastrointestinal nightmare.

That did it. Junior started to choke and tried to cover his face. He regarded his father through a net of fingers as his own embarrassed laugh began to leap across the table. The two sat there reeling in the putrid picture Berrick had painted, unable to get themselves together.

Finally able to speak again, Junior remembered fondly, "Dorena and I must've been talking out there for an hour!"

"At least!" Grabbing his aching ribs, Berrick started to laugh again.

A hood of seriousness slid over Junior. "Yeah, until the ambulance showed up."

Berrick's raving chuckle slid away as he assumed the same pensive manner. "How's Berta doing?"

"She's been out of the hospital for at least a week now. Gubbins, of course, fired her and Dorena, but at least it didn't take effect until after she was discharged from the hospital."

Berrick drew a circle around his mouth. "You said she had all that charcoal on her face."

"Yeah," Junior nodded his head, "charcoal treatment—the ER used it to absorb the booze."

His dad winced at the thought, which rated just as gross to him on the offensive scale as Paco's explosive diarrhea.

"All in all, she's pretty good for someone whose blood alcohol was a point-three-six. I think she's more embarrassed than anything."

"Why?" Berrick softly questioned. "She showed all those people what kind of jerk Gubbins really was."

"That's the problem," Junior summed. "They still bought LeisureFace from him. He still won."

Both of them sat in silence for a second, their sensibilities hurt by the reality Junior had just said aloud.

Junior shook it off and stood up. "Come on, let's go get something to celebrate!"

Suddenly, Berrick's memory gave him something else to be excited about. He got out of his chair, snapping his fingers. "Oh! Let's stop at Circle K and see if they have any more chocolate coins!"

As his dad went to the bathroom off the living room, Junior rounded up his father's bowl and cereal box. After going through some of the nastier areas of the local Comfort Inn, he thought it best to wash his hands at the sink. Drying them off with a tea towel featuring a glittery outline of Charlie Brown and his spindly, piss-poor Christmas tree, Junior noticed the flat card on the table, taking a few seconds to compute that it had been under his dad's bowl.

Picking it up, it wore a printed X in a box next to the initials C.L.L.—"POSITIVE" was typed aside it. Over the years, Junior had learned that anything his dad got from the doctor with the word 'positive' on it was anything but.

The toilet flushed and out came Berrick, ready for a congratulatory dinner and maybe some foil-wrapped Jewish chocolates for dessert. But as soon as he saw Junior standing there with his biopsy results, a blackness came over his eyes and pushed downwards over his frown. Berrick didn't know whether to cry or kick himself in the ass for stupidly leaving the card under his bowl.

"What is this? What is CLL?" Junior asked of the latest piece of his father's unending medical puzzle.

After a pause, Berrick figured it best to just answer truthfully, or, at least as truthfully as his mouth would let him. "Chronic Lyto...Lit—Lym-pho-cy-tic Leukemia." A terrible irony filled his lungs, peppering his explanation: "I can't say it, but I got it."

"When do you get this?"

"Yesterday's mail. I just got off the phone with them about 45 minutes ago, too."

Junior's volume got a little louder. More aggressive, but just barely. "Dad, when were you going to tell me about this?"

Berrick shrugged. "Twenty-sixth. You've been through enough, I didn't want to mess up your Christmas."

For a second, Junior turned away, the biopsy card folding over into his fist.

"They want me to start next week." Berrick confessed.

"Start what?" Junior's voice cracked and warbled. He tried to stay strong.

"Some more bone marrow shit, I don't know. Chemotherapy comes next. I guess they're setting everything up at Willamette Valley Cancer Institute." After a break, Berrick started up with a staunch resonance. "Supposedly will take about seven weeks, but I don't know if I believe that yet or not. But I did believe your girl."

Junior's flustered face rolled different shades as confusion rose atop the sadness and anger. "Wha'?"

"Dorena. She asked me a bunch of questions when we stopped that one day on the way to get the new meds. She made me promise to get another blood draw that day. I did," Berrick affirmed, "because, son...I think she knew."

A frightened frustration rose again in Junior. "I just...I don't know what to do first."

"Relax. Just relax. The military is gonna foot the bill, the leg work is already getting done, and I've been through a hell of a lot worse than this."

Junior appreciated his father's sunny disposition, but now wasn't the time for it. "Dad, this is cancer."

"Yeah! And all I have to do now is lie there and let a lot of people take care of me like their jobs depend on it. I don't have to be on my feet, alert. No water for two days. No sleep. Using hand signals and tap codes because I'll be killed if I speak." An uncanny peace came over Berrick's face. He surrendered to blind faith. And it felt good. "Just lie there. That's all."

"It's not just that. There'll be a lot of pain," Junior warned, not just his father, but himself.

"There's pain with everything eventually!" Berrick raised his brow. "Just like letting you go. But, Junebug, that's one of the reasons I gave those pills to Paco." He reached out and took his crumpled biopsy card from his son's hand, holding it up in front of him. "Even before I got this card yesterday, I was starting to realize that you need to go and be happy. It looks like I'm gonna be forced into it, because I should have let you go and do it a long time ago. And not just for you, but for me, now, too."

Junior began to cry, burying his piercing expression in the nape of his father's neck. Berrick stood firm, holding his son, and truly believed every word he was about to say as tears slowly pumped under both of his lower eyelids.

"I'm not scared," Berrick vowed. "I don't want you to be, either. We're a team. We always will be."

Though Berrick had to drag his son out to eat, ultimately both were glad they went. Over dinner, they came up with a game plan for the next week, and their hot meatball sub sandwiches were divine. Even better? Berrick was on cloud nine to find that the Circle K at the bottom of the hill had just put out their last case of chocolate Hanukkah gelt. Sixteen were left by the time they walked in, and Junior bought his dad every last yellow-netted bag.

Gubbins and his wife were snug in their bed, while visions of retirement danced in his head. They slept the sleep of babes, because the only thing better than steady cash flow was a single lump sum sitting in the bank with your name on it. Santa Claus turned out to be an entrepreneurial Black man in his 30s, and he had come early this year with one hell of a gift for the Gubbins household.

After getting up and dressing, they stood at the living room window, looking out at the clear and cold Christmas Eve morning. Filtered through the fingers of fir and cedar, the sun tapped over the top of the calm Pacific, and everything was as it should be. Gubbins was in such a good mood, he figured he'd give Geraldine an early Christmas present.

The bow was green and red with gold trim and—surprise!—it was a two three-day passes to the Crescent Treasures resort down on the California coast. Gubbins' wife thought it was the best present he'd gotten her in years. Facials! Massages! Relaxation! So thoughtful. Wasn't her husband just the dickens?

Speaking of dicks, the phone rang and Gubbins sprang up to answer it. "Excuse me, sweetie!"

He never imagined the present that was coming his way as he answered with a palatable "Hello?"

"Merry Christmas, you perverted, ancient piece of dog shit."

Gubbins' eyes darted to his wife, who was still too busy drinking in the glossy Crescent Treasures brochure to take note of his conversation.

"What do you want?" Gubbins straightened his spine and kept his voice lifeless, as if trying not to give away any clues as to whom he thought—no, he *knew*—was on the other side of the line. "Why are you calling me?"

"Just wanted to give you some seasonal greetings and tell you that, if you have any brains left in your fucking head, you better meet me in the Safeway parking lot in fifteen minutes." Casey figured she needed one more word to make her point. "Alone."

"If this is a business matter, I insist on doing it in my office."

"No, we won't do this in your office—"

"It is Christmas Eve and I'm home with my wife!" Gubbins rumbled through clenched teeth.

"—and I can make this everybody's business, including radio, newspapers, and TV if you don't get your ass to Safeway in fifteen minutes."

The phone line went dead.

Gubbins' pulse began to race. Hearing Casey's militant tone stirred up a whirlpool of emotion in the linear space between his heart and groin, but the danger of *'radio, newspapers, and TV'* whipped his prurient mind into coming up with the best and fastest excuse possible for his wife.

Without fail, Cles Gubbins had manipulation ready for any occasion.

"StileCorp found some stray paperwork that needs initialing, and Brody needs it right away," he sighed.

Geraldine turned away from her vacation leaflet. "Oh, honey! But it's Christmas Eve!" she pouted with disappointment.

"I know, I know. I'll be right back." Gubbins was already starting to gather up his keys, his wallet, and his coat while keeping an eye on the clock. He still had fourteen minutes. "It'll only take a few minutes, so go ahead and figure out which of the spa packages you want while I'm gone."

"Oooh!" she swooned, turning over the brochure before waving goodbye. "Andy, be careful!"

"I will," Gubbins fumed on the way out the door.

Though it was the kind of frosty morning that would normally keep coastal residents home until the afternoon, it was still Christmas Eve, and so the Beaver Lake Safeway was positively berserk. Inside, it was butts-to-nuts, all the way from the produce section in the front to the meat department along the back wall. However, the real horror-show was out in the parking lot. Cars were squeezing into every spot they could find, and so Gubbins' Mercedes slammed to a halt in the red-striped fire lane fronting the entranceway. Casey stood there waiting, right in front of the payphone.

Gubbins smirked as he stepped from the car. "So, Miss Morris, how's the new job hunt?"

The arrogance of her former boss was insufferable. "Probably about the same for any of your former employees."

Gubbins put his hand on his hip. "I don't see why we couldn't have done this in my office." Considering how much his imagination had magnified the potential cruciality of their meeting during the red-light-running, thirteen-minute drive here, he thought he was doing a remarkable job of keeping calm under pressure.

"I wanted to do this in a public area," Casey smoothly volleyed.

"Why?" bellowed Gubbins. A few last-minute cranberry sauce and eggnog shoppers turned to look at him as they entered the store.

"Because, believe it or not, I don't trust you very much," was the natural response.

"That saddens me," Gubbins admitted as he walked closer, "because I'm just a retired old man now. I have no reason not to be trusted."

"Ha! Maybe you can sell that shit to StileCorp, but they don't know you like I do."

Gubbins' wrists began to ache. The phantom sensation of the handcuffs tickled him for a few fleeting beats of his hot, horny heart before Casey's fingers flashed the picture in front of him. The humiliation of two weeks earlier hit Gubbins like a freight train, heightening every one of his feelings.

Even though he knew, his ire couldn't help asking, "What is that??"

"It's pretty small," a humorless Casey punned. "You'll have to come closer."

"You give me that this instant!" Gubbins roared, overpowering the young girl and easily tearing it away from her.

"Keep it," she said coolly, reveling in the fact that last-minute shoppers were starting to take notice of them as they flitted to and from their cars. "Mr. Gubbins, did you ever use the color copiers at the Beaver Lake Library? They're amaaaazing. Very good detail!"

"You're a sneak. And a cheat... And a tease," a panting Gubbins squeaked as his throat gave out on him, "...and the WORST CUNT I ever had the misfortune to meet, Miss Morris!" The former CEO wiped his nose, probably because, by now, his brain was leaking out of it. Rich men aren't used to losing, especially on such a grand, ass-kicking scale.

"Then you won't find it too hard to never look at, call, or contact me in any way, ever again," Casey rattled off with ease.

"You'll never—!"

"And—here's the important part, so you better goddamn listen to what I say—if I ever hear of anyone not getting a job because of their affiliation with LeisureFace, that picture goes straight to the internet, do you understand me?"

The only thing left for Cles Gubbins to do was bluff. "The internet won't care."

"If not, your wife will." Those beautiful blue eyes bore holes in Gubbins' soul. "And she'll take you for everything you just cashed out."

Gubbins looked down at himself: mouth open, the north wind slicking his salt-and-pepper pubes to the left part of his abdomen, shirttails and tie flapping, and, finally, a penis not really big enough to flap at all dotted the spot right above his tightened, windblown nutbag.

His umbrage was so pronounced, it almost bent the door pins as he headed for the driver's seat.

"Do we have a deal, Mr. Gubbins? Oh, excuse me—'Cles'?"

Madness from an untapped vengeance scorched Gubbins' face. "This isn't over."

Casey shrugged. "That's up to you."

"How do I know you won't just lie?" Gubbins asked with a morbid, intrinsic curiosity.

Casey reached into her pocket, bringing out what must have been two dozen copies of the very picture Gubbins held in his white, sweaty hand. She fanned them out effortlessly, as if they were the cards from her tarot deck. "I got proof, Mr. Gubbins. I don't need to lie."

From that moment on, the agreement was kept. Gubbins convinced himself that acquiescence on his part was a small price to pay, and, therefore, he never gave Casey a reason to drop the hammer on him.

They never saw each other again.

ACT THE LAST

[UNTIL WE MEET AGAIN...ALOHA]

With Christmas Day being a Monday, it would've been a three-day weekend had anyone still had a job. The day passed without a lot of fanfare anywhere in Beaver Lake—it was probably the quietest day for everyone since finding out that LeisureFace was on the auction block.

The first thing Tuesday brought about was an early-morning appointment for Berta. The doctor checked on her recovery from the concussion and answered a few questions she had regarding COBRA, for which she was getting ready to submit her first payment. The cost of the premium was outfuckingrageous. However, she didn't have much of an option at the moment, and would have to funnel her unemployment into continuing her health insurance for the time being.

Berta had just gotten home and managed to pluck off the first few ornaments from her tree when the phone rang. Chilled from being outside, she hopped into her slippers on the way to the receiver.

"Hello, Mancari residence, this is Roberta speaking," her unassuming voice answered.

"Berta? This is Hal Weinrich from Work Warriors!" Berta's head-hunter chirped.

"Hey there, Hal. Hope you had a good holiday." Berta said back, fidgeting with her lighter to start up a smoke.

"Oh, I did! The family and I just got back from Reno last night. Good times!"

"Glad to hear it. So, what's new?"

"Well, it looks like you might have a happy new year."

Cringing against the desire to read too much into Hal's sentence, Berta simply opted to ask for some more information. "What do ya mean?"

"The Olympic Elk Lodge I mentioned out in Sandy? On the Mount Hood Highway? They want you for their Housekeeping Supervisor."

Berta held her breath, mid-puff. "Are you serious?"

"Totally!" Hal yelped. "I knew they were really, really aiming to hire as many people as fast as they could. It turns out they finished building the property a month sooner than they thought!"

"For real?!" Berta coughed as she finally remembered to exhale.

"Yeah! They were impressed by your supervisory work at LeisureFace, and they already confirmed your work history with someone there."

Berta's nose crinkled and her mouth broke into a sarcastic rictus. "No shit?!"

"None at all! They want you to start on the twenty-ninth of January. It's still only a month away, though, and I know you'd have to get everything moved up here in the next few weeks." Hal was hopeful, but his doubt clearly showed. "Is this something you could pull off?"

Mashing the receiver into her shoulder, Berta clamped her hands on top of her head. She glanced around the room, thinking about every factor, all at once. Her medication, her bankbook, boxing up her stuff, moving her indicas, finding a new place, Portland, the city, the traffic, everything! She figured she needed to buy some time and began asking questions as her brain did what felt like jumping jacks behind her sinuses. "Uh...tell me, what's the hours?"

"They would want you full-time, Sunday through Thursday, of course for the big Sunday morning checkout," Hal reasoned. "Forty, forty-five hours a week. You'd be building a crew from the ground up over the first two weeks because they want to open in the first half of February." Hal's cadence had a nudge-nudge-wink-wink wrinkle to it all of the sudden. "Valentine's Day! You know what I'm talking about. Long President's Day weekend, too. There's a lot of potential moneymakers for them right off the bat if they open then instead of March."

Nope. She still needed more time. Think. Think. Think. Berta served up another question.

"Salary?" Her mouth issued the diversion as she continued to scramble for a happy medium that would appease Hal for a while. Hell, for just the rest of the afternoon, if nothing else. She envisioned all her belongings stacked up by the front door in a wall of boxes way bigger than she ever dreamt. This little mirage certainly didn't help her nerves any, let alone her decision.

"Sixteen-fifty, which is a smidgen over four more than what you were making at LeisureFace. To be honest, the Portland area is more expensive, so, in essence, you'll probably be a little ahead of where you are now, even to start. It's a lateral move at worst, really." Hal sounded a bit sheepish in his odds-laying, but at least he was being honest.

"Trust me, Hal, I can live with lateral as a worst-case scenario," Berta replied, never imagining that she was now placing the highest importance on something other than her pay: "What's the medical?"

"Medical and dental is one-hundred percent employer-paid. No vision right now," Hal offered a verbal shrug of sorts, adding with some optimism, "but it's a cheap add-on if you decide you want it."

"Immediate or ninety days?" Berta's question was fraught, as if it was being asked as a tie-breaker. Maybe that's because it was.

"Ninety days. Sick time and PTO are out of the same hopper, and it starts to accrue after ninety days, too." Hal made it seem like a solid offer overall.

Berta looked down and noticed her ashes had gotten nearly an inch long since she last took an inhale off of her cigarette. "So, how long do I have to decide?"

"Well, not long," Hal laughed. "They want an answer A.S.A.P. I'd say definitely by close of tomorrow."

"Alright, give me till tomorrow, okay?"

"Absolutely. It's a big consideration, I know." Hal was courteous and understanding. "And hey, like I said, you're going to be building your own crew, so if you know anyone down your way, or up here, or whatever, that you could bring with you, all the better."

Berta froze. "Yeah. Yeah, I think I might."

Less than two minutes later, the phone not far from Dorena's head rang. She'd taken to lying on the floor to watch T.V. because Paco had just moved the couch with him to Eugene.

For the first half of the conversation, Dorena could barely understand anything Berta was saying because her ex-supervisor was talking so fast. Ultimately, the directions were clear: meet her at the Sandmark Lounge in an hour...and bring her little sister along.

Berta was already having a celebratory White Russian when Dorena and Casey bounded through the door. The three screeched like schoolgirls, taking turns hugging as Berta kicked out their chairs so both sisters could have a seat at her table. The waitress brought them some drink menus, which Dorena took hold of as soon as they made it to her underage little sister's hands.

Dorena marveled at Berta's appearance. "Shit! You're looking better than ever. How the hell you do that?"

"Thanks, I feel good," Berta affirmed. "So good, I can resume what the doctor calls 'light physical activity'. That includes power walking and a stationary bike."

"Oh man, fuck that shit!" Dorena laughed.

An honest smile came across Berta's clean olive skin. "It's amazing what being unconscious a week straight can do for ya."

"I'm making that my New Year's resolution," Dorena joked. "We only got a few minutes, but we wanted to hit you up on the way."

"Yeah, what's up, what's up?!" Casey cried, unable to contain herself in her chair. "Dorrie almost pulled me off the toilet, we got into the car so fast!"

"I got big news," Berta wagered.

"Big. How big?" Casey wondered aloud what both she and her sibling were thinking.

"Bigger than my hospital bills!" Berta cracked a laugh in the round. "You're never gonna believe this."

After the past few weeks, Casey was assured in her response. "Try me."

Dorena lit up a smoke, sliding the ashtray closer to her as she added with a rising jitter, "What is it?!"

"I just got an offer from the new Olympic Elk Lodge in the foothills outside Portland. Basically, I have to find a new place and move in the next three weeks."

The congratulations the sisters wanted to give was eclipsed by the fact Berta would have to leave the area if she took it.

"Damn, they don't mess around, do they?" Dorena frowned, pushing her lighter back into its hiding place.

"Nope, especially when the place wants to open a month earlier than planned," Berta said behind a swallow of White Russian. The cubes tinkled around as she put it back down on its chipped cork coaster.

"So, have you given them your answer?" Casey's paper-thin hope was buried there in the doubt that enveloped her voice. "Are you taking it?"

A serious air floated from Berta's eyelashes as she nodded, but it was just coy enough to let the two sisters know something great was about to come of it. "And since I have to build a team from the ground up before February, I've decided the best thing to do is take my existing crew with me."

Casey yelled so loudly, everyone in the Sandmark turned and looked at Berta's table. The younger of the two sisters jumped up and down in such a hilariously enthusiastic way that the patrons couldn't help in share in the thrill.

Berta started rattling off the specifics because she knew they wanted the details. "Sunday through Thursday. I'm not sure of the money for you guys yet, but I'll find out."

"Saturdays off!" Casey squealed in a deliciously cute way.

It got better as Berta rolled out the remainders. "Probably start the beginning of February. Paid time off and medical after ninety days."

"So, you'll get coverage before COBRA runs out?" Dorena computed.

"Exactly!" Berta said, high-fiving her partner-in-crime. "Also, I'm looking into some financial assistance for my meds to help cushion that blow, too."

Casey bent her back over the top of her chair. "Oh my God, this is the fucking SHIT!"

Berta breathed in the symptoms of victory. "Gals, we have made it."

Dorena could only shake her head. She held off looking up till the very last second. "...I can't do it."

Casey's innocent face went a sickly, mute white at her sister's suggestion.

Berta nodded. "Yeah. I know."

Casey finally realized the hurdle. Turning to her sister, she began to plead. "Oh, come on. It's not that far from Petey. You can come down here for the legal stuff, can't you?"

Berta's sad eyes darted between the sisters as they talked.

Dorena pledged, "I'm the closest I've been. This may be my last shot. Mom and the state have a microscope so far up my ass, you could probably see Mars with it. I've already started rehab here, which is where I gotta be in fifteen minutes! I got welfare jokers looking for me a job and transpo since Paco took the car with him. I already promised them I'm staying put at least till the lease runs out in March because the place is big enough for me and Petey both. You know I have no money, let alone enough to do a move." Though the tears were visible as she turned and looked straight at Berta, there was a steadfast shine in Dorena's eyes. "But I'm close. And I can't fuck this up now."

There was a sweet consideration in Berta's assurance. "And you won't. I just wanted you to have first crack at the offer." A smile that could only be fully appreciated by Dorena rose up between them. "You know, you were one of the only people who helped me try and stick it to Gubbins. That means a lot, thank you."

Dorena calmly nodded and ditched the grey from the end of her cigarette. A huge lump was gulped down as a curtain of curls shaded her face.

"Speaking of Gubbins," Berta went on, "I don't know how the hell he gave me a decent referral."

Dorena, having regained her tough exterior, blew a wad of grey, hazy mess up to the rafters. "He didn't get a concussion, too, did he?"

Taking another drink, Berta thought it sounded plausible. "Hey, these days, anything's possible."

"Dunno," Casey opined, never tipping her hand. "Maybe he learned a little something from all this?"

"Riiiight!" they all said in unison, but there was something different about Casey's contribution and the way that she smiled. If Gubbins didn't learn anything, at least she had.

Dorena checked her watch. "Oh shit, we gotta go."

"Oh no, so soon?" Berta asked as the two sisters bent down to give her a quick hug.

"Yeah, Little-Miss-Whitebread has to play by the rules for a while," an unenthused Dorena admitted.

Berta pointed to Casey. "And you need to get packing."

"Yes!" the youngest said, pumping both fists.

"Call me tonight and I'll give you some listings of places I found in the eastern parts that aren't too spendy—Sandy, Troutdale, Gresham."

A smooth adrenaline pumped through Casey's body at the thought of a new start. It was horrifying, but cool. "After dinner-time okay for ya?"

Berta nodded as she chugged the last of her White Russian and they said their goodbyes, with the two sisters jumping quickly into Casey's car and pulling back out onto 101. The television above the bar could barely be heard, but it was the graphic next to the talking head on Northwest Cable News that caught her attention. Berta could barely hear it over the clank of the backroom glasses, forks, and plates, and strained her ears for the specifics.

"And a happy day for a family in Seattle today. A quiet breakfast turned into a gold bonanza as a West Seattle family found the coveted gold nugget in a contest held by the popular new cereal, Arizona Munch."

"Ah, shit," Berta griped just as the waitress walked up.

"Yeah, I hear ya! I probably gained ten pounds in the past month alone eatin' that cereal and lookin' for that nugget!" The waitress let out a whoop so big, she nearly lost the pen from her apron. She pointed to the empty, sweating glass in front of Berta. "You want another one, baby?"

"Sure." Berta had a look over her shoulder to the 'Gimme Five' pull tab banner. She reluctantly pulled a twenty from her purse. "And you might as well give me four Gimme Fives, too." As the waitress nodded and turned toe, Berta recalibrated her investment decision. "Actually, just give me two."

Just a few seconds later, the waitress strolled back with a brimming White Russian and two slick, oversized pull tabs. "Oh hell, sweetie, I forgot your change. I'm so sorry. Hold on, I'll be right back," she apologized, slipping the new glass atop the coaster. She re-snapped the barrette holding up her grey hairdo as she headed back behind the bar.

Berta turned her attention to the pull tab as a new customer showed up and diverted the waitress' attention for a few extra moments. She looked down at the afroed kitty cat, half-listening to the sounds of the guy behind her ordering a beer and the cash register opening. Berta wasn't surprised at all when she broke open the first tab on the card to find a not-even-close combination of banana-cherry-orange underneath.

She was, however, surprised to find the three yellow 5's underneath the second tab. There was no mistaking the words written aside it: *INSTANT WINNER! - * $55, 555 ***

It was only a few seconds, but to Berta, it seemed like half of her life. All the struggle. The ridiculous odds. The money wasted. The prayers. The optimism. It was right there in black and white—actually, black and yellow.

She had a new job and a new start. Her meds were going to be taken care of, and the long-standing worry about her insurance lapsing was gone. Even building a new housekeeping team was going to be easier now that Casey was coming onboard. Those three little fives were the only thing in the world that could make her realize the habit she really invested in: worry. Something even more worthless than the paper all the losing pull tabs and Arizona Munch boxes had been printed on.

Berta didn't need a jackpot anymore to save her. She was going to be just fine.

Tapping a ten-dollar bill on Berta's shoulder, the rushed waitress served up an extra mea culpa. "Sorry there—here ya are! You need anything else right now, sweetie?"

It felt so good to shake her head, and the answer she gave was one she'd waited her whole life to say. "No," Berta said. "Not at all."

For the next few days, conversation was strained as everyone was assholes and elbows packing to go on their next big adventure. Adventures that would, for good or bad, take them away from Beaver Lake, at least for a little while. Details to one another were in fits and starts as doctor consults, recruiter questions, and long hours of driving to look at apartments brought them all less sleep than usual.

Berrick wrangled up everything for the cancer institute, only to have to enlist Junior help move it to two separate boxes. His checklist of things to take with him ultimately got way too long to fit into any soft-sided Samsonite bag.

Berta found a new apartment—a nifty split-level duplex just this side of...Boring. Boring, Oregon. It's true, the town wasn't a hotbed of entertainment, but her place was only about a 15-minute drive to the Lodge where she and Casey would be working.

Speaking of Casey, she, too, landed a place just a couple of days later. It was in the thriving burb of Gresham, which was close to a lot of things nineteen-year-olds hold dear. Barely 450 square feet it, nonetheless, felt like her own private palace.

U-Haul was charging exorbitant prices for cardboard, so Casey went on a quest to every grocery store, liquor store, and electronics store in the west part of Lane County in search of boxes, preferably with lids. The sisters took to keeping Vaseline within reach due to their fingers getting so dried out from handling all of the corrugated bastards. Once they were full, Dorena would tape them up and stack them by the front door. Unlike Berrick's bloated roster of bring-alongs, the sisters were surprised by how little Casey actually owned. Deciding to leave her bed behind for Petey to use, she would easily be able to fit everything in her little Toyota and probably have room to spare.

As she was filling one of her last boxes from her bedroom end table, Casey found a stray copy of Gubbins' picture. Having not seen it the best part of the past week during the flurry of interviews, 200-mile apartment jaunts, and packing, she felt a strange distance from it when the campy example of middle-aged nudity tumbled out of the drawer housing her metallic purple vibrator.

"God, I made too many of these," Casey censured herself, stuffing the renegade smut into her purse.

Fittingly, New Year's Day turned out to be the busiest day of the year for Junior. After spending his introductory half-day at the Comfort Inn filling out employment paperwork and helping pump the heavy rain waters out of the flooded first floor, he had to drive over to Eugene to see his dad one more time before his treatment was slated to begin the following day. Berrick was nervous but in great, talkative spirits, especially after Junior showed up with a VCR, which was fed "The Fog" the minute it was hooked up to the room's wall-mounted television.

One last present from his son remained for Berrick: a printed-out picture Junior had taken of their patio, dotted with three of his dad's raccoon friends. Berrick clutched it to his chest and banged his heels against the mattress as if he'd already been cured of what ailed him. The photo stayed taped up to his bed rail the entire seven weeks.

Junior checked his watch as he fell back into Nuggetz's driver seat and began making his way west again. The skies cleared just enough to begin seeing rays set over the translucent orange and bruise-purple ridges ahead of him. He was hoping to make it back to Beaver Lake, and his date with Dorena, just before dark.

A beam of low-level light was warming Dorena's face as it made its descent. The final few minutes of daylight were only strong enough to warm her lips and brow bone as she waited for Junior on a cedar bench that faced the happy, playful set of oncoming waves.

Beaver Lake City Park was puny, but beautiful. It catered to the kind of folks who wanted to beachcomb or storm-watch from benches behind its matte silver railings. Gentle green slopes pushed out to a precarious horseshoe-shaped stairway, each direction leading down to the beach. For a second, the thought of wandering the marshy, packed sand seemed intriguing, but the dying light and fatigue from helping Casey pack for the past few days kept Dorena's butt firmly on the bench. It was a good choice since she could start to hear Junior's Firebird slowing to a stop in a parking space not far away. A few grains of sand lifted in the curling winds, rubbing Dorena's knuckles as she pinched the cherry off her cigarette.

As always, Junior didn't want to seem too forward, so he jumped up to take a seat on the thick railing, making himself as comfortable as he could. At least he had the gusts at his back. "Hey, how long you been here?"

"Casey dropped me off just a few minutes ago." Right off the bat, Dorena sounded tired and not quite up to speed, but, in contrast, the omnipresent edge to her diction was missing. She sounded happier. "I guess congratulations are in order."

Between Junior's chilly cheeks came a self-conscious wrinkle of laughter. "Yeah, thanks."

"So, how was the first day at Comfort Inn?"

"Mostly paperwork, thank God. It was just a half day. The real test will be tomorrow." There was a peculiar double-meaning to how Junior said it. He went on to explain the duality. "Just finished getting Dad ready for his first round of chemo in the morning." Junior's voice was preempted by his own lack of something to add. Grief, hope, strength, and an absence of understanding all floated in the gap.

"Yeah?" came Dorena's curious reply, hungry for emotion and depth.

The quaver in Junior's voice was sullen but straightened out to become seemingly unbendable in the wake of some long odds. "He found out a few days ago that he has leukemia, but you already knew that, didn't you?"

Dorena nodded.

"Thanks for making him get that latest blood test. Actually, he told me to thank you for making him get that blood test." Both of them smiled with a sense of solace. "I don't know if we would've caught it in time otherwise."

The knowing grin only got bigger, and Dorena's teeth shone a bright yellow in the light of the sunset. "Well, as long as he stays out of Golden Cedars, he'll do fine."

"Yeah," Junior looked down, bashfully agreeing. "I hope he does."

"Guess what?" Dorena spun the subject to comfort her date just a little, "Casey found a place."

"You serious?"

"Gresham. Her and Berta are both leaving tomorrow." The usual edge to Dorena's voice was back, front and center.

Junior noticed Dorena's discomfort seeping in and tried to lighten things up. "What are the chances that they'd get jobs at the same place two hundred miles away?"

That edge became a scared uncertainty in Dorena's throat, which she was trying hard to swallow down. "Everyone's leavin'."

Junior's attempt to cheer up Dorena wasn't working, so he opted to just shoot from the hip. It seemed to have much better results. "Paco gone now, too?"

"He left a few days ago. It's better for both of us." Dorena paused, the compressed sunlight making her squint as she turned up her face to Junior. A type of crooked humor was added to her next sentence. "At least, that's how I feel."

Junior couldn't hide his enthusiasm, and it ended up fueling the ice-breaker that he had been searching for the past few minutes. "Now that he's in Eugene, maybe he'll run into Stacey-Lynn's ex."

A grim giggle tumbled out of Dorena. "I have a feeling he will." She stopped, empowered by the far-reaching emptiness everyone was leaving her with. Dorena found herself having a problem with seeing all this as a positive—an endowment of independence and choice—but, somehow, she was unearthing the determination to make it work. "I ain't gonna lie, I'm not looking forward to the legal battle, I don't have any cash to do it, and I wouldn't be surprised if getting Petey back means that my mom cuts ties with me. I know it sounds whacked, but," she paused, truly believing what she was about to say, "I feel good."

"You should." Junior's intended encouragement hit a winning bulls-eye, offering up the two best words of support Dorena could have asked for.

"Yeah?" Dorena wasn't quite convinced yet. "There's still one prob-lem."

"What?"

She blew her hair out of her face. "I need a job. Fast. Comfort Inn isn't looking for a housekeeper, are they?"

Junior shook his head. "Not that I know of. Ever do any mainte-nance?" he joked. But, just there under the surface, he was half-serious.

"Well, I did put those Life Savers and bouillon cubes in the shower-heads," Dorena side-eyed with perfection.

Junior slid off of the railing, his new work boots smacking the con-crete. The sun had gone, and so was its sliver of warmth. Things were getting cold quickly. "You hungry?"

"Gettin' there." Dorena stood up, pulling the zipper on her coat up to her neck. They started toward the Firebird.

"New Year's. Probably nothing open," Junior said with a disappoint-ment that his date resisted.

"I got a lot of leftover pizza in the freezer," was the optimistic suggestion.

All that disappointment melted in the wake of a temping possibility. One with toppings. "What kind?" Junior asked.

Just to screw with him a bit, Dorena pretended to think about the question a few seconds longer than she needed. "Pineapple and Canadian bacon."

That was probably the best moment in Junior's life, and he would remember it forever.

The next morning started early for everyone. Almost too much so. It was still dark out when Casey's alarm clock beeped her out of a dead sleep at 6:30 AM. Dorena was in shambles from too much pizza and late-night fun with Junior, but still got herself together enough to help her little sister load up the Toyota after breakfast.

Berrick was being wheeled down the hallway to his first chemotherapy treatment at the same time his son was starting the first full day of his new job. And though it was tough to concentrate on propositions of hiring part-time landscapers, buying new carpet for flooded first-floor rooms, and even where to stash his lunch in favor of thinking about his dad, Junior made it through. Happily, so did Berrick, who proved cranky that first night. Not from the fatigue or pain of the chemo, but because the nurses had taken away his chocolate coins, citing them as 'too fatty and rich'.

Berta was the one who got the luxury of waking up the latest that morning. She had loaded everything in the small U-Haul moving truck and hooked up her car trailer to it the night before, allowing her a leisurely start to an otherwise grueling day.

Lined up on the bare kitchen counter were the keys to the house, the keys to the moving truck, and her meds for the morning and evening, divided up best as she could into little sandwich bags. Crunching the last of her Arizona Munch, her paper bowl and plastic spoon found their way into the top of a bloated Hefty bag. She marveled at how much trash you generated when you were moving.

Groaning as she realized that she'd forgotten to keep a cup out, Berta had no choice but to down the first of the two pill bags by cupping her hands under the tap. Though it was only going to take about four hours to get north to Boring, she had an impatient itch to get on the road. She didn't know if she was running from Beaver Lake or running towards a new start, but she wanted to get it underway, whatever the catalyst, reason, or excuse happened to be.

The Hefty bag gave a fat whoosh as it plopped into the trash can, which was rolled out to the curb where Berta's Christmas tree laid, its needles starting to brown underneath a wisp or two of tinsel. The clouds had mostly slid inland overnight, affording a chilly start to the morning. At least she wouldn't have to worry about dragging her car and everything else she owned 200 miles through a downpour.

The truck's engine jumped alive, and Berta disengaged the emergency brake. Remembering all the things that were stacked up on the other side of the wall behind her seat, she eased into the accelerator. Relief misted her face as she saw her car in the side view mirror, tagging along like a mechanical pet. Berta had planned the trip out well, so she would only have to make one stop on the way, and it was just down the road.

Casey and Dorena's apartment was, mercifully, on a pullout just off the highway, with more than enough space to make a U-turn without the worry of shearing anything in half. Berta pulled over as close to the row of mismatched mailboxes as possible, but since the truck rode so high, she still had to step out to throw a sealed pink envelope into the metal box marked: MORRIS.

Berta didn't just do fine with the U-turn, but the whole trip, as well, buoyed by a sense of completion and that she had done the right thing. The calm she felt inside was the reward she had looked for all along, and it stayed with her long after the boxy orange truck and bopping, tagalong car disappeared from town.

Not long after was when Casey started feeling the pressure to get on the road, too. It was already past lunch, and since she didn't have a ton of confidence in her way around Gresham quite yet, she wanted to get there before dark.

Dorena followed her little sister out to the Toyota. Its trunk and backseat were weighed down with so much, they were surprised the muffler wasn't dragging on the ground. Neither of the flinty sisters had ever been handy with goodbyes, let alone to each other.

In yet another step towards adulthood, Casey opted to admit her anxiety as she opened up the car door. "Paco leave behind any of that hash?" she asked with breathy lungs but no trace of embarrassment.

Dorena rocked on her heels. "I put it in your purse." Casey didn't seem to want to get in the car yet, so she indulged her for a bit longer. "Don't go pissin' off Berta now."

"I won't, I won't!" Casey heaved, thankful for one more diversion.

"Count the acid washes. And you know how she likes her vinegar in the rinse cycles to keep the towels fluffy."

"You know I got a lock on this!" Casey grinned.

"Yeah. I do," her big sister agreed.

They hugged each other for the last time in what would end up being quite a while. The next few months would be tough. Both of them had some hard work to do, and no one else could do it for them.

The Toyota puttered to life. A part of Casey wanted nothing more right now than the mellow she got from smoking a bowl, and that's what made her check her purse for the promised hash. Seeing the top of the Zip-Lock bag was enough of a reassurance.

What she wasn't ready for was the picture of a naked Cles Gubbins she had mindlessly stuffed into her purse while packing a few days earlier. It popped up merrily over her hand as she headed for the shifter. Casey stayed the car, her foot rising from the clutch, which made the feathered roach clip hanging from her rear-view mirror sway slightly as she sat there in neutral.

A giddy smile hit the left side of her mouth as she pulled out the picture and positioned it right in the middle of the clip's pinchers. At least she had someone to keep her company on the trip up to Gresham.

Dorena waved as Casey drove away, with the transmission sounding smoother as she upshifted, finally becoming silent as the car headed out of sight. A humid cloud eked out of Dorena's mouth as she gave a sad sigh. She decided to grab the mail on the way back to the house.

About 30 seconds after she shut the front door behind her was when Dorena Morris' life changed forever.

And everyone on the block probably heard it.

"HOLY FUCKING SHIT!!"

With no coat, no shoes, and no keys, Dorena bounded out the front door, hoping somehow her sister's car would still be there. The open pink envelope trembled in her left hand. In the other, a small greeting card and the Gimme Five pull tab everyone in Oregon had been trying to buy.

The inside of the card read in curly, feminine cursive, *"Petey needs this more than I do. Go buy him something special!"* The signature was in the bottom right corner: *Auntie Berta.*

Dorena put her hand to her mouth, blissfully unaware that she was screaming and crying and laughing, all at the same time. With all the exuberance of a maniac who'd just made it over the asylum wall, she ran back into the house with such a clamor that her neighbors started to populate their doorsteps to see what all the commotion was about.

Casey was almost to the business loop by the time her sister had become the biggest pull-tab jackpot winner in the state's history. But not knowing this, a frazzled grief squeezed at her heart as memories toppled and grabbed Casey on her way out of town. The raw, scratching emotions welled to the surface, stacking and piling far higher than any of the belongings wedged into the backseat behind her.

Beginning to break, she glanced over to the passenger seat, which was where her crutch invariably rode shotgun. The silken lump of her tarot deck sat there, waiting to give answers to the questions Casey was always too scared to find out on her own. Before going any farther down the road, she knew what she had to do.

The accelerator took more pressure, and the tiny, old Toyota panted in its highest gear. Fifty. Fifty-five. Sixty. Her thin, appealing fingers moved off the shift knob, flicking back the silk. She rolled down the window in a fitful series of cranks, not wanting to take her hand off the wheel for too long.

Careful as she could, Casey stretched her reach, bending the pack against the wind that blasted by. All 78 cards popped and blurred as they caught the clearing afternoon sea breezes, billowing up to fill the air with a stunning, psychedelic blur of dancing symbols and colors. A triumphant howl spilled onto the highway—it belied the petite body it came out of and echoed against the shore with a zesty spirit she'd never had before.

Casey was so in tune with the wonder of the cards flapping and dropping and spinning in the whirlwind that she didn't notice one had inadvertently whisked itself on a backdraft and ended up on the passenger floorboards, inches from its starting point. As soon as she saw it, her two feet stomped clutch and brake, and she steered to the dusty pullout on the side of the road.

It was facedown. The thin blue and white lines that made up the deck's backing design beckoned her to touch it. Casey grappled with the gear shift, and the car idled in an even, ticking pattern as the defroster kicked on. Though the deck was back there on the road—stuck in the guardrails, embraced by the soft needles of tall fir branches, getting run over by 101's lunchtime traffic—it looked as though it had one last thing to say to her. Unable to resist the persuasion, Casey braced herself as she overturned the thin paperboard.

It was the Ten of Cups.

The fortune she felt knocked the wind clean out her. For a spell, it left Casey catching breaths only here and there. Finally, her lungs grew strong enough to punch holes in the giggles of gratitude that spread across her dashboard. She lifted the card and placed it between the little jaws of the feathered roach clip, covering up Gubbins' picture as it took its rightful place.

A boisterous gust of dirt shot up from the Toyota's tires as Casey merged back onto the road. She made her way past the business loop where the LeisureFace logo lay dismantled on the shoulder. A flash of the bold StileCorp insignia, towering atop the company's freshly-erected sign, was the last thing Casey saw in her rear-view mirror before breaching the Lane County line.